SHADOWMARK

(RAVEN CURSED BOOK 4)

MCKENZIE HUNTER

McKenzie Hunter

Shadowmark

© 2020, McKenzie Hunter

McKenzieHunter@McKenzieHunter.com

ISBN: 978-1-946457-15-8

ACKNOWLEDGEMENT

With each release, I am increasingly grateful for my readers who make this possible. Thank you for reading my books and following Erin's adventure.

Each book is the result of a lot of wonderful people who helped me tell the best story: My editors: Meredith Tennant and Therin Knite. My beta readers: Elizabeth Bracker, Márcia Alexandra, Robyn Mather, Sherrie Simpson Clark, Stacey Mann. Cover artist: Orina. Needless to say, my family and friends for their support and checking to make sure I leave my writing cave.

CHAPTER 1

*B*ecause of me, Arius was dying, or whatever it was that was happening to his body.

His reddish skin was ashen. The tip of the arrow remained lodged in his body, unable to be removed despite the various spells Elizabeth and Nolan tried. The wound refused to heal. Cory's shoulder, once we'd removed that arrow tip, had fared much better, responding to his healing magic.

"The Immortalis," Elizabeth said, her lips downturned into a painful looking frown.

"You think they did this?" I asked.

"There were two. We thought they were both trying to break the ward, but the woman's magic was directed at Arius, not the ward. It was a simple distraction. They knew they wouldn't get past a ward that either Nolan or I made. But once the arrow was in Arius, they didn't have to get past the ward to invoke the spell." Her eyes flicked to Cory and his bloodstained shirt. "If they wanted me involved, they needed to hurt Arius. I don't care about you. Whether you live or die is of no consequence to me. But I do care about Arius. So that's what she used against me."

Cory flinched at her rudeness. I rolled my eyes; she was making it hard to feel sympathy for her.

Elizabeth paid close attention to the infrequent and shallow rise and fall of Arius's chest.

"'Fifty years, I picked up some things,'" Elizabeth said, repeating Malific's parting words. "What things did she learn? This is like nothing I've seen." She looked up at Nolan. "Have her skills and knowledge surpassed mine?"

Nolan looked dejected.

"I'm sorry," he said. It was the only thing he offered but it sounded like a condolence. It sparked Elizabeth's ire.

"Too many apologies and not enough action. This is on you!" She stood, dropped the ward that had separated us from Malific, and snatched up the blue, glowing, diamond-shaped piece of metal that my mother had left as her calling card.

"Elizabeth," Nolan snapped. His voice was sharp and chastising as he switched to their language.

She responded in English, making sure I heard every word. "I will not put Malific's daughter's life before his. Do not ask me to."

Even when Nolan hissed at her in their language, she responded so I could understand.

"You want me to get rid of the pharus?" She lifted the blue calling card. "You find a way to heal Arius, because if you don't, I'll use it. Don't ask me to care about Malific's daughter, because that, brother, is beyond what our love can endure."

Cory pressed his hand against my back and gave me a gentle supportive smile. Madison glared at Elizabeth. I could see her mind turning over Elizabeth's response and her mood becoming hostile and retaliatory. She took on the offense of Elizabeth's unwarranted resentment that I no longer had the energy to let bother me. After the initial jolt of umbrage, Cory seemed to be able to let Elizabeth's insults roll over him in the same manner I'd adopted. Madison was having a hard time doing the same.

Cory winced at the slightest movement of his injured arm. It wasn't responding like a typical injury and kept reopening. Each healing spell healed it only a fraction of what we were used to; at this rate it would take days for his arm to be fully restored, and the constant spell casting wasn't sustainable without significantly weakening him.

I looked at Elizabeth. "I can't right the wrongs of Malific, nor will I entertain your misguided resentment. But I will do everything possible to help Arius survive," I promised.

Elizabeth's chin jutted in defiance.

"I'm not doing this for you," I clarified. "I just don't want Malific to have another victory."

Ignoring Elizabeth's heavy glower, I turned my back on her. Taking my phone from my pocket, I reviewed my contacts through the crack in the screen that must have formed when I dropped to the ground to avoid being hit by the assassin's arrow.

"Erin," Mephisto rushed out, answering the call on the first ring. "Is everything okay?"

"No," I admitted. "Things are bad." I told him the unabridged version of what had occurred: the assassination attempt by the shifter, my mother killing the shifter for his failure, and her making a deal with Elizabeth to cure Arius in exchange for killing me.

"I need your help," I added.

"You believe Elizabeth will use the pharus despite her commitment to her brother?"

I made a half-turn, taking a furtive look at Elizabeth. Her ginger-colored eyes held something far darker than the thick coat of mascara on her lashes. Desperation and anger gleamed in them.

"Definitely," I said. "Malific said that she had learned

some new tricks, but I'm not sure if they're new or just undiscovered. I'm hoping you can help."

There was a long moment of silence. I didn't think he'd decline but I did wonder what was going through his mind. Mephisto was pragmatic; perhaps he was debating if Arius's death would serve a purpose for him and the Huntsmen. Would Elizabeth's anguish lead to a valuable ally?

"We'll be there," he finally said before I could suggest that he bring the Mystic Souls. "I'll bring everything I think can help."

While we waited, we continued to brainstorm solutions. Cory was a good spell weaver, yet he hadn't been able to weave anything that worked against the active spell. Every so often, worry cast a shadow over his face. Did he feel that something was off about his magic? Or perhaps he worried that the wound would never heal.

Madison and I pulled our eyes from Cory to the Huntsmen who were approaching with their graceful determined walk and the indomitable look of warriors. A wave of magic accompanied them. Mephisto had abandoned his suit for dark jeans, a black t-shirt, and boots. The others were similarly dressed, as if it were their unofficial uniform. They glanced at the beheaded body of the hawk-shifter assassin as they moved past it. It didn't seem to disturb them. I'd been avoiding looking in that direction since it happened.

"I wouldn't be happy if they were coming for me," Madison said, taking the words out of my mouth as we watched the dark warriors approach. My attention was drawn to Benton, who flanked Kai. *What is the world's worst employee going to do? Slurp coffee and read a book while the others worked?*

Mephisto's lips lifted into a half smile at the inquiring look I gave Benton. I didn't say it, but my face certainly did: *Seriously, this guy?*

When we were face to face, Mephisto leaned into me, his

breath warm against my ear as he spoke. "I said I'd bring what I thought would help, and I did."

How's the laziest employee ever going to help? I kept my voice low. "I don't think coffee is going to help." There was much-needed humor in my voice, but it didn't lift my spirits.

His hands dropped to mine, stroking them. "He's a druid and was our advisor in the Veil. His knowledge is extensive and far superior to ours."

Advisor? He didn't look old enough to have lived here for fifty years and to have advised them during the years they were in the Veil.

"He is our advisor," Mephisto repeated in such a way that it had significance and yet was missing something. I searched my mind for everything I could recall of druids but found nothing that would justify Benton having immortality. He had to have it, since he looked to be in his midforties but had been with the Huntsmen both here and in the Veil. As with elves, there wasn't extensive knowledge about or accounts of druids' existence, other than them being known as educators, protectors of harmful and destructive magic, and advisors. They were attributed with the compilation of many of the magic books. Like elves, druids were thought to no longer exist, or at the very least no longer be practicing.

In a world of magic, when your own magic is limited, it's easy to be considered irrelevant.

I looked over at Benton, who'd followed Simeon, Kai, and Clayton to where Arius lay. Clay's attention was split between me, Mephisto, and Benton, who was assessing Arius's injuries. Distracted by the new information, I was trying to reconcile Benton being a druid.

"I've never met a druid before," I admitted.

"I'm sure you have but didn't recognize what they were," Mephisto explained. "They have no place here. You have the STF, who manages your most dangerous magical objects. The magic here is just a fraction of ours, so there's not as much use for druids here. I suspect on this side of the Veil they live a human existence. Benton's our pledged advisor. Although his magic is weaker, his knowledge is worth the pledge we share with him. When he's no longer willing or able to serve his purpose, the pledge will be severed."

Answering my inquiring gaze, he added, "Their pledge is linked to our magic and our immortality. When they are no longer willing to honor the pledge, they are laid to rest. Because most of them have outlived the mortal life. But I'm sure Benton will stay on for the next Huntsmen. For now, he's pledged to us, which is why when he was exiled, he found us and has been with us ever since. He's invaluable. You know, druids discovered the praseodymium metal that's used to make Obitus blades."

"Is it the metal, or are the symbols on them bespelled to make gods vulnerable to the Obitus blade?" I asked.

A modest smirk peaked and vanished before his tongue slid over his lips and his teeth gripped his lips. *Come on, this isn't the time to hold back information.*

"Which one is it?" I urged.

"The symbols usually found on the blade or the grip designates it as an Obitus blade. It's the metal that kills. The symbols are just a denotation. If a blade can kill us, we'd like to know."

What the hell.

If I ever got hold of an Obitus blade, I wouldn't have it marked. The element of surprise, I thought, dropping my eyes to the floor and hoping my thoughts wouldn't show on my face. But when I looked up, Mephisto was scrutinizing me.

"So undeniably Erin. You do own up to your dirty fighting," he said softly, without a hint of judgment. Perhaps there was some honor in admitting a person would do anything to walk away alive. Although he hadn't cast judgment, I did. Where was the line between trying to survive and violating the rules of engagement, something Malific was infamous for?

The sun was setting, and Benton must have directed them into the house because Simeon picked up the massive creature Arius with the ease of lifting a small child. Elizabeth sneered in my direction. Even with the offered help from the Huntsmen and a druid, I'd curried no favor with her. Her unforgiving gaze sharpened and was split between me and Nolan. On him, it softened, displaying an unconditional sibling endearment with remnants of empathy and affection. I was given none of those feelings.

Mephisto's jaw tightened as he cast a disapproving look at her.

She scoffed. "Hunter, don't be so possessive of Malific's daughter. She has her mother's gift and her empowerment of lure. You're not the only one she's enchanted."

We followed her gaze to Asher, who was trailed by a small but menacing-looking army of shifters. Asher scanned the area, looking at Elizabeth, the assassin shifter's body that we hadn't moved, and the bloodstained ground. His face tilted and he inhaled. From his expression, I assumed he knew the gist of what happened.

The contentious look that Asher leveled at Mephisto had me quickly meeting him before he could get to us.

"What's going on?" I asked, doing a quick head count of the people with him. Twenty-five.

"What's going on? I called and your phone went to voicemail."

"It must have died," I told him. It had been nearly out of charge when I called Mephisto, and the cracked screen couldn't have helped.

"There were reports that you looked distraught leaving your home. You've been here for hours. I was concerned." He looked back at the body.

"Concern is bringing one person, maybe two." I stepped

closer, hoping that only he could hear, and whispered, "Twenty-five people is an act of aggression." I found myself trying to use humor to slice through tension so thick and heavy it was suffocating.

Asher's eyes snapped to Mephisto. "I'm feeling pretty damn aggressive. Erin, what's going on? The smell of blood is overwhelming and the unfamiliar magic can't be ignored." He shot another glance in Mephisto's direction before turning to look at the body again. His attention finally moved to Nolan, who was standing a few feet from Elizabeth.

"Your heart is racing and you reek of fear," he noted.

"Stop smelling things. Stop smelling me. Do you have any idea how unsettling that is?"

"Do you know how unsettling it is to have to rely on those things to know you're in trouble, because you keep me in the dark?" Anguish and hurt edged into his voice and revealed themselves even more in the way he looked at me.

"You know the whole sordid tale, Asher. My mom's an Arch-deity. I'm the result of a plan she has to use my death to release her from her prison. My dad wanted to use me to weaken her as punishment for killing his people. She's free now." Recounting the situation left me with a dank feeling.

"How did she get free, Erin?"

I frowned and rubbed my hands on my face. He took hold of them and brought them to his lips and kissed the backs of them, then rested them against his chest.

Why the hell is he so calming? I was convinced there had to be more to their magic than just shifting.

"How was she released?" he asked again. Previously, he'd accepted it was a confidence that I couldn't share, but now his tone indicated that was no longer an acceptable answer.

"It's complicated."

"I have time."

"I don't."

Frustration coated his features and he inched in so close, I thought he was going to kiss me. I was prepared to turn away. But Asher's focus snapped to the person behind me. Based on Asher's sneer I knew who it was. Mephisto.

"Erin, I'll be in the house if you need anything," Mephisto offered from behind me.

I nodded. But he didn't move until I acknowledged it aloud.

The Mephisto-provoked sneer remained on Asher's face. "Erin, there's a dead body just a few feet from us."

"She killed him," I blurted. I hated my voice for breaking. And I despised that the thought of Malific doing the same to me caused me so much fear. Angry tears welled in my eyes and an urge for retaliation against Malific rose in me.

Asher waited patiently for me to continue and I told him about Malific's parting words to Elizabeth.

"I need to stay, to make sure Arius is okay."

"If he's not?"

"I don't know."

Asher nodded. "Exactly," he said. "If you come with me, I promise Malific won't hurt you. No one will." He said it so earnestly, I knew he truly believed it.

"This is because of me. I have to stay and make it right."

"No, it's because of your sociopathic mother and your father's misguided mission for revenge. You owe nothing to anyone other than yourself. Get Cory and Madison and let's leave."

I gave him an inquiring look. How did he know they were here? They'd followed Simeon into the house.

He gave me a wayward grin.

"Scent?" I asked.

He nodded.

"Cory's injured, too. A small one. The arrow went into his shoulder. It's not healing properly." He had to know that I would do anything to make sure Cory was okay.

"Come with me, we'll figure out something."

"I have a better chance of figuring it out with Mephisto."

Asher flinched as if I'd slapped him, and part of me felt like I had.

"Because he's like your mother?"

I stilled, trying to ensure my body language wouldn't betray me. "Ask him?"

"I don't need to." Asher stepped back. Despite my effort, I had inadvertently given him the information. He moistened his lips and several beats of time passed before he spoke.

"I'm not going to let you be killed because of misplaced guilt. You have twenty-four hours to fix it…" The command lingered in the air.

"Look, Asher. We have the same goal. We're both on 'Team Keep Erin Alive.'" My frustration was misdirected and I knew it, but it didn't stop me from reacting. "You don't *tell* me what I need to do. I'm not your pack. I don't follow your orders."

"You'll follow these," he responded in a low, ominous whisper.

"*Really?* So, I have twenty-four hours and then what? You're going to make me go with you?" It came out in a heated rush before I could tamp down my frustration. The moment it spilled out of me, I wished I'd worded it better. It was a challenge that pricked at the primality of his wolf. Never challenge a wolf and definitely not an Alpha.

He turned slightly to the small army in his command.

"Yeah," he said with such undeniable confidence that I knew without a doubt he'd successfully do it. He spoke with the self-assurance of a man who commanded hundreds and, if needed, he could enlist the help of the cat shifters.

"We're immune to magic. We have you to thank for that. I am indebted to you." Then he shrugged. "It's not just the debt. I like having you around and have every intention of keeping you alive because it's what I want. Before you even ask, yes, my want trumps your will." With the slightest move of his head, the shifters, with unified precision, turned and left.

I wanted so desperately to give him a piece of my mind for slathering his Alpha-ness all over everything. His brand of caring and intervention was pissing me off. It needed to be known that he was doing it wrong. I stood seething at his back.

"Well, that was dramatic," Cory said, walking up to stand beside me.

I blew the strands of loose hair that fell into my face. When that didn't work, I shoved them out of my face.

"He's so stubborn. So demanding," I complained. "I appreciate his help and concern, but he's Asher-ing the hell out of it. Why does he have to be that domineering and arrogant? It's so frustrating."

"Frustrating? Save your frustration for the unexpected. This is who he is. He's shown you that, so believe him. You're acting like it's your first time meeting him. He's just being Asher. Either you accept it or you don't."

"I don't remember him being like this," I said. That wasn't the truth. It was that my tolerance for it was lower. Usually I just dismissed his directives that were said with the confidence of a person who'd never been told no. Cory was right. Asher wasn't being any different. It was me. With everything quickly spiraling out of control, I was trying to grab hold of anything that I could handle.

"Are they having any luck?" I asked as we headed toward the house, aware that the Asher clock was ticking.

"No. Benton created a spell and they were able to return Arius to his imp form. He hoped it would neutralize whatever is happening with him."

From the rigidity in Cory's voice, it hadn't. Placing a hand on his arm to stop him walking, I examined his injury. It looked better than it had.

"Simeon was able to get it to close more, but it's still in a fragile state. Benton said the arrows had bane, a poison that slows healing, especially if whoever it hits doesn't have the ability to magically heal. So, it's better that it hit me than Madison. But even I couldn't heal it completely. Erin, the arrow was intended for you. A less-skilled magic weaver wouldn't have been able to heal it."

Which was even crueler, leaving an injury that wouldn't heal.

"Do you think it will heal completely?" I asked as we continued toward the house.

Before he could answer, I saw Arius's small pallid body lying on the sofa. The wound remained open. His breathing was labored and irregular. Elizabeth clasped his hands in hers as if she was offering her final goodbye. Her sorrow-filled eyes met mine and my chest clenched with guilt. It wasn't my fault, but I couldn't shrug off the burden of it.

CHAPTER 2

*B*enton stood in the kitchen studying the various books, including Mystic Souls, placed in front of me. Occasionally he examined the heads of the arrows that had struck Cory and Arius. His face twisted in concentration, Benton seemed to have aged years in the hours he'd been there.

Elizabeth stood and started walking toward Benton, changed her mind, and headed out the back door. The Huntsmen were in the corner talking; occasionally I could feel their eyes on me. Madison was seated on the sofa opposite Arius, dividing her attention between Benton, Cory, and Arius. The impassive look on her face made it difficult for me to read her thoughts. Was she afraid of what Elizabeth would do if Arius died? Or was she thinking about Malific? Catching me looking, she made an attempt at a reassuring smile, but it faltered and fell away.

The helplessness of not being able to do anything caused me to watch Elizabeth through the various windows as she slowly paced in circles around the house. Her lowered head and sagging shoulders made returning the hate she felt for me impossible. After giving her some time alone, I went after her. She was in the backyard, near the garden, peering at the fallow land I'd created when I found out she'd stolen the Amber Crocus—a plant that could kill vampires—from the Lunar Marked witches. They'd made the Amber Crocus and had been extorting the vampires for the purchase of it.

"I'm sorry this happened to Arius," I offered in a whisper.

She searched my face then let her eyes drop to the destroyed land. "Sorry? I knew that your birth would have consequences, I just never expected that they would affect me in this way." She forced a wan smile. "There are hints of my brother in you, but how much of who you are can be attributed to Malific?"

"None. Because neither one raised me. I'm a product of the people who did."

She made a small sound. "Yes, they did raise you. Your magic is elven and god. No matter what you choose to believe, Malific and Nolan are your foundation. Your magic. And you are the reason Arius might die." She inched closer to me, acute interest tethered along the lines of bemusement and fascination. "Where your mother uses violence to influence, your ways are diametrically different. You have charmed the cold and the callous." I assumed she was talking about the Huntsmen. "And tamed the wolf, giving you access to a very powerful pack." *Tamed the wolf? Asher?* Did she have any idea what tamed meant?

Her eyes traveled languidly along my face, assessing me. It was as if she saw layers of me and was attempting to pull them away. Not to see any depth; on the contrary, she appeared to be looking for something to support whatever was going through her mind. I kept shifting my eyes away from her intense scrutiny. It was a relief to see Nolan open the back door.

His brows drew together. "Are things okay?" he asked.

Expressionless, Elizabeth nodded. "They will be." She whispered something in their elven language and Nolan was thrown back into the house. A wave of patina encapsulated the house like a cocoon. I ran toward it and hit the field. Noticing the pale-yellow substance surrounding the house, I realized that her walk hadn't been to clear her head, to mourn and grieve in silence, but to imprison the people in it. Dropping to my knees, I tried to break the pattern, but with the ward erected, it remained cemented to the ground. The wispy magic that Nolan had previously used on me began to twine around me, luring me into slumber.

In a hurried move, I came to my feet, covered my ears, and erected my own ward.

"Erin, it's not the words that bespell you, it's the invocation. Cover your ears if you must, it won't stop the spell," Elizabeth informed me, walking around my sphere of protection.

"Elizabeth," Nolan yelled, pounding at the magical prison. He said several sharp things to her in their language and she returned it, the harshness of her voice matching his.

My searing look of anger had little effect on her. Her lips drew into a tight line and she shook her head at Nolan. "Your vengeance became your debt, your humanity your weakness, especially when it comes to magic. Your magic has never been a match for mine."

Mephisto had joined Nolan at the door, their faces contorted with strain as they attempted to break through the ward.

"Erin, I need you to say this," Nolan yelled, rambling off words in his language. I attempted to repeat them while keeping a careful eye on Elizabeth, who had resumed her trail around the circle of my ward. I felt confident she couldn't get through it, until she continued with her spell, making it difficult to concentrate on Nolan's words.

"You have your mother's arrogance," she taunted. My ward dropped. A heavy blanket of magic shrouded me. I was wrong; it wasn't the enchanting sleep that my father had lulled me into. His spell was a lullaby. This was a thrash of magic that hit me, knocking me to the ground with a thud.

CHAPTER 3

I awoke to near darkness, only the failing light of a glowstick giving any illumination. There were several inactive glowsticks tossed at my feet. Waving my hand, I attempted to use magic to draw them to me. Nothing. My stomach roiled with fear. I didn't have magic, and I was positive it had to do with the manacles on my arms. I patted for my phone. It was gone and so were my weapons. Picking up one of the glowsticks, I could make out that one of the manacles looked like my Palladium cuffs, and I was willing to bet the other restricted god magic. I tugged at the metal to the point of exhaustion, as if I could rip the cuffs off me. Giving in to the futility, I slumped.

But I refused to be helpless.

"I'm going to fucking kill you!" I screamed at the top of my lungs, doubtful that either my mother or my aunt could hear. But it was a promise that I had no intention of breaking. I snatched up the glowsticks and thought of the many ways I could do it. I was in a shed. Maybe near a farm. I thought the smell was compost, but the odor was too acrid. There wasn't anything but the rough plywood floor and a small sun window at the top of the building that I estimated to be eight feet above me. Even if I could reach it, I couldn't get through the window.

I sniffed again. The smell wasn't compost; it was crenin, used to distort a shifter's scent. A product I had placed on my list of tall tales. Crenin was effective but dissipated quickly, delaying an object being found for maybe a half hour at best. Perhaps that was what Elizabeth was counting on, since I was provided with a blanket, four large bottles of water, and a bag of trail mix. Nothing more than that. Maybe she expected me to be found by then.

Would Asher look for me? He'd given me twenty-four hours. Would anyone call to let him know? Cory would, even if it was through Alex.

I screamed louder, banged at the door, yanked on it, but it wouldn't give.

Knocking against it, I tested the thickness. And kicked. Nothing. I kicked again. Nothing. My kicks came harder, driven by a rage that consumed me. When I was done, there was just a small dent. I kicked again, harder. The door wouldn't give.

Don't just kick wildly, Erin. They have to be targeted strikes.

I struck the same area again and again until my heel ached and my muscles cramped. Slipping into the corner where the supplies were, I opened the water, assessed my limited supplies, and again tried to figure out a way to escape.

I was sitting on the ground, taking a sip from one of the water bottles, when the door opened, a dusting of particles moved through the air, and a breeze of strong magic filled the room. It didn't surprise me in the least to be enclosed in a barrier.

Elizabeth sauntered in and eyed the enclosure she'd placed me in.

When she finally spoke, her voice was a barely audible whisper. "Arius is fine. I've confirmed it with Nolan. But I have made an enemy of the Huntsmen, or rather of the one who goes by Mephisto. I could hear his threats over the phone." She blew out a sigh. "I suppose, if I make an enemy of one, I've made one of all." Her lips beveled into a frown as she paced idly. "I've been companions with Arius longer than you've been alive. He followed me here when I could no longer tolerate being in the Veil, reliving the horrors of people like me being murdered. It's like the earth has a way of keeping the memory of it in the soil, in the air. The pain carries on the wind. So I'm here. Living as much as one can in this world."

Her scowl deepened. No one who experienced the Veil seemed to be fond of living on this side of it. I knew of its beauty. Mephisto had helped me see it, but he'd also told me of the horrors that dwelled within the Veil. Yet the horrors didn't seem bad enough to stop its former inhabitants from yearning for it.

Elizabeth stopped pacing, her head canted as she studied me. "I don't quite see the appeal. You're attractive but not a true beauty. I've seen the type of ethereal beauty who enchants men in such a way they would destroy cities in her honor if it'd satisfy her. You don't possess such beauty." She moved even closer to the barrier. "Perhaps some may find your ways charming, proven by the fact you've beguiled both Mephisto and Asher. I find you crude and lacking a certain je ne sais quoi that would make you even remotely fascinating. I just don't see the appeal. You're lauded for your ingenuity and tenacity, but can't the same be said of vermin?"

Her gaze traveled from my feet all the way back to my eyes, where she held my gaze in a cold grip. "I wish I could see what intrigues them so. I see nothing but a woman capable of great violence. Just a lovely brute."

"Well at least I have lovely going for me." I smirked, enjoying the irritation that skimmed across her face.

She sneered. "There's no sophistication in your humor."

I felt every pound of her heavy judgment as she backed away.

"I suppose you possess a dedication that can be admirable, and an ability to love intensely. But any monster is capable of that. Malific once loved, yet it never tamed the monster within her. Just made her a terror who managed to suppress it when dealing with one person." She shook her head slowly. "Nolan is convinced you are so much more. I wish to see it, but I don't."

"Are you finished?" I asked after a period of silence had elapsed. I took her cold response as an implicit yes. "You're a bitch. And I say that with all the unsophistication and crudeness I possess. You may not have done the things that Malific has, but you've done far worse than I ever will. You're handing me over to her, knowing that once she has her full power, she'll return to her old ways. You've built a life on cruelty and trickery, providing help only after the person has made a fool's deal that leaves them in situations far worse than necessary, and all for your barbaric satisfaction. There's nothing savvy or remarkable about your ways. You're just a trickster." I sneered at her. "You can prance around in your eclectic clothing, but you're nothing more than a savage in a tuxedo." I went on to relay every rumor I'd heard about her, every instance of her cruelty.

She'd settled into a dark calmness, a slight curl to her lips as she listened.

"Since you felt the need to attack me, let me tell you that you're a self-indulgent woman-child with an unearned confidence and sense of entitlement. We've all been through things. I'm a living example of that. Yet you sit in judgment of me. Since I'm feeling pretty pissed and exceptionally petty, let me tell you this as well: In the wrong lighting, you're no prize yourself. You wouldn't be out of place among the *Lord of the Rings* hobbits. Yoga pants aren't flattering on everyone, especially when you have a pancake butt."

Okay, the last part just made me seem juvenile, but I didn't care. Her insults had grated into me so much, I was raw.

She scoffed. "As I said before, unsophisticated and crude. For your information, my foolish and ill-informed niece, it isn't tricks and snares. It is justice. If they come to me in an attempt to circumvent a debt to a demon, I remove the debt, but I leave an indelible mark to let others know of their transgression. One asks for my help with a failed or ineffectual love spell, I grant them the wish but leave them spelled, unable to see the other person's beauty. When they look at them, they see a vile creature that now loves them. They attempt to take away that person's volition, I take away something from them. I'm more than the WIB misnomer. I'm the justice, the balance needed in a world where magic exists."

I waved a hand at the cage she had me in. "How is this just and balanced?"

"I will make it so, not for you but for my brother. It is his affection that drives my decision, not Malific's daughter. We've wasted far too much time, so I need you to listen to me. I'm about to remove your cuffs." The hard coolness in Elizabeth's gaze remained. "You, daughter of Malific"—I cringed at the accusation and disdain that weighted the title she gave me— "have two options. You can fight me, which will be your natural inclination, or you can allow me to help you and offer me an opportunity to make it right with Nolan."

I shifted my gaze from her, refusing to allow her look of sorrow to tamp down the anger and rage I felt toward her.

"When she gets here, I will remove your manacles." She tossed a knife to the ground, the one she must have taken from me earlier. "Remember its location because you will need to get to it quickly." Then she held up a piece of paper in front of the barrier. "Read it."

The four words on it weren't familiar. I assumed they were elven and just sounded them out.

"Again." She corrected one of the words, and after I'd said it to her satisfaction, she let the paper fall next to the knife. She quickly whispered a spell and the knife and paper became invisible.

"I must hold up my part of the oath, which is to give you to her. When I tell you to, prick your finger, say the spell, and you will be cloaked." She bent down and I watched as she made quick work of putting sigils in front of me. "Remember the location of the knife and the spell," she said again.

I studied her, wishing I possessed the ability to detect dishonesty. Should I trust her? I remembered the many looks that she and Nolan shared. They loved each other. I couldn't ignore her sorrow at the realization that she might have irreparably damaged their relationship.

"Trust me or not, at least I'll know that I tried to help you." Her lips formed a tight, defiant line.

"I don't trust you, but I don't have a lot of alternatives."

"I don't think you're worth saving," she snapped in return.

"Such hostility toward my daughter." Malific's melodious voice held a hint of amusement. "Have you diverted your hate for me toward her?"

Elizabeth scanned the area behind her. "You're alone?"

"Just as you requested. This level of distrust can't be good for you."

"When you trust a viper, you can't blame it when it strikes."

"I take no offence. It is the viper's bite that is most feared. That bite gives them power. It precedes them in tales and serves as a warning. A viper never requires an explanation for its actions or offers apologies for what it is. And I make none for what I am."

"Of course you don't. But I've protected mine; that's all that matters to me."

It was hard to hate Elizabeth at that moment. Her words served as a reminder of the lengths to which I would go to protect mine.

Malific breezed over to my magical cage, studying me with the same regard one does an ant scurrying across the sidewalk carrying a piece of food. She unsheathed her sword with a level of dispassion that made her seem devoid of humanity. A violence-seeking, power-lusting, callous husk of a person. How could a mother hold so little regard for her child? When she looked at me there wasn't a semblance of compassion. Could she not see even a glimpse of herself in me or remember that I was the child she carried and bore?

"You *are* the monster that I was warned about," I snapped, looking at the sword. She planned to kill me while I stood before her defenseless. Hate wasn't a strong enough word for what I felt for her.

"You're old enough to understand that one needs to be the king among lions. In the Veil, it is predominately lions, and if you don't ensure that you are the king, then you just become prey. Surely, if you are as close to the Huntsmen as I've been led to believe, you know of what I speak. They did everything possible to ensure they were predators and never prey."

"They did it because it was their job."

Her smile was cruel and her look condescending. "When one is that good at their job, it's not because they enjoy justice but rather because they revel in domination. The thrill of the hunt and glory of the kill. Same beast, different label."

Hiding the disappointment was difficult and I struggled to mask it. I was tired of the dark complexities of the Veil spilling into my life.

Elizabeth slid between me and Malific.

"You will not murder her in cold blood the way you did

the shifters and…" She left the elves unsaid, but the ache in her voice said it well enough.

Elizabeth dropped the barrier and slid closer to me, then re-erected it with enviable deftness and speed. I wondered if that level of proficiency was a result of needing to feel protected at all times. She removed my manacles with narrow-eyed apprehension, as if she expected me to attack. Then she backed away.

"I'm dropping the field," she announced. When she did, the restricted magic surged through me. I thrusted it into my protective wall.

"This is not our deal. You have not given her to me, if we are separated by this," Malific hissed, waving her hand at the protective field. Sheathing her sword, she pressed her hands against it. Her face strained with exertion. The wall undulated, a multitude of little bubbles forming along its border, but it held.

It was a bad time to taunt her, but oh, how I wanted to. Out of my periphery, I could see Elizabeth giving me a nod. Her hand pressed against my protective bubble, shattering it into fragments that drifted in the air like debris. I went for the knife, cut my hand, and recited the spell. The sleeping serpent that wound around Elizabeth's arm came to life, quickly striking Malific's arm, leaving a trail of blood as words spilled from Elizabeth's lips.

I moved, thinking Malific wouldn't see me. Her cruel eyes snapped in my direction and followed my every movement, like a predator ready to pounce. Elizabeth had lied. I wasn't cloaked. Malific drew her sword. Magic clung to the air, forming a heavy blanket. I couldn't see the magical twines that formed a network of lines between me and Mother Dearest, but I could feel it. Malific's face flushed; she bared her teeth and whipped around. Her anger was explosive.

"You deceitful bitch." Her thirst for violence and vengeance was palpable as she readied her sword to strike, only to be restricted by her magical oath. She was unable to hurt Elizabeth once the agreement had been satisfied. I speculated that the agreement had been that she had to give me to Malific, which Elizabeth had fulfilled.

Elizabeth closed the minute distance between them, her face bright with satisfaction. "One only has to feel the sting of the viper's bite once before realizing that their only protection is to become its mirror image. Go ahead, kill your daughter." She turned her back on Malific, who glared at her. "One strike, two birds. You two are as one now. If she dies, so do you. If she hurts, so do you."

Malific's eyes closed and her features hardened. "I vow to find a way to break my oath to you, and when I do, the very people that you sought to protect will feel my wrath. Everyone with even an ounce of elven blood will pay for your betrayal. And Nolan will be the first. I will kill him in front of you. You will be the lone survivor, forced to carry the burden of their deaths and know it was because of you."

Elizabeth scoffed. "Get to know your daughter. You were right about her; she is a clever one. And her aptitude for violence and chaos rivals yours. I suspect that she'll find a way to unbind herself from you before you discover a way out of your oath. And when she does, your wrath is something I won't have to worry about for very long. If not her, the Huntsmen will do what they do best. You won't live long enough to be of any consequence." With that, she pressed her hand to a stone secured around her neck and disappeared in a swirl of magic.

I shoved the knife into my waist sheath and started out the shed as well. Malific blocked my way.

Emboldened by the new situation, I said, "Move."

"Do you believe you have the upper hand, girl?" she snarled.

"I believe you're not going to kill me. You want to, I can

25

see it in your eyes, but you won't. So, move the hell out of my way."

Malific hissed in a breath and yanked the knife from my sheath. She drove it into her hand, holding my gaze the entire time. The pain nearly collapsed my legs. I looked down at my own hand to see an open wound. Blood gushed from it and ran down my fingers. My stomach lurched. I gasped back the bile that rose in my throat. Tears from the pain gathered in my eyes. There was no way I could have prepared myself for her action. Her cruelty. The seemingly symbiotic relationship she had with pain. She was a martyr to it, seeing it as a means to an end.

I doubled over and swallowed before sucking in a few rough breaths as the agony dulled enough for me to heal the wound. I restored my hand and in turn, the magic repaired hers as well. I wasn't sure if Elizabeth had done me any favors or had penalized me for the sin of being Malific's daughter.

"Find a way to unbind us," Malific hissed. "You're just a novice in the art of battle. I am master of it. Don't make me show you the many ways I can best you."

She grabbed me by the hair, pulled me close, and kissed my forehead. Before I could react with the punch she so rightfully deserved, she was gone.

CHAPTER 4

I dropped to the ground and sat as everything that had occurred over the day rampaged through my mind, trampling my will. Exhausted and emotionally depleted, the motivation to leave wasn't there.

Elizabeth's pronouncement that I'd kill my mother taunted me. Living in the many shades of gray had only confirmed what she believed me to be. It was overwhelmingly ironic that Elizabeth had forced me into a situation where I would have to be as cruel and ruthless as Malific in order to defeat her.

As unrealistic as I knew it was, I just wanted to lie back and will my life to be simpler. Instead I sat with my face resting in my cupped hand.

Erin, you can't stay here, I coaxed.

I knew that, but where did I go from there?

I forced myself to stand, my legs quivering with fatigue, then I trudged out of the shed and took in the surroundings. I had no idea where I was. I could make out a small house about twenty yards away, but seeing how unkempt the tall grass was and the crowd of trees, I wasn't inclined to go that way. I was sure if I walked long enough, I'd come to a road, then I'd have a better grasp of my bearings. The sun was still in the sky, and since I didn't know where I was, I went east.

I had to force myself to speed up. Each step felt like a death march, causing me to move molasses slow. I gave myself unenthusiastic pep talks. *You can do it, Erin. It's fine, you've seen and dealt with far worse than Malific. Once you get home, you'll devise a plan and everything will be right as rain.*

I was feeding myself pure BS. Usually, I looked at the potential for defeat, gave it the finger, and soldiered through. I wasn't sure that was possible this time. I hadn't dealt with anyone nearly as bad as Malific, who could walk through fire as if slipping through a waterfall and plunge a knife through her own hand without flinching. Once I got home, what was going to miraculously happen to make things right and feasible?

The pep talks weren't working and I was spiraling. I would call Dr. Sumner once I got home. As I walked and made actionable plans, the light-melon color of the sun eclipsed. A shade fell over me. I turned around. Commanding the sky, large cerulean wings intermingled with the various hues of blue, making them look ombre. Kai descended. Once grounded, his wings snapped away.

"I found you."

Okay, let's just go ahead and state the obvious: You have beautiful blue wings and a seraphic face.

"Hi," I said. "You're just flouting the rules and flying around the city, huh?" It was a poor attempt at levity.

He fell in step with me. "We always flout the rules when it comes to you." With his voice neutral and his face indecipherable, I didn't know what to make of his statement.

"Sorry."

He shrugged. "You don't look well. I should get you home."

"I'm fine. Just tired and hungry," I said, giving him a half-truth. I wasn't fine. My hand still throbbed despite healing it;

I needed to learn to take away the aches and pains the way that Mephisto did. Tired was in the rearview and I was barreling toward exhaustion. Feeling overwhelmed and deflated wasn't something I enjoyed.

"Let me get you out of here," Kai suggested.

"The reason you don't fly outside is so you're not discovered, right?"

He nodded. From his profile, I could see the pained yearning. Was this why they worried about him? Were winged people predominately in the sky, and walking everywhere made for a pitiful, mundane existence?

"I appreciate you finding me, but we should walk. Call Madison or Cory. They'll pick us up."

"No need. The others will be here." He increased his pace, using the few inches he had over me to devour stretches of ground. Keeping pace was a challenge. He looked back periodically, and finally, when I had fallen too far behind, he moved in that dreadful way they did and was suddenly in front of me. He scooped me into his arms.

I would not end my day being damseled and carried out to the main road, for all to see, by an ethereal-looking winged god. It felt like I had surrendered to Malific.

"Put me down."

"You're tired and moving slow. It's slowing me down. And I don't like the look of your face."

"Thanks. Sorry my face is so offensive," I shot back, squirming out of his hold.

"You were grimacing. Since you live in a pen of filth, I know there isn't much that bothers you, so I know that something is wrong with you now."

Pen of filth? Why don't we have some quiet time? You keep your insults to yourself and I promise not to junk-punch you.

"Carrying me like this makes me feel—" My voice broke. "I'd like to walk."

He quickly put me down and stepped away. The heaviness of his appraisal made me avert my eyes. He turned around. "You can cry now."

"Don't make it weird, Kai." I started walking, moving quickly ahead of him. Spite was a good motivator, and having him pick me up and cradle me in his arms made me determined not to let Elizabeth or Malific reduce me to that.

Eventually I fell back behind him, watching him navigate the unlevel terrain with his earthbound grace, a reminder that he was reduced to walking when he usually soared in the air. We moved along the barely discernible path to a single-lane road, where we were met by four awaiting cars.

Mephisto in a matte-black Range Rover was expected. Clayton was in the passenger seat. On the opposite side of the road were three cars filled with shifters, Asher's 911 in the front.

Instead of looking at them, I focused on Simeon across the street, partially visible through the thicket of trees, hanging out with a family of deer. I was going to hang out with Bambi and her family and an animal-whisperer god.

Traversing the street, I gave a small wave, intended for everyone, feeling the intensity of Asher's gaze as if he was staring at me through a scope. Mephisto's look was hard and penetrating. It wasn't that I didn't want to make a decision, I just had no idea which one to make.

When I was scared and locked in the shed, Asher was the first person who came to mind. He commanded hundreds of shifters who were immune to magic.

Mephisto, a god, had violated their established rules and practices by allowing Kai to fly, for the second time, to find me.

I couldn't choose one without insulting the other.

Instead of addressing the problem, I became overwhelmingly interested in the family of deer and whether I could communicate with them. It was just magic. I could turn into a cat; was it too big a leap to assume that I could speak with animals?

At my approach, the smallest deer of the group of three looked up with wide-eyed fear, readying to bolt, until Simeon said something. It continued to scrutinize me but lowered itself to the ground.

"Pet him," Simeon suggested. "Gently." He covered my hand and guided me to apply the right pressure and technique. For a bunch who lived in the forest and ate leaves, they were quite finicky about the way they were touched.

Out of my periphery, I saw Asher give a small signal, and the row of cars parked behind him left. He stayed.

"Which spell is it that allows you to talk to them?"

Simeon considered it, as though what he did was so interwoven with his magic that it was absurd that it would be linked to a spell.

"It's like Wynding and glamours. You either can do it, or not. I wish to speak to them, and I can."

Cool. I wished to speak to Bambi because he was freaking adorable and... Nothing. A whole lot of nothing.

We sat in silence for a long time, me willing a conversation with Bambi.

"You speak in English?" I asked.

"Whichever language I choose, they will understand it."

I willed it again and then said, "Hi, little one, will you stand?"

Black marble eyes looked back at me and he didn't move, but I had the distinct feeling me concentrating so much on trying to communicate with him was changing the way I was stroking him and he didn't appreciate it.

Great, my deer was high maintenance. What were mama and papa deer like? Maybe they wouldn't be so judgmental about my petting skills.

"Maybe you should practice more," suggested Simeon.

After several moments, my can-do spirit was met with

31

failure. And as I continued to try to communicate with my judgy diva fawn, I couldn't ignore Simeon's withering gaze.

"I don't think I can do it," I said.

"Yet your goal has been achieved. You've delayed making a choice."

It wasn't as if I believed my actions weren't as transparent as glass, but did Mr. Observation have to point out the obvious?

"I'm curious about my abilities," I countered.

"Perhaps, but discovering this one was only secondary to your true objective."

Returning his attention to the deer family, he said something in what I recognized as the language Mephisto had used with his lawyer. The family stood and gave their good-byes by nudging him with their noses before walking deeper into the forest.

"Choose the Alpha wolf," Simeon suggested, coming to his feet and dusting the dirt from his pants. I studied him.

"Is that what *you* want or what you think is best?"

"Both." Mr. Observation tended to be blisteringly tactless and brutally truthful. I finally stood. His suggestion only made the decision harder. People have that little stubborn jackass problem-starter that dwells deep inside them: when someone insists they go left, it sparks every desire in their being to go right. My problem-starter was a cantankerous bi-yatch and was pushing me to run straight to Mephisto just to spite Simeon.

Before I could ask about what was really concerning me, which was why the Huntsmen were so committed to keeping me and Mephisto apart, I spotted my car easing up the road. Madison was driving and Cory was in the passenger seat. Once it was parked between Asher and Mephisto, I fought the grin threatening to emerge. And held it even as I saw Cory's brow hitch, his eyes bouncing between both men who were out of their cars and leaning against them.

The men tracked my movement with unabated concentration. I glanced in their direction once after feeling the weight of it press into me.

Even Madison gave them both a cursory look before driving off. "That was intense," she admitted.

"More intense than when Elizabeth finally let us out of the ward?" Cory asked.

"No, that was a crapfest. Violent promises, magic, and rage."

"What happened?"

Cory huffed. "Elizabeth had the audacity to come back and get Arius after he was healed. Benton had come up with a spell and had me, Nolan, and Mephisto try it. Then at the same time, a metallic smoke puffed out of Arius. His wounds and the one on my shoulder completely healed. He sat up, giving us one of his disapproving self-important looks. You know, his favorite one where he looks down his nose. Then an hour later, Elizabeth glided into the house as if she hadn't abducted you and imprisoned us. She had what I guessed was one of Malific's henchmen with her. I don't think it was an Immortalis. He escorted Arius out and Mephisto told Elizabeth she should say her goodbyes to him and Nolan because she may never see them again." Cory scratched at the light hairs on his chin. "I thought he was implying that Malific would betray her. He wasn't. He looked scary as fuck."

My mouth dropped open. I had a hard time imagining him saying that. Or did I? They'd killed the Immortalis, and people in the Veil feared them, so was it impossible to think he'd make a threat and not follow through? Remembering Malific's comments about the Huntsmen, I wasn't sure.

"Are we sure they were the good guys behind the Veil?" Madison asked.

I didn't respond and she noticed.

"I really thought he was going to grab Simeon's blade and

take off her head. I'm not confident he wouldn't have if not for the others putting distance between them."

It was hard to feel sorry about threats against her, especially recalling her laundry list of insults.

"She told Mephisto that she hoped his last words to you were good because if he touched her, he wouldn't have to worry about Malific killing you, she'd do it. As things stood, Elizabeth planned on returning you home. That stopped the threats and had everyone waiting. Then she told Nolan she had protected him, and you, and that he had to trust her," Cory said.

"After being locked in the house by her magic," Madison added when Cory paused, "we weren't exactly in a trusting mood, but Nolan seemed to believe her. It eased some of the tension. They said something we didn't understand and then he wished her safety."

"She was gone before he could respond. Mephisto tried to Wynd out but her ward kept him from doing it. We spent a little over an hour still locked in," Cory provided. "Then the ward fell. I assumed it was once things with you had been finished. After we were released, I called Alex and told him to tell Asher you were missing. I hoped he'd get to you before Elizabeth could. I trust him a hell of a lot more than I trust Elizabeth. But since you're here, I guess she was being honest."

"Sort of. Technically she did give me to Malific to satisfy the oath, but then she bound us together." I went on to tell them about Malific's big-girl tantrum, her promise to break the oath, and her threat to kill anyone with any elven blood in them. I didn't go into detail about the binding, saving it for later. It needed to be explored in depth and I didn't want to relive Elizabeth's deception at that moment.

"Damn bloodthirsty psychopath," Madison ground out.

"A sadist, too. She drove a knife through her hand, just to

make me feel pain. To show me it doesn't bother her as much as it would bother me."

Madison slammed on the brakes, pulled to the side of the road, and put the car in park. She squeezed between the seats and looked at my hand.

"Erin, no." Her eyes glistened and she blinked several times. "I'm sorry. We tried to break the ward and get to you." She looked at my healed hand and her brows inched together in question.

"I have my own magic, remember?" I'd lived so long without it, people were bound to forget I now had it. And that they didn't have to worry about me struggling to obtain any scrap of magic. But unfortunately, me getting magic came with Malific issues. "I'm fine, Maddie."

All the sympathy and misplaced and unnecessary guilt didn't stop her from glaring at me for the name.

"What do we do now?" Cory asked.

"I'm bound, which means Malific won't kill me. In fact, she'll protect my life. But after our exchange of words, I have a feeling that when I am killed, she wants to do the honors."

Madison had started driving again. I inserted a lot of nonchalance in my shrug, but I could tell by their faces they understood the gravity of the situation.

CHAPTER 5

*B*ecause Madison's preferred cheese and black olive pizza tended to send Cory into connniptions, I thought we were safe getting burgers. I'd gotten so used to the way she ate her burgers, it never dawned on me how truly odd it was until a baffled Cory watched her remove the top bun and place a neat grid of fries atop the burger before covering it again with the bun. I grinned as Cory's lips puckered, fighting the urge to comment. Madison, feeling his gaze on her, lifted her eyes to meet his as she took a bite.

Cory had given me his fries and had settled for a lettuce-wrapped burger. A. Lettuce. Wrapped. Burger. And he had the audacity to judge Madison. Getting injured by an assassin, watching my mother behead said assassin for his failure to do his job, and being imprisoned by my aunt hadn't warranted a cheat day?

"No one eats their fries like that!" he finally said.

"That's demonstrably wrong. I do. And the last time I checked I am a 'one,'" Madison countered in a cloyingly sweet voice that only served to further irritate him. It seemed to be a tacit agreement that we would have a moment of peace while eating and not discuss the day, so our conversation was pure frivolity.

Once the table had been cleared, we meandered, putting off the inevitable. It wasn't until Madison moved from the kitchen to the living room and took a seat that Cory and I joined her in the room.

"What happens now?" Madison asked, folding her legs under her on the sofa. Too wired, Cory wasn't able to sit. Within minutes of taking a seat he was up again, walking the length of the room and straightening pictures.

"What happened with the binding? I need to know everything," he said.

I went over it all, watching their expressions become increasingly grim.

"You helped with the spell?" Madison asked.

"Not knowingly. I thought Elizabeth was cloaking me. Instead, I helped her bind me to Malific."

"Do you remember the spell?" Cory asked.

I shook my head then pulled out the paper and placed it on the coffee table. "This was my part. I couldn't make out the spell she invoked."

Both Madison and Cory stared at the piece of paper. Madison's brows inched together as she attempted to make out the words. After studying it for a few minutes, she shrugged.

"Elven," I said. Something I couldn't translate, but I knew two people who could. It forced me to ask the question I'd been debating since they'd picked me up. "Nolan didn't want to come with you all?"

"No," Cory offered. "He blames himself for Elizabeth's actions and he didn't think you'd come with us if he was present."

Giving me a wry, joyless smile, Cory sat next to me and placed his hand on my leg. "I know what he did was all types of screwed up, but I don't think he's a bad person. Revenge, grief, anger, they can blind anyone. Sometimes their actions are controlled by that. It isn't a reflection of who they really are. You have to know that."

It wasn't hard to see he was including his violent response to Harrison trying to give me to a demon. But it was a reflection of Cory. He had the ability to be violent when angered.

Part of me wanted to forgive Nolan and let bygones be bygones. If only it were that easy. I had lived my life wanting and needing magic. My adult life was spent thinking I was capable of murder and missing an important portion of the night of the *incident* because of it and unable to share that fact with anyone. And the knowledge that my birth was nothing more than a calculated move of Nolan's to exact revenge was unforgivable. How could I wipe the slate clean and pretend it never happened? Or have him in my life in spite of it?

In response to Cory's look, I gave him a noncommittal nod.

"Do you think we can do this spell and add 'Rescindo' to reverse it?"

I shrugged. "How would we know it worked? I don't think we want any ambiguity with the unbinding spell."

"Then you need to talk to your father. He might be able to help."

"Nolan," I corrected. Cory's lips pursed. "I'm not going to call him father. I have one."

"You have two," Cory corrected. He gave me a wry look when I didn't respond.

"I'll try to contact him tomorrow." It was a half-hearted commitment. Nolan was gone and I didn't have a way to contact him, and for some reason, he didn't strike me as the type of person I could find on social media. Tomorrow I'd do my own research. Maybe I'd find some way to contact him, maybe a global communication spell of some sort.

"May I stay here for a couple of days?" I asked Madison,

standing to stretch and diverting my gaze from them. I knew without seeing their faces they had matching suspicious expressions.

"Of course you can. But do you want to tell me who you're hiding from? Mephisto or Asher?"

"Malific." It was a BS answer, but I was willing to use her as a scapegoat. "If she strikes again, I want someone with me." I took the lie too far. When I looked at Cory and Madison, lips were twisted and faces held disbelieving glowers.

"You don't believe that for one moment," Madison challenged.

No, I didn't. Malific was about shock value and showmanship. A violent virtuoso. Her pleasure was in seeing others' response to her violence and demonstrating her tolerance for pain. It was her badge of honor. And an audience was a form of currency for payment for the show. She wouldn't hurt me without others there to witness how unaffected she was by the very pain that caused me to react.

"Why do you want to stay with me, really?" Madison asked.

A half grin lifted the corners of Cory's mouth.

Their scrutinizing eyes tracked my most minute movement.

"Does it have anything to do with the Alpha and the god waiting for you earlier and how gloriously happy you looked to see us drive up?" Cory coaxed.

Pushing away an errant strand of hair didn't offer nearly enough of a distraction. "No," I lied.

"Fatigue has made you bad at lying," Madison teased.

"It's not just them. They're a distraction—"

Cory beamed. "Yeah, they are," he said, his voice husky and laden with innuendo.

"Don't be proud of that," I scolded him. "I don't know what to do and they're less likely to show up here. I'll have some peace," I admitted. "And we can problem-solve the Malific situation uninterrupted."

"Oh my, both a god with seemingly limitless power and resources *and* a werewolf Alpha who's immune to magic and has an impressive reach and unchecked control in this city, want to protect me and are all up in my business?" Cory whined in a dramatic, high-pitched voice. "What *ever* will I do?" He threw his head back on the sofa and draped his arm over his forehead in the overly theatrical way some women did in old black-and-white films when they fainted onto a chaise.

"No one thinks you're funny," I barked, despite Madison's snort of laughter. "I didn't say it was a problem. It's complicated. Is Mephisto's interest in this selfless? Malific's the reason they're confined here. Asher and his pack are immune to magic, but so were the shifters in the Veil. Before I get them involved, I want to have a clear objective."

It was a good enough excuse and close enough to the truth. I did want a clear objective, but I had a feeling that Nolan and Elizabeth would be a significant part of the plan, not Asher and Mephisto. In fact, they might hinder more than help.

"Does it matter if Mephisto has an ulterior motive? He's a powerful god who has access to three other powerful gods. I don't see the problem," Cory said.

"There isn't a problem. I just need to have a plan. And this binding was done with elven magic. What can they do about that?"

"They have the Mystic Souls book. Maybe there's something in there," he suggested, but I had a feeling Cory just wanted to get his hands on the book again to get a few more spells. Even people who didn't use dark magic or who abided by the tacit agreements between covens and magic users wanted the advantage.

Whether they accepted my answer at face value or not,

their faces didn't betray it. Without further questioning, I went to the garage to grab my overnight bag out of the car trunk and quickly headed to the guest room to take a shower, positive that no matter how tired I was, I wouldn't sleep.

Sitting on the bed, I decided to do a quick search for Nolan on Facebook, which was useless because I didn't have a last name. A light knock on the door announced Cory. I placed my phone on the nightstand and invited him in. He was hesitant at first, his lips twisted to the side as he stood with a look of deep contemplation.

"We saved you from that choice, but eventually you're going to have to make it, Erin," he finally said, coming into the room and closing the door behind him.

"What?"

"Oh come on. I saw the relief on your face and it had nothing to do with you being locked in that shed."

I lay back on the bed, and he crawled onto it and lay next to me.

I stared at the ceiling. "I don't want to read more into it than there is. I know Mephisto's interest, but Asher…is it really anything more than him being grateful that I helped him with the animancer fae?"

That Cory was taking time to consider my question confirmed to me that my skepticism wasn't ridiculous. Asher and I had worked together for years and occasionally flirted, but Asher was known for flirting. I couldn't deny that there was something primal and captivating about shifters that was notably untenable. It made people cautious around them. The ambiguity of shifters and their ability to both lure and repel made dealing with them complicated. Questioning whatever it was that existed between me and Asher wasn't irrational.

"I don't think it has anything to do with the fae," Cory finally said. "If that was the case, he'd just compensate you financially and be done with it. The panic of you being missing was more than just a person appreciative of a favor. And then there's M."

"I think Clayton's the only person who can call him that."

Cory scoffed. "He's not here. I'll call him M if I want." But I knew he made a mental note not to irk a god over a name. "It's very obvious how he feels, but none of that matters because it's about you."

I huffed out a breath. There were more pressing things I needed to focus on.

"Or," Cory began slowly as he rolled onto his side to look at me, "you don't choose. Float the idea of polyamory and see what they say."

Even I didn't expect my laughter to end with me snorting.

"Okay, Ms. Puritan," he said.

I rolled onto my side to face him. "You know my views are far from puritanical."

Cory and I had very few secrets and our boundaries were nonexistent. Dating a vampire for any stint of time will abolish any limits a person may have. Me being, or having been, an adrenaline junkie as a way of dealing with my magic addiction made my adventures with Grayson salacious, even pretty damned tawdry.

"You've met them, right?" I asked Cory rhetorically. "Do you think the 'hey, let's be a throuple' discussion is going to work?"

"This coming from the woman who lives by the belief that you never know the answer unless you ask."

"In this case, I do know the answer." He did, too. "Besides, a throuple is three people dating each other. I've seen Asher and Mephisto together, and I can assure you they have no desire to date each other. I don't think they're bi."

Cory slapped his forehead. "Of course they're not gay or bi. They've met me, and who's choosing you after meeting me?"

If only I could convince myself he was joking.

I glowered at him, then rolled my eyes. "Well, I have modesty going for me. You'll be surprised how many people find that attractive."

"That's not true. That's a falsehood equivalent to the tired cliché of confidence is sexy. Yeah, confidence on an average or attractive person is sexy. Confidence on a trollish-looking person is just confusing. You can't help but wonder what that person has to be so confident about." He grinned at me.

"Looks fade. What are you going to do when your self-proclaimed model-good looks are gone?" I teased.

"Really? Total package here. Eyes, face, personality. I'm going to be appealing at ninety." He lifted his shirt to reveal defined delineations in his stomach that made up abs. And gave me a look that made me want to dispute it just out of sheer spite. Then winked. "You're trying to change the subject," he chastised. "So, who?"

I closed my eyes, but I didn't envision Mephisto or Asher. My mind drifted to Malific and her stabbing her own hand. How could I be dwelling on something as trivial as men while being bound to her?

Flashing a toothy smile, I kissed the tip of his nose. "I choose you."

"Clearly, I'm the best choice. But not an option. Answer the question, Erin."

"I don't know and I'm not sure I'm in a good headspace to make that decision," I admitted in a whisper, feeling the heaviness of the day come over me.

Giving me a tight smile, Cory nodded once and I closed my eyes, feeling the bed dip as he got up and only just hearing his soft goodnight as he closed the door.

CHAPTER 6

I was met with a low murmur of voices as I descended the stairs the next morning. I recognized Madison's laughter but not the other voice and was surprised to see her and Clayton seated at her kitchen table and a pastry box in the center of it. Kai was in the corner, quietly wiping down the newly installed bookcase. Madison was enjoying an old-fashioned donut.

Dear fates, don't let them all be cake donuts.

"Morning," I said, opening the box and immediately seeing a cinnamon bun. "Is this for everyone?" I asked, eyeing the oversized box. It was enough for us and the neighbors, too.

"Of course." Clayton's smile was tight and obligatorily polite. He shifted forward toward Madison to ask if he could try a piece of her donut.

Come on. It's an old-fashioned. The dullest and most unimaginative of donuts. It's the last-resort donut when all the frosted and filled ones are gone. No one needs to try it. Just imagine half-sweet boring dough. There you go.

While I poured myself a cup of coffee, Clay broke off a piece and made eating the most unimaginative donut a lot more interesting. He popped it into his mouth, his tongue gliding over his supple bottom lip and licking whatever was left off his thumb. Madison's attempt to avert her eyes from him lasted a whole three seconds.

"How was it?" she managed to eke out in a wispy rasp.

How was it? It seems like you two should be rolling over onto your sides and spooning. That's how it was.

Clayton was leaning forward to take another piece from her donut, when I wedged my way between them and looked into the box. "Oh, there seems to be four more old-fashioned. Here you go." Grabbing a napkin, I picked one and placed it in front of him.

"Thank you, Erin." Based on his smirk, he was on the receiving end of his own antics.

He took a small bite and ate it in stark contrast to the donut seduction that Madison had received. It was a good thing I intervened, because her nose and cheeks were contoured with the glow she got whenever she was embarrassed. Her gaze wandered back to him. With his long locs tied back, there was an unobscured view of vivid chestnut-colored eyes, appealing razor-sharp cheeks, and a broad face. Madison kept having to drag her attention from his full lips that delved into a bow.

Are you remembering the donut seduction or what? Stop looking at him.

It wasn't until she caught me watching her that she decided to refresh her coffee.

Splash yourself with cold water, too, Maddie.

"This is where you've been hiding," Clayton said, scrutinizing me. "M has been a little irritable today and I suspect it's because The Raven is missing."

"I'm not missing. I wanted to spend some time with Madison."

Madison's face went blank when he looked at her.

"How long do you plan to stay?" Clayton inquired.

I shrugged.

"Call him," Kai urged.

If he cared, I couldn't tell. His inflection was so casually neutral it seemed like an afterthought. Standing in front of Madison's new bookcase, he admired his work. It was beautiful. Modern-style molding at the top and bottom, recessed lights, and nickel hardware that complemented her décor. It was customized for Madison and her home and I couldn't imagine her purchasing one more fitting. It was so impressive I considered cleaning my place in hopes Kai would deem it worthy of a nice bookcase, too.

Madison managed to pull her eyes from Clayton. With a cinnamon roll in one hand and coffee in the other, I approached Kai, Madison close behind.

He gave my hand with the cinnamon roll a sharp, disapproving look. *I am so not getting a lovely new bookcase.*

"Do you like it?" he asked Madison, looking over his shoulder.

Madison stood next to him. "I love it. I can't believe you made it so quickly," she said, running her fingers over the details.

While she appreciated the craftmanship, Kai evaluated the room, as if looking for another project. This was his outlet. Would it be so bad if he could take to the air more often?

Both Clayton's and Kai's eyes snapped to the door when someone knocked. Was it Mephisto? Had they notified him? The idea irritated me. I was more relieved than I was willing to admit when Madison opened the door to Cory, who was carrying a tote of books and holding several pages of papers.

Cory stood in the middle of the room, silently assessing the situation and, I assumed, deciding if he should share the reason for his visit and whatever was on the papers. As the moments ticked by, things became increasingly awkward.

Kai and Clayton took the hint and gathered their things.

Before they could leave, Madison grabbed Kai's hand. "Thank you for the bookcase. It's beautiful. I feel awful not compensating you for it."

"It was my pleasure." His hand covered hers and the silence became palpably uncomfortable under Clayton's keen observation.

Breaking the silence, Clayton said, "We'll leave you to…" He trailed off as he discreetly looked at the papers in Cory's hand. Cory slid them into the tote bag.

"We're just weaving spells," Cory offered, a partial truth. That was my goal: to figure out how to undo the binding.

Kai, who seemed disinterested in anything that wasn't lumber—and maybe Madison—gave me a pointed look of disbelief as they left.

CHAPTER 7

*C*ory looked at the large box of pastries, then frowned at me when I shoved a donut into my mouth after finishing the cinnamon roll. Then he sneered at Madison, who had returned to the table and was picking at her cake donut.

"What! Why do you always have a problem with the food I eat?" she groused, taking a bite and making it obvious it was for his sake.

"Because whatever you eat is unnecessarily weird. Seriously, who eats a pizza with just black olives? And no one under seventy eats cake donuts. It's a waste of carbs."

Madison pressed her lips into a challenging glower. "I'm under seventy," she said, then took a big bite.

He smirked, leaned over, and kissed the top of her head. "It's a good thing you have the Disney princess thing going for you or you'd be terrifying," he said.

He dismissed my glare with a wink. He knew where to hit her. With her round face, nub nose, heavy-lidded round eyes, and skin that didn't have any visible pores, she was undeniably what people considered cute. A description she hated.

Her looks didn't make being taken seriously as head of a

department any easier. It was the reason she had cut off her full head of tightly coiled sienna curls, which were rapidly growing back. She tended to compensate by intentionally looking severe. A quasi-resting bitch face accompanied by a cruel smile, when needed. When relaxed it returned to full suppleness.

He'd struck a nerve. She glared at him as he got himself a cup of coffee and raised it in salute. A cake donut soared across the room and smacked against his head. It was only then that she returned his salute and raised her cup to him.

Their playfully contentious relationship would probably be more combative if it weren't for their shared affection for me and the lengths they would go to protect me. Madison did it because she loved me like a sister and technically, with all that had been discovered, should have been my sister. And she appreciated Cory risking his life by loaning me magic to ensure I'd never take it from anyone else.

After a long drink from his coffee, Cory blurted, "Shifter."

"What?" Madison and I responded in unison, obviously not privy to the train of thoughts that led to the outburst.

"Shifters are immune to magic, and they can't perform magic. The only thing they can do is shift."

"What does that have to do with anything?" I asked.

"If you and Malific were turned to shifters, wouldn't it break the bond?"

I considered it. How easy was it to change a person to a shifter? I was sure a bite would be involved, but there had to be more to it, otherwise it would be done more often. Asher had offered to change me, but the process was as mysterious as most things that involved the pack. The Alphas worked as a network, keeping information available about them minimal. I always wondered if that was the reason them coming out hadn't been as well received as other supernaturals. It was hard to trust such a surreptitious group.

Was the shifter change the same as the vampire, where the physical body died and you were reborn as a vampire?

After long stretches of tension-riddled silence, Madison said. "It's not a terrible idea. If a god can be changed, we'd successfully accomplish breaking the bond and divesting Malific of her magic."

"The question is, can a god be changed? Can any magical being be changed? Vampires can only change humans, so what if it's the same with shifters?" I countered. "We do that and it fails, what happens to the shifters? Once again they'd become Malific's target. What if it doesn't break the bond and she dies?" I said it softly, thinking out loud.

After shelving the shifter idea, Cory pulled out the papers he'd stored in the tote. "I've gone over the spell you gave me. It just didn't make any sense. There's nothing in my books to suggest we can remove it. But if we have spell books, I'm sure elves do, too. We need to speak with Nolan or find someone who can translate this spell and then we can find a Latin or English alternative. Or weave a spell." He made a face. "I'm not confident there's a reversal spell that you can do alone. I suspect you'd need another elf to help you remove it. That's why Elizabeth tricked you into helping. The binding spell required more elven magic than she possessed." He blew out a heavy sigh. "How are we going to find more elves when the general assumption is that you're all extinct?" Cory started pacing, thinking out loud. "How do we find more elves and their spell books?"

"Nolan and Elizabeth." Madison voiced what we were all trying to get around.

"What if Nolan can't do it either?" I argued. "The reason Elizabeth was able to be the WIB was because her magic wasn't like anyone else's. What if the binding spell required elven and fae magic, which is why she needed me to help with it?"

"Or a combination. Between your magic and Elizabeth's, you two check a lot of boxes."

He was right. And if it was a woven spell, we'd have to make a counterspell.

Exhausting all avenues, we reviewed every magic book of Madison's and the ones Cory had brought and came to the very obvious conclusion that if we were going to get anywhere, we needed someone well versed in elven magic. We needed Nolan.

I thought I'd skate over frozen ice in hell before visiting Elizabeth's home again, but there we were, going through the labyrinth of trees that spilled us out at the entrance to her home. We moved over the bridge unobstructed. The toothed fish were gone and the fastidious Arius wasn't stationed as sentry, using his riddles to determine if a person was worthy of meeting with the Woman in Black. No sounds came from the house. The door was locked, but with a little magical incentive we opened it. I had expected a ward to keep us out, but there wasn't anything. There were vacant spots on the bookshelf where books had been removed. Magic inundated the air along with traces of ginger, tannin, fennel, and other less-identifiable scents. But everything else was as it had been the first time I'd been there, with the exception of the pompous and obnoxious elf/fae hybrid Arius.

I left Madison and Cory in the house while I searched outside. Out back, my sights were set on the fallow stretch of land that was once a garden. Not knowing what I was looking for, I made note of everything. The pale-yellow powder that had circled the home was gone. There wasn't a trace of lingering magic. Finding nothing of interest, I started back toward the house but glimpsed a green spiral notebook shoved into the dry, unusable dirt. I pulled it out and read the scribblings. "Cloaking spell," "Mirra," "Adligatura, a neutralizing spell" had been hastily written. After the spells, there was "I don't know how to—" but it ended abruptly. And he simply signed it N.

He must have had to write in haste. But why? Was he forced to leave? If so, by Elizabeth? Malific? How thorough and protective was the oath?

Nolan knew me well enough that he had placed the notebook in the garden for me to find. I pressed it to my chest and gave him a silent thanks. Forgiving him didn't seem like such an unrealistic thing to do. He was trying.

I nearly crashed into Cory and Madison as I rushed back into the house, looking over the elven spells again.

"What's that?" Madison asked.

"Spells. Nolan left them for me."

There was no mistaking Cory's I-told-you-so expression that took up permanent residence on his face. Every time I looked up from the back seat, it was there. Even after I kneed the back of his seat, it was there.

CHAPTER 8

"It works, disengage it," Cory demanded, standing in the middle of the circle I'd scribed, similar to the one Elizabeth had placed me in to ensure that I couldn't borrow her magic. We were on the small concrete landing behind Madison's house, mimicking the sigils Nolan had written for me. I'd invoked the spell, rendering Cory magicless.

His breathing was becoming more labored when he made an attempt to leave the circle or use his magic. Having his magic restricted was causing him to panic. I had to release him soon. It was like placing an iridium cuff on a witch. The brace itself meant nothing; it was being divested of their magic that bothered them. Magic was so interwoven into their existence that taking it away felt like taking a part of them. It was their breath, the beat of their heart, and the ability to move of their own volition.

I released the magic from the circle and looked in Madison's direction. She didn't seem as reluctant as Cory. Again, I invoked my magic. It surged through me, along with the elation of using magic. Elven magic. Something I had never experienced. Even when I'd borrowed magic and after my restrictions were lifted, I had been using universal generic magic—magic shared between all magic wielders. But this was exclusively mine. The magic pulsed, the markings blazing orange before fading out, and Madison stood in the middle of the circle, making futile attempts to use her magic. Even the novice ability of just moving an object was gone.

Madison and Cory both tried to perform spells to invoke the circle and neutralize it. Nothing.

"But will it work on a god?" Madison asked, moving out of the circle once I'd disengaged the spell.

"Mephisto said that elven magic is the only magic comparable in power and equally different," I said, repeating his statement verbatim because it was for that reason Malific had destroyed the elves when they wouldn't ally with her.

"You'll need to test it on Mephisto," Cory suggested.

"I will." I returned my focus to the notepad but didn't miss the look that passed between Madison and Cory. Rolling my eyes, I said, "I'm not hiding from anyone or distancing myself. Can I just do this? Explore magic without the reminder of Malific?" There it was. I'd made the confession out loud. Mephisto, Asher, Nolan—they were all reminders of Malific's cruelty. The reason Elizabeth considered me an abomination. I wanted a break.

Madison gave me a small sympathetic smile and Cory sat next to me and gave my hand a squeeze. "What's next?" he asked.

"Cloaking spell."

There was no denying it worked. The moment I invoked the spell, a heavy magic draped over me like a blanket, and I moved throughout the room undetected. It didn't require blood to invoke, as Elizabeth had led me to believe. But when engaged, it did restrict my ability to perform magic.

Cory made several unsuccessful attempts to reveal me. So, my wards and the cloaking spell were my best defenses against Malific. For now.

We were interrupted from practicing the Mirra by a knock on the door. Madison answered, made a face of surprise, and mouthed that it was Alex, Cory's boyfriend. He had a bag of food in one hand and two bottles of wine in the other. Cory rushed to him, planted a kiss on his cheek, and helped him take everything to the kitchen.

"What are you doing here?" Cory asked, removing the food from the bag and setting it up. The smell of oregano, cheese, tomato sauce, and garlic filled the house, reminding me that we hadn't eaten since morning and that breakfast had consisted of pastries and donuts.

Alex shrugged. "You were sporadically responding to my texts and I knew you were working, so I figured you all hadn't had a chance to eat." He made an assessment of the room.

"Excuse the place. We've been working and I haven't had time to straighten up," Madison said, busying herself with tidying displaced pillows and gathering the discarded papers where Cory had jotted down woven spells. I looked at the "mess" she was explaining away. It was cleaner than I usually kept my home. No wonder they thought my place was a sty. I was surrounded by cleaning overachievers.

The disarray didn't bother me, but I got the impression it might bother Alex. I studied his meticulous appearance. His dark-brown hair was neatly cut, not a strand out of place, and his after-five shadow looked groomed. The cuffs of his crisp, cream-colored shirt were folded to mid-forearm with ruler-like accuracy. And his shoes were polished. I assumed his home was just as scrupulously cared for.

"Thank you for the food," I said. His eyes glinted as he raised the bottles. "And the wine," I amended.

"Take a break and have dinner. There's more in the car."

Before leaving he gave Cory a long kiss, and for a moment, I think they must have forgotten we were there, or just didn't care. Cory looked down at the floor and his skin flushed.

Instead of giving Cory a well-deserved teasing about his PDA—something he always adamantly railed against, although I guessed his position changed when it was *him* and his hot shifter boyfriend—I couldn't help but be suspicious of Alex's appearance. Was it a coincidence? After all, he was the Northwest Pack's fourth. Was Alex the considerate significant other, or was he doing recon for a certain nosey Alpha?

Alex was gone for longer than it should have taken to just get another small bag of food and some cans of Sprite. My stomach rumbled at the sight of the food, but my suspicion was too heightened to eat. Excusing myself with my phone in hand, I went to the guest room and called Asher. Convinced that I'd be able to tell if he wasn't being honest, I used video.

"Erin," Asher drawled in a low husky voice. "To what do I owe this pleasure?" He flashed a smile that managed to be roguish and charming. And I was having none of it.

"Now you have Alex spying on me?"

His brows inched together and he looked genuinely surprised. "Alex is with you?"

"Not with me. I'm at Madison's and he came by with dinner."

"Well, that was nice of him, don't you think? Or are you calling because my wolves are too polite? That complaint would be a first."

"It's nice if he's not spying. Be straight with me, okay?"

"Of course. Have I ever not been?"

"Salem Stone?"

"Was I secretive about that, or did I take it from right under your nose? I did in fact wave at you as we passed each other, after I had it in my possession, correct?"

He didn't need to remind me. That day was burned into my memories. His smug smile as he left the cave in South

Dakota where the stone was rumored to be. I'd found the Salem Stone gone and an angry troll.

I glared at him. "I want you to be upfront with me. Please. I just need that, okay?"

He canted his head, his brows still furrowed. "Haven't I always been? When it's pack business, I tell you I won't tell you for that reason. When I had you followed, they did it in plain sight. Do you think for one minute I'm not able to have you tailed without you knowing?"

This guy. Ugh, and I could do without the smug grin.

"Ms. Harp?" I challenged.

"I never asked her to spy on you." His smile widened. "I just never discouraged her from passing on information. You've seen her technique. She's neither sly nor covert with anything she does. I'll even go as far as to say she's not even savvy at it. She snoops for all to see. The cane? Alleged hearing aid? The frail geriatric persona? Anyone around her for a minute knows she doesn't need the cane. No one has ever seen the purported hearing aid. And the frail geriatric act she loves to don whenever it suits her lacks any panache. She is definitely not a spy. She's unabashedly nosey and she's a fan of mine. She offers me information because she wants to, and she's aware that I care about what goes on with you. So, no, Erin, I'm not spying on you." He winked. "But thank you for letting me know where you are. Ms. Harp mentioned that you hadn't returned since you left two days ago. I really appreciate you keeping me updated. Go eat your dinner, it's getting cold."

The arrogance drifted off the phone and the twinkle of satisfaction in his eyes didn't falter no matter how hard I glared.

"That was the purpose of my call. I wanted to let you know I was okay," I asserted, trying to wrangle some semblance of control over the situation. I wasn't fooling anyone, especially Asher.

"Of course," he breezed out.

I huffed. "Bye."

"Bye, Erin." My name rolled from his tongue in a low purr. What, was he a cat now? I took a quick look in the mirror as I passed, hoping the embarrassment hadn't shown on my face. I was slightly flushed but I think that was just Asher-rage returning. I knew he needed to be confident to succeed as an Alpha, but was the hubris necessary? I huffed again, then, once my frustration subsided, returned to the kitchen to eat.

CHAPTER 9

I had spent two days at Madison's, practicing. The cloaking spell was now effortless for me to engage. The neutralization spell wasn't something I could consider as a defensive option, only as a last resort. It wasn't as passive as Elizabeth had made it look, tugging at my magic the entire time it was erected. By the time I'd finished with it, I was exhausted, and it made doing the cloaking spell so difficult that I didn't have enough energy to attain it and move throughout the room.

Forming the Mirra was the most challenging of the spells. Mine looked like Elizabeth's, erected to stop Malific, but neither Madison nor Cory was willing to walk through it to tell me how it felt. We could all feel the heat radiating from it. Each time I tried to put my hand through it, the Mirra fell. I wasn't able to both keep its form and walk through it. Or maybe it was a safety precaution for anyone foolish enough to erect one and then walk through it.

Despite the new arsenal of spells at my disposal, relaxing was impossible knowing that a sadist had a direct connection to whether I'd be subjected to pain. Alone in my home, the knowledge that she enjoyed an audience wasn't enough to comfort me, because it had been two days and she'd been quiet. Silence wasn't good for people like that. The ease with which she'd stabbed her own hand was chilling, and she'd accepted the pain as though she was taking a dip in a pool of cool water on a sweltering day. The similarities in our appearance didn't deter her, either. Why didn't that disturb her?

Instead of fixating on Malific, I practiced my magic nonstop. Wynding just didn't seem like it was going to happen. A hernia or hypoxia was in my future if I didn't stop straining to produce wings. I couldn't Wynd like Mephisto, talk to animals like Simeon, or produce wings like Kai. Unlike it did with Clayton, the weather wasn't responding to any of my invocations, even the ones laced with a colorful litany of swear words. And "rain, damn you" wasn't an actual spell. Calling the wind four-letter words did not make it respond to my commands.

Trying to invoke a glamour made me look like I was having a neurological incident and in need of immediate medical attention. Nothing good was going to come from the faces I made trying to achieve it. Almost all the spells in the witch books, I'd mastered. I'd kick ass against a witch, mage, or fae. But against a god or an elf, how would I fare?

A familiar ache tugged at me at that realization, quickly morphing into frustration because I had no way of contacting Nolan. I needed more.

I wasn't surprised that the person at the door, interrupting my thoughts, was Mephisto. He'd texted twice to check on me and I'd responded, telling him I was fine, and when he called, I ignored the call.

I greeted him with a weak smile. His body brushed against mine as he entered my apartment. His steel-gray suit and obsidian-black shirt matched the cool darkness in his eyes that traced my face while he maintained distance between us.

"You've been avoiding me."

"No, just busy." I waved my hand at the books, notepads, and crumpled papers from my efforts to weave spells.

His attention breezed over them before returning to me.

"Elizabeth and Arius have gone underground. I believe your father—"

"Nolan."

"Nolan, is with them, but I don't believe he went willingly."

I'd figured that, seeing how the spells looked as if they'd been written in a rush. He hadn't even completed his name. Being more powerful, Elizabeth probably took him in the same manner she did me.

Mephisto swallowed the distance between us in a flash of movement, something I was still working on. I'd manage to accelerate my movement, I thought, or maybe it wasn't magic; it was certainly unimpressive enough to be just a basic run.

"What did she do to you? How did you survive being handed to Malific?"

"I'm not sure if I really survived. Once again, I was used as a tool."

I told him everything, excluding Elizabeth's insults and my pancake butt counter-insult, which I was strangely proud of.

Taking my hands into his, he stroked the backs of them and then turned them palms up, pressing his warm lips to them. I sucked in a ragged breath before he delivered the same tender touch to my lips. Tentative soft lips pressed against mine, searching and enchanting. His tongue glided gently over my bottom lip as he walked me back to the wall, pressing me into it, his kisses becoming more impassioned as he explored my mouth, our tongues caressing.

"My demigoddess is fine." He breathed out the statement with such reverence, it seemed like a prayer.

He slipped his hand under my shirt, splaying it across my back and sending shivers through me as his nails grazed my skin. Arching into him, I sighed. The warmth of his body enveloped me; the intensity of his touch spoke to a need that was explicitly Mephisto. His hardness pressed against me. He moved his hand from my back and laced his fingers through my hair. With a light tug, he bared my neck to him, where he planted kisses and nipped lightly.

My breath caught as his finger brushed my taut nipples. The kisses were becoming more voracious. And the minute space between us seemed too much. Need blazed in me. Panting, I tugged at his shirt, pulling it from his slacks and letting my fingers run along the defined muscles of his abs and the V of his waist. Just as I started to unfasten his pants, I remembered Elizabeth's words—her pain is your pain—but what about pleasure? Malific drove a knife through her hand and I felt it as my own. Would she feel…well, Mephisto and whatever he made me feel?

I nudged him away. His hot-coal eyes raked over me.

"I'm bound to Malific," I reminded him. "I feel what she does. She stabbed her hand and I felt it. Bled, too."

Taking my hand, he caressed one of the fingers with his tongue before leaning into me and pressing another hard, passionate kiss on my lips, tracing the hardened pebbles of my nipples with his fingers. "Where she brings you pain, I'll give you nothing but pleasure."

He showed me by pressing his lower body against me. Need rampaged through me again. I wanted to forget I was linked to Malific but I couldn't. I pushed him away, again. "I'm linked to her."

His lips lifted into a wicked smile. "In a few minutes, you won't be thinking about her," he said. Tousled hair, exposed abs where I'd unhooked several buttons, and the outline of him pressing against his pants was making Malific a distant thought. But I yanked the images of her back and when he attempted to move forward, I extended my hand to keep some distance between us.

"If we do this, I don't think it'll just be *us*." I grimaced at the idea of Malific feeling everything I did. *Yuck.*

When Mephisto stepped a little closer, I shook my head. "Look, my kink threshold is pretty high, but I'm not having a three-way with you and my mother."

Mephisto's eyebrow rose as he gave me a roguish smile. "Is it?" he asked in a deep growl, his tongue moving slowly over his lips.

"I said a lot of other things before that comment. Things that are *really* important."

"I think this is a good time to let you know we're out here," said Clayton's voice from the other side of the door.

Please and mercy to all the fates, let that not be something they heard. Please! But from the amused tone in Clayton's voice, they had. If, for a moment, I pretended they hadn't, Clayton's smirk confirmed it. Simeon's look was indecipherable and Kai was too distracted by the state of my apartment to care. Kai's expressive eyes went to the pile of books, crumpled paper, the pizza and its crumbs that dusted the table, and the end crust discarded on the table. Then they crept back to me. Being judged by the seraphic man with the entrancing wings hit just a little harder.

Clearing away the blankets on the sofa, I made room for Clayton to put down the backpack he was carrying. He immediately focused on Mephisto.

"When you weren't home, M, I knew this should be the next place to check."

A look passed between them, and possibly silent words, because the intense look lingered too long, and Kai and Simeon were observing them in the manner one did when watching an argument unfold.

Clay gave Mephisto another sharp look, then turned to me, his easy manner restored.

"Malific's free and wants you dead. Let's not make it easy for her," Clay said.

"She can't kill her," Mephisto told them, shrugging off his jacket and laying it over the sofa before coming to me, his hand pressed against my back, urging me to tell them why.

Retelling the situation, I watched their faces go from neutral to shock and finally wary frustration.

"If you die, so does Malific's spell, and Laes's spell will be broken," Clay pointed out.

A weighted, murky cloud of tension filled the room as the Huntsmen shot furtive glances at each other. Lifespan, including immortality, was linked to magic. Gods didn't age out of life, but they could be killed, as could vampires. Witches and mages lived longer than humans but eventually died. The same with shifters, but their lifespan was about twice that of most humans, some living to be close to two hundred. The books that I studied about elves reported a similar life expectancy as the shifters, some living up to three hundred years. But me, quarter human, quarter elf, and half god, what was my expectancy?

The sly looks that continued in my direction should have deterred me, but didn't.

"I'm probably not immortal, am I?"

"No, you're human. You have inherited the brevity of human existence. Although I suspect you will live much longer than most," Mephisto provided.

So just like before I got my magic, I could die just as easily with a regular knife.

"But you have elven magic, and that gives you an advantage over us and Malific. So, let's see what you can do," Clayton suggested. He was speaking to me, but he kept a tentative eye on Mephisto and the attention he giving me.

I listed every spell I could do, which was extremely long and included telling them that I was positive I didn't have wings, couldn't talk to animals, and when I Wynded, I just turned into a cat. That had all of them giving me the WTF look.

"Hybrid magic is complicated. When mixed with humans, it's simple; the magic is usually less potent, but with other supernaturals, it's a toss-up," Mephisto explained. Which wasn't necessarily true. Shifters trumped all. Ms. Harp seemed to be the only exception.

"Is speaking with each other telepathically something you do just between each other or is it a gift all gods possess?" I asked.

All eyes turned to me and widened.

"I figured it out," I explained. "You all get these intense looks and I can tell there's a conversation happening. And"— I turned to Mephisto— "you contacted them once without using a phone." I crossed my arms over my chest and raised my brows. "So, how do I get in on this group chat?"

"It's not that simple," Kai explained, folding one of the blankets he'd picked up off the floor. "It's not because we are gods, it's because of other things."

Despite me knowing what they were, they didn't seem open to admitting to it, as if calling themselves Huntsmen outside of the Veil was blasphemous.

Abandoning the topic of their special communication abilities, Clayton questioned me about my magical skills while he pulled books out of his bag. Answering him, I became acutely aware of the concerned looks they kept casting at Kai, at the slow, tightly coiled way he stalked through the room. Mephisto appeared increasingly concerned, always moving to stay between me and Kai, fixing him with a hard look of disapproval until Kai stopped and positioned himself across the room near the door.

The fierce exchange of looks made it obvious they were holding another conversation that I wasn't privy to. The hardening of Kai's features and the steely cut of his eyes when he looked at me made me very aware that my death would allow the Huntsmen back into the Veil. There wasn't any doubt that Kai was thinking about it.

I scanned the room, calculating how long it would take to get to my weapons, despite it being a futile plan. My speed was no match for theirs. Magic. We both had it and my only option was my protective wall. With all the practice, could I erect it before he struck?

It pained me to think that Kai, the type-A winged Huntsman with the lumber obsession and angelic appearance, was considering how better off he'd be with me dead.

Self-preservation had me distancing myself from them all as I pretended to peruse one of the books.

With a look of resignation, Kai asked, "What happens now?"

"I need to figure out a way to unbind myself from Malific. She's been quiet lately, but it won't last. She wants the bond removed more than I do." Ignoring the uncomfortable silence, I said, "I know how to do a cloaking spell and a neutralizing spell, but I need to determine if it can withstand hers." I knew that they couldn't undo elven spells, but could they be subverted by a god? Would a neutralizing spell even work on a god?

Mephisto moved forward first, but Clayton placed himself between us. "I'm at your service."

Next time you and Madison are together, you won't get within an inch of her.

Clayton's rakish smirk had me wondering if I'd made my threat aloud. "Go ahead. Do the cloaking spell first."

Because of my relentless practicing, the words for the spell fell from me naturally. Clayton kept careful eyes on me. When I moved to the right, they didn't track me, nor did the others. Clayton's lips moved ever so lightly as magic cascaded over me and through the air, but their eyes scanned the room, searching for me. I became overly confident that

66

my movement would go undetected, when, with a flash of movement, Kai appeared directly in front of me. His hand grasped my throat. My breath whooshed out of me at his sudden movement and I stilled, aware that his grip could get tighter and deadlier. It wasn't constricting or even threatening, but the look in his haunted dark eyes was a reminder of what my death meant to him.

Everyone in the room was motionless.

"You can still be heard. Move quietly when you do. Cloaking is no good if others can hear you," he instructed. His voice was low and rough and the pressure of his touch noticeably increased.

Moving with stealth might not have been perfected, but I had a light step. Unfortunately, Kai had exceptional hearing. Both times I was lost, they'd sent him to find me and it was now clear that it wasn't just because of his ability to fly. I released the cloaking spell, and in the same strike of movement, Kai had moved to the door. A light hiss from the collective exhales from Mephisto, Clayton, and Simeon filled the room.

The hard knock on the door provided a needed distraction, but I didn't move toward it until Kai put some distance between us.

Ms. Harp beamed up at the peephole.

"Hi, what's up?" I asked through the small crack I created, giving her just a view of me.

"Nothing," she chirped, hip-checking the door to barge her way through. "I noticed you had company, so I thought I'd bring over some cookies."

I looked down at the unopened bag of *store-bought* cookies. She didn't even demonstrate the slightest show of propriety, the barest of couth, or the minimum of effort it would have taken to put them on a plate and microwave them for a few seconds, to pass them off as homemade.

Shoving the package into my chest, she said, "If you put

them in the microwave, they'll be warm and tasty for you."
Then she swept past me, quickly giving everyone and everything a once-over.

No. She. Didn't.

Mephisto was met with her slit-eyed scowl.

Clayton shifted, his massive frame blocking Ms. Harp
from seeing what was on the table or anything past him.

Her cordial smile pulled into a tight-lipped one.

"Ms. Evelyn Harp, this is Clayton, Simeon, Kai, and you
already know Mephisto."

Ms. Harp repeated each of their names, undoubtedly
committing them to memory so she could give Asher a full
report.

The Huntsmen greeted her with casual ease. Mephisto's
eyes flickered with amusement and his lips twitched as he
fought to keep from laughing at a frustrated Ms. Harp
trying and failing to inconspicuously see behind the human
wall.

"Seems like you all are busy," she offered, backing away.
"Is there anything I can help with?"

"No, we're fine," I said.

She did another sweep of the room, then grabbed the
cookies out of my hands. "You're probably going to be too
busy for these," she said as she pranced toward the door.

"It's good to see you getting around so well without your
cane," I said, my smirk so rigid it couldn't be hidden if I
wanted to.

She shot me a cheery faux smile that hinted at the
mischief she was causing.

"Yes. Asher"—she invoked his name like it was a power
word—"suggested I try getting around without it." She
kicked her leg out and every incident of her hobbling around
on a cane that she didn't need ran through my mind as she
stood on a single leg like she was about to perform a ballet
passé. "He was right. I don't know why I ever doubted him."

She turned from me and pinned a hard gaze on Mephisto. "He's right about so many things."

And off she went, having given us one of her practiced appearances of innocence while leaving behind a little grenade of trouble.

"She's... interesting?" Clayton said, taking a seat after she'd gone.

"She's something. I'm not sure if *interesting* is the right word," I provided.

Ms. Harp's interruption only momentarily distracted us from the undeniable issue that persisted and that Kai wore profoundly on his face, in his movements, and in the intensity of his gaze that kept wandering in my direction.

"I don't think I need to be here. You all have a handle on things, right?" Kai finally said.

Mephisto relaxed and gave him an appreciative nod. Simeon didn't bother to give an excuse, just followed Kai out with a look over his shoulder, his attention skating over Mephisto before landing on me.

"The cloaking worked on us, but will it on shifters? It's something you'll want to find out. Perhaps that local Alpha can assist you with that. If your mother used shifters before, it's likely she'll do it again. It's best to know the boundaries of your magic."

Simeon missed the sharp look Mephisto leveled in his direction, but Clayton didn't.

"Now for the *adligatura*," Clayton suggested, standing.

Neutralizing spell, fancy pants. The black chalk was dark enough to leave the necessary markings for the spell. Not as confident with it as with the cloaking spell, I had to keep referring back to Nolan's notes. Once the circle was complete, Mephisto stepped into it.

I made a note to make it bigger next time. When I stood in front of him, he leaned into me. "The roles will reverse and I'll be the one without magic," he teased. Feeling the warm breeze of his breath, I leaned into him, our lips almost brushing each other, just as Clayton nudged him back.

"You have to be *in* the circle. Your toes are over it."

Words were definitely exchanged and there was no way, based on the daggered looks, they were words of love and endearment.

I invoked the spell and Mephisto attempted to perform magic, without success. But he was able to walk right out of the circle, something Cory and Madison couldn't do. Once the circle was formed, a wall had risen around them that they couldn't pass. The Huntsmen were impervious to the wall. It was good information to know.

"Do it again," Clayton requested. Once the spell was invoked with Mephisto in the center of the circle, Clayton tried to disarm it. He couldn't. Powerful magic thrashed through the room from the spells and magic he used. Nothing worked.

He smiled. "Good."

"Not great if he can just walk out of it." But if I made it wide enough, I could give myself the advantage. I did it again, finding that the larger the circle, the greater the strain on me and my magic. When it was over, I needed a break. Sitting on the chair, I wished I had that bag of cookies.

Hours had passed and I still hadn't managed to modify the neutralizing spell or prohibit Mephisto or Clayton from exiting the circle. I never imagined I'd get exhausted from using magic or have no desire to use it. But I'd reached that point. Shifting to a cat during another effort to Wynd had Clayton curious about that ability. I didn't see the shift to be of any benefit unless I wanted to soar through the air and claw someone's eyes out. I put that down on the last resort list.

The cloaking spell worked against the Huntsmen: score one for elven magic. The neutralizing spell didn't work on gods and was too time consuming to create. But I was happy to have established that before putting it in my quiver to use against Malific. Clayton pointed out that my magic seemed most effective against "lesser magical beings." I smiled wryly at that; neither Cory nor Madison would be happy to learn that gods considered them lesser beings.

I could break gods' magic wards, but it was exhausting. I was on the floor, slumped against the wall, resting after I'd crashed Clayton's ward. It felt like I had physically shattered a brick wall using a sledgehammer.

Clayton had packed up his things and was by the door. "Just waiting on you, M," he said when Mephisto didn't move from his spot against the wall.

Mephisto's eyes lifted to meet his but he remained silent.

Clayton made a mirthless chuckle, whispered something. Observing their *non-fight* and geniality would have been entertaining if I'd had some clue as to what was being said between them. Although, looking at their hostile posturing and body language, maybe I didn't.

"Reconnect," Mephisto ordered out loud.

"Nah, I don't want to hear you raging in my head. You want to be rude, say it in front of Erin." Clayton's smirk became an infectious smile. I'd never seen Mephisto flustered; Clayton was apparently talented at getting to him.

"We should go. I'm sure Erin would appreciate some down time."

"I'll make sure she gets the down time she needs," Mephisto responded.

"Cool, we'll make a night of it." Clayton shrugged off the bag and let it hit the floor.

I needed a moment away from the Huntsmen and I definitely didn't want more hours of their restrained arguments, their faux smiles during their silent fights, or Clayton being the chaperone from hell and running interference anytime Mephisto came within a foot of me.

"Rest," Mephisto said, hesitating before approaching me. The kiss he pressed to my cheek was so chaste we might as well have been related. A controlled, unemphatic touch. Clinical. Although his fingers trailing along my cheek sent a shiver through me, a reminder of the way he'd touched me earlier.

He didn't look back at me or at Clayton as he moved past him to leave.

Before Clayton could leave, I stopped him.

"Yes?"

"Can we talk?"

CHAPTER 10

*C*layton's easy manner and warm smile made it difficult to be angry with him. The hard-set resolution in his eyes made it easier. He pushed his long locs out of his face before resting against the door, his arms crossed over his chest.

"What's your problem with me?" I asked.

He shrugged. "I don't have a problem with Erin Katherine Jensen. Nor do I have a problem with you as a death mage, a *Naut*, or someone who could navigate through the Veil and find the Laes to lift our restriction. That Erin is fine, and if she and M want to have a naked tumble, I don't care. It's M being with Malific's daughter that bothers me. The daughter of the woman who forced us to be here for over fifty years. Who killed Oedeus, murdered a pack of shifters, and created an army for the sole purpose of death and destruction. Your mother put us here."

He turned his head away but not before I saw the same look on his face that I'd seen on Kai's. My death could free them.

When he lifted his eyes back to meet mine, I saw more than resolve: there was concern, frustration, anguish. "Our anonymity has served us well. Simeon doesn't have conversations with animals in front of people, I don't control the weather or do bizarre things with water at beaches and lakes, and Kai"—yep, there was definitely anguish—"doesn't take to the sky. Something he did daily. He's not meant for land. And the only two times those restrictions were lifted was to find you. M used to be totally committed to our anonymity, to living this life until we could return to the Veil. Until you. The precautions we took to protect ourselves have been bent to the point they are unrecognizable, holding by a tendril, because of you."

"Everyone's holding me responsible for things that aren't in my control. I had no say in being here or who my mother is. I'm as much a pawn as you all are. Do you think I like being linked to her and knowing that's the only thing keeping me alive? Do you think I wanted an aunt who hates my guts and tried to enlist you all to get rid of me?"

"I don't. You asked a question and I think you deserve the truth. We don't belong here among people who aren't suited for the Veil." At least he didn't call us unremarkables, a term Mephisto used to describe people on this side of the Veil. "Imagine if we are discovered. Gods living among the masses, immune to your magic, only able to be killed using an Obitus blade. I don't think we'd be revered. In fact, we'd be feared. There are only four of us. The city, we can deal with. The world, I doubt we can."

Wait. Was he implying that the four of them could take on a city? Maybe he wasn't speaking from a place of arrogance but rather experience.

"The vampires are immortal and not easily killed either, and people are fine with them. They might not be gods, but they seem to have godlike egos."

He chuckled. "You think we have egos?"

I considered it for a long moment. "As powerful as you all

74

are, you have more humility than I'd expect." I paused. "I'm still a *Naut*. I'll go to the Veil and find the Laes."

"It won't do any good. I suspect it's with Malific. When she was imprisoned, we could have found it. We've lost that chance now."

I swallowed and couldn't believe my next words until after they'd spilled out of my mouth. "You used a necro-summoner spell to save me when I died. Can you use that spell or something similar to get back into the Veil?"

"Not if M has anything to say about it. I suggested that today, but the likelihood of finding another Tactu Mortem is slim. I suggested other spells, but he wouldn't consider any of them because he feared they would be too dangerous to you."

So, while I was perusing spell books and practicing, they *were* having debates and probably talking Kai down.

"We'll find a way," I said, sounding far more optimistic than I felt.

"I see M's intrigue. You're very..." He smiled, seemingly searching for the right word.

"Undeniably Erin," I offered with a plaintive smile.

"Yeah," he breathed out, scrubbing his hands along his face. "You're like a chihuahua among wolves and yet you don't seem to realize it."

Being compared to a tiny yippy dog with a bad temperament wasn't necessarily an insult, but there was no way that was a compliment.

"I'm a demigod," I pronounced a little too confidently. It seemed like a humble-brag.

Amusement traveled along his features. "And I'm a god," he countered with far less enthusiasm. In fact, it was a very passive claim. It reminded me of a quote about a lion never having to tell you it's a lion.

Perhaps my pride was hurt. It was getting battered and bruised at every turn, and I was tired of it. Closing the distance between us, I erected the protective field around us. "Only one of us can get out of this," I pointed out.

"True." He bent down until his forehead was pressed against mine. His large hands rested over my balled fist, a reminder of his size. He gave a light squeeze, his touch gentle; I would even go as far as comforting. "Never trap yourself in a cage with a serpent without knowing if you are dealing with a garden snake or a black mamba," he whispered. I lifted my head and moved back slightly to look him in the eyes. His chestnut eyes had taken on a mild earthy tone that contrasted with the ominous note in his voice. Everything people said about the Huntsmen—the warnings, Elizabeth's confidence that once they learned of my existence, they would kill me—was very real. This was who they were.

His soothing eyes and comforting touch and the Huntsmen's infamy seemed diametrically opposed. Something portentous slipped through his demeanor, and I was faced with the dichotomy of the gods. Was I being fooled? Lured into passivity? A lion might seem gentle but were their claws any less dangerous?

I let the enclosure fall, feeling the breeze of magic from it, a reminder of how intense their magic was to me.

"I shouldn't have done that." It was an unnecessary power move that only proved his point. I was a demigod among gods. I possessed elven magic, but until I could harness its full ability, it was ineffectual. I had two parlor tricks: a ward that gods couldn't break and the ability to cloak. They protected me from harm, but they were nothing more than defensive tactics. The cloaking spell could be used offensively, but how effective would it be against Clayton? "We're on the same team," I reminded him. "I'll do what I can to help."

His look faded into a grimace. "Little Raven, we're not on

the same team, are we? Can you honestly say that our interests align? They converge because of M."

"Okay, I'm good with all the truth-telling. I've had my fill of blunt honesty and forthcomingness. You can start lying to me," I said, trying to lighten things, something I desperately needed.

"Okay." He chuckled. "This situation isn't complicated at all. It's a cakewalk. It happens all the time. We have absolutely nothing to worry about. Go, team." The effort he put into trying to seem lighthearted was abandoned midway.

He nodded. "Night, Erin."

It wasn't quite night and I was glad he didn't say goodnight because there wasn't going to be anything good about it.

CHAPTER 11

*T*he next day, I was still thinking about my conversation with Clayton and Simeon's recommendation to see whether the cloaking spell worked against shifters. Wards didn't. I fished out one of the three packets of cookies I'd purchased that morning. One grocery bag on my counter was filled with cookies and bacon, the other held three bottles of Kahlua. Ms. Harp was on to something with using it as cream in her coffee. So I'd gotten one for me and two for her.

She wasn't secretive about her nosiness, being president of the Team Asher club, or her intention to report anything she thought she knew, and I wasn't being sly either. The Kahlua was an out-and-out bribe: "Hey, nosey old lady, you stay out of my business and you'll never be without your favorite cream." But knowing her, she'd take the Kahlua with one hand and would be calling Asher with the other to give him the Erin report. It was worth a try. I thought the light knock at the door would be her, responding to my message telling her what I had for her.

It wasn't.

"What?"

"Erin," said Landon. "You sound hostile."

"Because I feel that way," I said through the door.

"We need to talk."

"I told you I'm not working for you anymore."

"Oh, I sincerely hope that is something we can discuss in the future. But this is in regard to an unfinished job."

"What unfinished job?" I said, yanking open the door. He looked out of place in the drab walkway of my apartment building, in his navy bespoke Italian suit, white shirt, and silk tie a few shades lighter. Standing with his hands in his pocket, he was styled and coifed, poised and exuding a level of self-importance and arrogance that could never be duplicated.

"Always so amiable," he said in a sultry growl that was the height of seduction.

I wasn't in the mood.

"Stop it!"

"Oh, Erin." He sighed. "Do you tell birds not to fly?"

"I would if they were trying to seduce me with their wings."

"If anything, if my mere presence leads to you feeling seduced or enticed, am I not the victim?"

I glared at him. He leaned in, his lips furled, waiting for an invitation into the apartment. Another misconception people had was that vampires needed an invitation. They didn't. It was just sheer politeness that they adhered to... when it suited their agenda.

Before I could invite him in and question him about the alleged *unfinished job*, his head snapped in the direction of Ms. Harp's apartment.

"Well, hello," he purred. *She's in her seventies, she doesn't want you!* Or maybe she did. Who was I to stop her fun? "Have I interested you?" Landon's voice held hints of delight as he gave Ms. Harp a crooked smile. Landon was a testament to his love for the arts: overly dramatic in presentation while simultaneously being mesmeric.

A flush crept up Ms. Harp's cheeks, and I wondered if it was from embarrassment or interest. No, it was irritation. She was used to me not calling her out, and now someone else was pointing out her nosiness and she wasn't having any of it. She did what she did best: She performed for her Oscar nomination. As she stepped out from her threshold, I saw she'd added props. Cane in hand, she even managed to tap it to the ground twice as she made her way to us.

"Don't you pay me any mind. I heard a noise and just came out to investigate. Erin and I make sure we take care of each other."

Do we? Or are you on an information-seeking adventure?

"She's such a nice person to take the time to watch out for this old woman. I'm sure it can be a bother sometimes."

Not at all, these performances are amazing.

"I'm sure you're not a bother at all," Landon said in a voice honey-sweet enough to give me a cavity. I controlled the eye roll, but it took a great deal of effort.

With waterlike fluidity, he moved to her side, tucking her free hand into the crook of his arm. Ms. Harp fully committed to her role as frail septuagenarian and held it tight. I cut my eyes in her direction and gave her a "you have to be kidding me" look.

Her smugness I expected, but the condescending eye roll she gave me was simply uncalled for.

"Where should I escort you?"

Nowhere. She's just checking you out, and in 1.5 seconds she's going to sprint to her apartment, probably holding the cane overhead like she's in a montage from a Rocky *or* Creed *movie.*

"Oh, nowhere. I was just checking on Erin, but she seems to be in good hands. Since I'm here, I'll just get the package she has for me. She's too good to me. She picked up my favorite cream. Can't drink my coffee without it. Asher Sullivan will bring me some when he comes to see her. Do you know him? Everyone seems to know who he is whenever I mention him. I don't think I'd enjoy that level of notoriety."

Yeah, you would, which is why you're name dropping. But please, do go on.

"Ah, yes, the Northwest Alpha," Landon offered, his tone losing its warmth for a fraction of a second and taking on the same coolness heads of denizens used when they dealt with each other. Always testing the waters of power.

She made a face. "I often forget he's the Alpha, when he's with us. It's something you just forget, don't you think, Erin?"

"Definitely. It's like dealing with a cuddly pup," I responded, sarcasm spilling into my expression.

I was sure she probably was running low on her *cream*. I opened the door wider to let them both in. Landon took a seat on the sofa in the living room as if afraid I'd toss him out when she left. I grabbed the bag with the Kahlua off the counter and handed it to her.

She made a show of checking the weight. "It's quite heavy." She looked at Landon. "Do you mind dropping it off when you leave?"

"I can do it now," he suggested.

"No, no, I have no desire to be a bother."

That's a super lie. But I knew exactly what she was doing and I let the knowledge show when we looked at each other. If he dropped it off when he left, she'd know the length of his visit, and if he took too long, she'd return.

Well played, Ms. Harp. Well played, indeed.

She took slow, careful steps with her cane as she made her way to the door. Any other time, she looked like she was doing her version of the moonwalk, but now she was wrapping Landon around her finger.

"See you later, Erin," she said, then turned to Landon. "And see you…" She waited for a name.

"Landon."

"Landon. See you soon, and if I don't answer, just leave it by my door."

She's not going to answer because she doesn't really like guests, but she loves the hell out of snooping.

After Ms. Harp bowed out of her performance and earshot, I crossed my arms over my chest and stayed close to the kitchen. It was nearer the exit than the living room, and I was hoping Landon's penchant for ignoring proper social distance would work to my advantage. He'd be closer to the door, and therefore easier to kick out.

"What do you want?" I asked.

He rose in a sweeping wave of movement. I exhaled a sharp breath when he'd moved to within an inch of me. I shoved both of my hands into his chest, pushing him back. It only put a few inches between us, but it was enough.

His lips lifted into a haughty smirk. "I paid you quite handsomely for the job with the witches and you failed to complete it."

"You paid handsomely because, for a brief moment, you had a spark of self-awareness and realized you're a pain in the ass. You paid me for that."

I remembered how quickly he'd stripped me of my weapons during one of our encounters. I had magic as an advantage, but the moment others knew that, I lost the element of surprise. This wasn't where I wanted to play my hand. Scanning the room for a defense strategy, I came to the conclusion that the best one I had was, if he attacked, I'd drop to my knees and jab him in his man giblets. It wasn't eloquent or pretty, and in some circles, it was considered distasteful. That line of thinking always escaped me. There were no rules of engagement when it came to survival. The only rule: SURVIVE.

Many opponents had tried to shame me for it being a weapon in my quiver, but that never worked. There was a difference between sparring, where I'd consider such tactics reprehensible, too, and fighting for your very survival.

"You need to finish the job," Landon informed me. His hand reached out, I suspected to stroke my cheek, but I knocked it away.

The dynamics had changed between us and it was weird. Usually, after you introduced a vampire to true death, if they weren't trying to exact revenge, they made it their goal to stay away. It subjected them to a humility that most weren't comfortable with. An immortal nearly dying? Not this century-old freakshow. The lascivious way his eyes remained on my lips, the dark allure that radiated off him, and the salacious way he leaned in and canted his head, was nothing more than vampire seduction.

"Turn it off," I demanded.

"I don't believe we are at any risk of you being lured by anything I'm doing."

"You're right, but you should save the good stuff for someone you'd have a chance with."

"After you finish your business with the witches, perhaps we can celebrate the actual conclusion of the job with—"

"Nope."

"You didn't let me finish."

"Don't need to. Even if you were going to take me to dinner in Paris, I'd decline." Visiting Paris was on my bucket list.

"Dinner in Paris is a no, but that's just a starting point for negotiations. What can I do to entertain you for one evening?"

Be normal. It would be such an endeavor for him that I'd be truly entertained. I didn't answer.

"I digress," he said after accepting he wasn't going to get

an answer. "Our last encounter left no opportunity for us to discuss closure of the job."

"You mean when I was forced to stab you because you were being an ass?"

"And felt just as inclined to feed me, thereby ensuring that I didn't have a true death." His tongue ran languidly over his bottom lip, and I really wasn't sure what was more appealing to him, me stabbing him or me feeding him.

"What part of my job with the witches do you feel was left incomplete?"

"The agreement was that the land be destroyed. I've been informed that it is still intact, and they had the audacity to have planted on my land."

"It's not yours," I corrected. "Their house, their land."

"Part of the two-million-dollar deal was for it to be destroyed. As far as I'm concerned, it is mine and nothing can be grown on it."

Rolling my eyes, I knew he was beyond reason. He was exerting a level of control, self-importance, and power that he assumed he was entitled to, all while doling out master-level triviality.

"They agreed never to grow Amber Crocus—" I started to remind him.

"No, they didn't agree willingly. It was under oath and it was agreed that the land would be destroyed. I expect it to be enforced."

True, that was part of the agreement, and if doing it would conclude the job to his satisfaction and end any more interaction with him, I'd enforce it and be rid of him. If not, it would leave an opening for him to keep coming back. I wanted Landon out of my life.

"Fine, I'll handle that. You'll receive pics as confirmation. I'll contact you. And after it's complete, we're done. Do you understand? No involvement from you or anyone in your camp, are we clear?"

I figured finishing the job would require a high level of diplomacy, and after his stunt of sending Dallas to kill the witches if things didn't go as planned, I was positive they wouldn't want to have anything to do with Landon.

He understood, but instead of agreeing, he responded with a sly smile. Starting for the door, he looked over his shoulder.

"My niece will be performing next week. Shall I purchase two tickets?"

"Sure. Her company will appreciate the money."

"Wonderful. You'll be my guest?"

"No. You asked if you should buy two tickets. I simply urged you to do so. I never agreed to go anywhere with you."

He turned in a sharp whip of movement, moving so close to me, reflexes had my hand readied to react with magic, but I caught myself in time.

"Don't be coy. You knew exactly what I was implying. Let it be a celebration of the closing of another job between us," he offered in his low husky voice that spoke to more than just the ending of a job but the beginning of something else.

"Don't forget Ms. Harp's bag." I handed it to him.

"Of course we can't forget our curious little friend. She must have been quite the actress in her day."

It felt odd sharing a laugh with him.

"Why don't you ask Evelyn when you drop this off? I'm sure she'd love to go."

His eyes glinted darkly, and I wasn't sure if he'd taken it as a challenge or just refused to let me get the best of him. Lips curling into a smile, he took the bag, taking my hand into his in the process and lightly kissing it. Perhaps the snarl I gave him would ensure that he'd never try that again. But if staking him in the chest didn't get rid of him, I wasn't sure what would.

"Pardon me while I ask Evelyn to join me next week for a night I'm sure she's not likely to forget."

She won't. It's not often she'll meet someone so utterly enthralled by himself.

I watched him approach her door, wondering if I'd just sent my elderly neighbor on a date. It would be a peculiar May/December coupling, especially since the man who looked to be in his late thirties was the wintry one.

CHAPTER 12

*A*t the desk in my office, I looked over the lease renewal agreement. It was the first time I'd considered not renewing it. After Landon's visit earlier that day, I wasn't sure if having an office on the opposite side of town was serving its purpose. It was supposed to keep the reprobates away from my home, but it seemed that having a second location simply made it a challenge for anyone who wanted to meet me to find my home address and just show up.

I liked to keep work and home life separate, even if only in concept.

When the door crept open, I looked up and quickly drew my eyes back to my computer, to roll my eyes at it and not the wizard robe-wearing witches who had just entered. I couldn't be the only person who found their clothing choices absurd. Did anyone else look at Stacey and Wendy and ask what the hell was wrong with them?

I wasn't sure which was more obnoxious: seeing one with a robe, or two.

They sauntered into my office, their robes swishing,

while I kept everything rigid to keep my expression from showing my thoughts.

I'd been surprised when Stacey contacted me before I'd had a chance to contact her about the Landon situation. I'd figured it was to get me to intervene with Landon, who I was sure would insert himself into the situation despite my request.

He was being a little petty by wanting the land destroyed. Or perhaps he wasn't. He'd paid two million dollars for the Amber Crocus and he had every right to want all aspects of the agreement fulfilled. Maybe destroying the land was a deterrent, although sending an assassin after the witches should have been enough to warn them off ever trying to extort him again.

"You wanted to see me?" I asked, approaching them. As their arms remained stiffly at their sides, I decided against offering a handshake. Tension, along with the feel of readied magic, swarmed through the air. That they both had their wands with them put me on edge. Instead of mocking them, I studied them with apprehension. Stacey's face was relaxed, but Wendy's was pinched with uneasiness.

A look passed between them and finally Stacey spoke. "Why does a demon have a capture bounty on you?"

The shock must have shown because the tension fled from Wendy's face.

"You don't know why, do you?"

I shook my head; the only thing that went through my mind was Malific. But we were bound, so she wouldn't want me dead, not now.

"He's offering the Black Crest grimoire for your capture. Do you know what most witches would do for that book?"

I paused for a moment to think. My only encounter with a demon had been during the visit with Harrison when he summoned Dareus to assist with finding out about the markings on my arm. It subsequently led to Harrison offering me to the demon in payment of an outstanding debt.

"Is it all demons, or one in particular?"

Wendy nodded. "He goes by the name Dareus." Something about the downcast of Ms. Wizard Robe's eyes made me curious.

"How do you know there's a bounty?" I inquired, my gaze homing in on her.

Almost simultaneously, their lips pressed together as if they were afraid a confession would spill out.

"You summoned a demon. The two of you are using dark magic," I accused.

"No, not at all," a flushed Wendy blurted.

I waited for their explanation, which I was sure would be intertwined with enough convoluted tales and excuses to try to distract me from knowing they were dealing in dark magic. If it got out, their reputation would be tarnished. Wendy wouldn't be able to participate in magic fights, she'd be ousted from their coven, and most witches wouldn't associate with them.

It felt wrong disparaging them since, essentially, they'd warned me about the bounty, but I needed to know how involved they were with dark magic.

Wendy looked defiant. "Not all magic is black or white. There's gray magic. Demons are well versed in it and for very little payment, they'll share some of it. Most comes from the Black Crest grimoire. People are afraid to consult demons. Operating out of fear is self-limiting," she said. From the jut of her jaw and her stance, she believed her defense.

"Making deals with demons is dangerous, too. Don't forget that little tidbit," I reminded her. Her argument seemed oddly familiar to the one Harrison gave to justify his use of dark magic. Anything could be twisted and contorted until it sufficed as justification, if needed.

"What does he want with me?" I asked.

"He seems to think you're elven-touched. Guarded by the elves, which means that you know where they are. I thought they were extinct, but after meeting you, he believes otherwise."

They were looking at my ears the way that I'd looked at Nolan's. I only knew hybrids, so I didn't know if the pointed ears thing was just a myth.

"He said you were marked on your arm and that there are pictures. He even directed us to Harrison." Wendy's face twisted in disgust at the mention of the dark magic-peddling witch who summoned demons.

Her hypocrisy was a perfume that wafted off her. My thoughts must have shown on my face.

"Clearly he and I are different," she said. "I don't peddle in dark magic. I dabble occasionally in gray."

Isn't gray magic just a coffee stop on the way to dark magic? Then I remembered that Cory had used gray, or grayish, magic in the past. Or maybe I'd consider it opaque.

"Harrison showed us the picture of the mark and said it's on your arm."

"I don't have any markings."

"Can we check?"

"Of course." I extended my arms to them, fully aware that even if the mark wasn't a magic restriction, it could only be seen with Mirra fire or similar.

Stacey grabbed my arm and held it tight. Wendy sprinkled a blue dust over it and whispered an invocation. Hellfire erupted. I howled in pain and before the pain could stop, I had ripped the push dagger from the necklace, lunged at Wendy, and pressed it to her throat. I was so close to pushing it in, when I remembered Elizabeth's description of me: violent, tenacious, known for explosive fits of pique. But this was justified. My arm was throbbing and had turned red from their version of a Mirra.

She glanced down, but I was too close for her to get a

look at it. When she moved, she could only feel the point of my blade at her throat. Fear filled her eyes. I could see her calculating whether she was faster with her magic than I was with a weapon at her throat.

"Please, don't hurt her," Stacey whispered. Remorse clung to her words, but I wondered if it was because I was just seconds from doing serious damage to Wendy, or whether Stacey was actually regretful for what they'd done. Anger had me rooted in place. It was a conflation of everything happening, and my emotions were a rubber band pulled to the point of snapping. Unfortunately, Wendy was on the receiving end. It should have been Malific.

I released her. Wendy eased away from me, her eyes narrowed. She lifted her chin. Had she felt my magic, sensed something? Diablerie magic? Had I released a magical charge?

"Dareus showed us the spell we needed. Now that we know it's not true, we'll alert others. It's good that we checked. If it's our word against his, people will believe us," Wendy assured me, inching farther back from me. "But it doesn't explain why he wants you. Even if it is a lie, why would he tell such a grand one? What gave him the impression that you're elven-touched?"

I shrugged.

"He's met you?" Wendy asked, skepticism etched in her words and in her narrow-eyed stare.

"Harrison summoned him for a job, and before you ask, I'm not at liberty to disclose any of the information."

"Client?"

None of your damn business. What is this, a cross-examination?

Stacey chewed on her bottom lip. "Harrison had the picture. Why would he make up such a thing?"

"He's indebted to Dareus. He attempted to give me to

Dareus as payment. He'll do and say anything to clear that debt."

After several minutes of quiet deliberation, they seemed convinced. Nodding, Wendy started to back out of the room with Stacey close behind.

"Who did you borrow magic from?" Stacey asked me casually.

"What?"

"When you attacked Wendy, there was a spark before you doused it. You're a death mage. Who are you borrowing magic from and should you be this far from them?"

"You're mistaken." I pulled one of my electric pellets from my pocket and dropped it. "That's what you saw."

There were too many lies being told. I needed these witches away from me, and I needed to remember what I'd told them so that I could keep things consistent.

Before they could leave, I reminded them. "We need to discuss the situation with Landon."

They both stiffened.

"What more does he want? He set out to kill us. That has more than satisfied our debt." Wendy fumed, her movements of waving away any further dealings with him made more dramatic by the excessive movement of the sleeves of her robe. I couldn't get past the unnecessary wardrobe.

"You're missing several scenes before that attempt took place. Remember you blackmailed him out of two million dollars, and when he asked for an oath, you sought another buyer. Don't claim innocence."

Wendy glared at me, my synopsis bringing a frown to her face. "Things didn't go as expected. We were robbed. We're the victims here," she huffed.

Okay, Ms. Drama. That's enough of that. She was wearing a wizard robe and carrying a wand. There had to be a cap placed on weird. She couldn't be a drama queen, too.

"Are you willing to return the money?"

They looked scandalized at the very suggestion. I just wanted one day to pass where I didn't get treated to dramatics.

"If you're not prepared to return the money, then you have to be compliant with the terms of the agreement. The land has to be destroyed."

"Fine, we'll do it tomorrow," Stacey conceded.

"I'll be at the house with Cory at ten."

"Will you be performing the spell?" Wendy asked.

My lips kinked into a smirk. *I'm not that easily fooled.* "I can't. Cory will do it."

There was the cool shadow of disbelief as they backed out the door. But they didn't have to believe me as long as they couldn't prove I had magic.

Once they were gone, I sent Landon a text notifying him of the arrangement. He immediately called me. I sent it to voicemail. After he called three more times, I foolishly assumed it was important.

"Yes, Landon." I managed to keep the irritation out of my voice. In fact, I sounded pleasant, surprising myself and him because I heard it immediately in his voice.

"Aren't you the face of diplomacy when dealing with the witches? Did they offer any resistance?"

Moments like this made it difficult to believe he was a century old. But I guess it took years to master this level of pettiness. "Did you want it to be hostile?" I asked.

Yes, he did.

"Of course not. I would have preferred to be there to drive home the importance of them never trying to extort me again. I'd like Elon or Dallas to accompany you."

"No. I'm not aiding your intimidation tactics. They're upholding the terms of the agreement. I'll send you pictures as confirmation and this job is done. *We* are done."

"Then we can celebrate the completion of such a distasteful situation."

"How about dinner at eight?" I suggested.

"That would be absolutely delightful. Do you have a place in mind?"

"You can choose because I have no intention of showing up. But pretend that I'm there. Perhaps that will put a stop to you repeatedly asking me out."

"Oh, Erin. Whatever will I do with you?"

"Nothing. I want us not doing anything, okay? Stop asking me out, stop trying to seduce me, and stop making me the recipient of your misplaced affections. The only thing about me that is appealing to you is that I once had a relationship with Grayson. I'm not going to be your ego-stroking trophy, 'kay?"

He was silent for a long time. "I understand the idea of me being beguiled by you is uncharacteristic. After all, it's *me*. Many have felt they aren't worthy. I think you need to hear this. Erin, you are worthy of me. Don't sell yourself short. *I* find you appealing. I find myself enthralled by more than a pretty face. I find myself enchanted by your tenacity, your strong will, and your feistiness." He exhaled an exasperated breath. "Listen when I say, you are enough for me, Erin. Don't let your insecurities keep you from enjoying... well, me," he provided in a tone drenched in arrogance and self-importance.

Enjoy this, you asshat. I disconnected the phone without responding and was prepared to do it again if he called back. But he seemed to have gotten the message.

CHAPTER 13

endy and Stacey met us with contemptuous leers as Cory and I approached their garden. Landon was right. They'd had the gall to have planted, and when we arrived, their jeans and shirts were stained with dirt from pulling plants from the soil. Wendy cut her eyes at us and I took it more seriously without the dramatics of the robe.

"I still feel that this is an extreme request," Wendy snapped, leaving a smudge of dirt on her face as she wiped her hand across it.

When Cory moved closer to get a look at what they had pulled from the garden, Stacey quickly rolled the plants into the wet paper where they'd been placing them.

"It's just Lilith root. We use them in sleeper spells and put a little in the candles we sell to the humans. Unless it's invoked in a spell, it doesn't do anything, but they like the smell. You know how they are. If they buy it from a witch, they believe it has magical properties." She shrugged, gathered up the paper, and placed it in the large tote next to her.

"Lilith root has small yellow bulbs on it." Cory's brow rose and his lips turned down into a disapproving frown.

"That looks like Willows Dawn," he said. "It's been rumored to force shifters into changing." He shook his head. "It's just a rumor. If you do a luna plena with it, you're just going to have a really angry and sneezy shifter. And that's it. Then you'll have to deal with them once they realize you tried to do a full moon spell."

I didn't bother to add that shifters were now immune to magic so the spell wouldn't even work.

"I know. We have no intention of doing anything with shifters," Wendy hurriedly and emphatically added. There might as well have been a flashing arrow in her direction calling out her lie. I had a feeling the witches were hoping to concoct something else that would give them a big payday. Greed was going to be the undoing of their coven. But I felt compelled to at least try to discourage her from whatever her plans were with Asher.

"You don't want to screw with the shifters, especially not Asher. Landon tried to kill you," I reminded her. I wanted to disclose what Asher had confided in me about another coven who'd extorted the Northwest Pack for a strand of wolfsbane that adversely affected them more than the regular version, but I'd be betraying a confidence. I was positive Asher wouldn't be as tolerant the second time around.

It was obvious Wendy was behind this, so I held her gaze. "Landon is indulgent." *And petty as fuck*, but she knew that and didn't need it reiterated. "His revenge is based on short-term gratification. His retaliations are quick and decisive. He doesn't play the long game. Asher isn't like that. You screw with the Northwest Pack, he's not going to immediately try to destroy you. He *does* play the long game."

"First, he's going to attack your coven legally and ruin you financially. I've seen him do it and it's not pretty. Then he'll really go to work on making your life a living hell. It will be horrible for you but just a game for him. He's at pro level. I advise you to open a store, sell love potions, sleep aids, and your herbs, witchy versions of weed and mushrooms, and make your money from that. Actually, instead, teach a class: 'Magic for the magicless.' Humans love that stuff. Many covens make an impressive amount of money from doing it. Leave the extortion gig alone. It won't end well for you, I can assure you of that."

As the witches packed up their things, leaving scattered dirt and holes in the garden, and headed for the house, I knew I hadn't made a convincing argument. They'd learn the hard way.

"You can let yourself out through the gate. Once you're gone, we'll erect the wards again," Wendy told me, closing the back door.

In other words, don't bother coming back and trying to lecture them about the Willows Dawn. They didn't have to worry about me; if they succeeded in making their concoction, I'd be around with popcorn in hand to watch how it played out.

"I can't believe Landon wanted this done. They can just grow a garden somewhere else," Cory said, kneeling to perform the spell.

"Because it's Landon and he's making a point. A trivial one, but one nonetheless." I texted Landon to let him know we were starting the spell and recorded the process. Magic poured over the area and into the soil. A dank smell of death bloomed in the air before the moisture pulled from the soil and a sheen of patina moved over it like a barrier to ensure nothing would ever grow from it. Just as I sent the video with the message "It's done," I heard whirring helicopter blades overhead, close enough for me to see Landon in the passenger cabin. What. A. Jackass. When my phone vibrated, I hesitated before answering.

"Good job, Erin," Landon praised in a condescension-laced tone.

Yep. Jackass.

I wasn't sure what disgusted me more: his triviality or his ostentatious waste of money. A freaking helicopter!

My adult side was urging me to deal with it with some semblance of decorum and dignity; after all, he was the acting vampire Master of the City. I put my phone down, fully aware that he'd be able to hear me, but just in case, I put him on speaker. Then I directed him to the destroyed garden. "See, it's all done," I said, using my special pointing finger. Not the pointer, but the middle, as I showcased the destruction with a wave of my finger.

Cory groaned. "Dear fates, she's giving the vampire Master the finger." He covered his face with his hands, unable to look at the display of immaturity and disrespect.

"He's the one being ridiculous," I asserted with a huff.

"Nice. We're children in the playground fighting ridiculous with ridiculous."

I'll admit it was juvenile, but it didn't make it any less satisfying to see the helicopter fly away and know that Landon was probably as done with me as I was with him.

CHAPTER 14

I would have missed it if I hadn't stopped at my door and checked my back pocket for my phone. A circle, right outside my door. Quickly backing away, I called Cory.

"What's this?" I asked, turning the video phone around to show him the faint chalked markings at my front door.

"Get me closer," he instructed.

I did and gave him a minute to look at all the sigils, then turned the video to me.

His jaw was clenched so tight it looked painful and his eyes blazed with anger. "It's a summoning circle for demons," he growled. Since our encounter with Dareus and Harrison, Cory had made it his duty to expand his knowledge on demons, summonings, and dark magic.

"Why would someone put it outside my door?"

"You say there's a bounty on you."

"I wouldn't say a bounty. Dareus offered to give them the Black Crest grimoire for me."

"What do you think a bounty is?"

"Why here?"

"They summon him the moment you're out, and he can snatch you."

"Screw this! I refuse to let this continue. I have a demon I need to chat with."

"What do you mean chat with?"

"I'm dealing with the whole bound-to-Malific situation. I don't have time to be dealing with mercenary witches attacking me over a damn book. This needs to stop and it needs to stop now."

"And your solution is to talk to Dareus?" Cory sounded incredulous.

"If talking does it, then we talk. If not, I need to find out how to kill a demon between now and the time I get to your house."

"Yeah, this sounds really well thought out. Great plan. 'Let's negotiate with the demon and if that doesn't work, I'm going to kill him Buffy-style.'"

"Who's Buffy?"

"I will disown you!" he snapped through gritted teeth. It was too easy. Pretending not to know cult classic shows and movies was my new favorite thing.

"Nope, I have no idea who that is."

"Well then, we'll remedy that. Seems like we need a binge-watching date. We can watch *Angel*, the spinoff, too."

I deserved that. Next, it'd be *Scarface*, *Dirty Dancing*, and *The Godfather*.

"I'll pick you up in thirty minutes," I told him.

"Good, it'll give me time to call Maddie."

I glared at him and added a snarl for good measure.

"I can never reason with you when you're like this. Perhaps she can."

This was equivalent to him threatening to tell my mother on me. Madison didn't need to be involved if it wasn't necessary.

"How should I handle this?" I asked.

"I'm not disputing you need to talk to Dareus, but going in guns blazing, ready to kill a demon—which we're only aware of one person ever doing, and you know what type of person he was—isn't a solid idea. Erin, I don't want everything that's happening to change you."

"Cory, do you seriously think I'll come out on the other side of this unchanged?"

"The Erin I know could."

He ended the call and my heart wrenched. That punch landed hard. He was wrong. I didn't think I was going to come out of this unchanged, no matter how hard I tried. I just wanted to recognize the person.

I made one call, Dr. Sumner, and left a message for him, then I cleared away the circle. Afterward, I stood outside my door and spoke just shy of yelling. "You don't want to try this again. Final warning. This is your free pass. If you dare try this again, I will find you and make you regret it. My life is worth more than a damn book!"

When Harrison saw my car drive up the dirt road, he turned and jogged into his trailer.

Cory snorted. "He remembers us."

How could he not? Cory had been sporting some dangerous magic and even more dangerous rage. If not for my intervention, Harrison would be dead at Cory's hands.

"Harrison, we just want to talk," I told him through his closed door.

"What part of never return did you not understand?"

"I understood it just fine, but I'm sure you're aware that Dareus has placed a bounty on me. He only knows about me because of you."

"You came to me for help and I gave it," he barked.

"No, you tried to hand me over as payment. Don't give

me your revisionist account. I need you to summon him because he and I need to talk."

"That's not going to happen." Harrison's breathing was labored, as if he was moving furniture or rushing around his trailer. There was rustling and scraping.

"What is he doing?" Cory mouthed. The window covering prevented us from seeing inside the trailer.

"Harrison, I need you to do this."

"No. Go away."

"Harrison," I implored. "Let's make a deal. You owe him, right? What do you think he'll take in lieu of a person? Maybe I can help."

"What are you doing?" Cory hiss-whispered.

"Negotiating."

"Sure, this demon freak wants a person. I'll also add we don't know the specifics and I'm sure I don't want to know. You plan to do what? Bargain him down to a cat?"

"I'm not giving him a cat. They're cute."

"What exactly do you plan to give him?"

"Don't know, but I'll figure something out when I talk to him."

"Wonderful. You're going to request that the demon remove your bounty, then negotiate the reduction of Harrison's debt, and your well-thought-out plan is to just wing it. Nice. There's no way this will fail. A totally solid plan."

I grinned at him. "I don't remember you being this pessimistic," I teased. "We both have magic, we got this."

My level of confidence surprised me. Worst-case scenario, we hightailed it out of there. Best case, I got the bounty taken off me and kept someone from being a demon pet or companion. I had no idea why Dareus wanted a person. Demons were known for using humans as subjects and practicing their magic and woven spells on them. But they eventually found humans too fragile and that abducting people made others less likely to summon them to strike deals. It also made them the target of revenge by the friends and family of the abductee. Witches and mages would summon demons under the guise of becoming a host, then when the demon was incorporeal, capture them in a phylaca urn, where they'd remain until someone was willing to release them. Which never happened. No demon had ever come to the rescue of another.

Several minutes passed. With my ear pressed against the door, I could hear movement. Smoke wafted through the door. He was pacing and smoking, which I took as a good sign. By the time Cory had gotten so restless he suggested breaking down the door, Harrison yanked it open. He took a long draw from the cigarette and then flicked it out the door past us.

"I've summoned him twice and he didn't respond. I can't make any guarantees," he said, widening the space to let us in. He kept a reproachful and careful eye on Cory. He looked haunted, with bags under his eyes and oily, straggly strawberry-blond hair.

"Try again," I suggested. Since Dareus had put out a bounty on me, he might answer in hopes that Harrison was making a claim.

Harrison moved his furniture to make more space in the limited area, then drew the circle. We carefully scrutinized his every movement to make sure there weren't any breaches in it. He said the invocation and moved to the opposite side of the trailer. Nothing. He cursed under his breath, moved closer, and said the invocation again. He didn't make it to the other side before Dareus showed up. If the level of fury and hate that blazed in Dareus's eyes had been directed at me, I would do what I could to get out of reach, too. Harrison retreated, fast, to the far side of the room, pressing his back firmly to the wall and looking as if he wished he could disappear into it.

Dareus's gaze tracked my movements with the same

caution and apprehension that I followed his. The circle was intact, but he kept inching precariously close to it. It was intentional; he was looking for any places of vulnerability. Not finding any, he focused solely on me.

"You're not going to find any way to get out or for me to get in," I told him.

"What's the purpose of this meeting, elven-protected?" His slitted snake-eyes pulsed with excitement at being near an elven-protected. That was the extent of what he knew about me. I had an elven magical mark and it was enough to put a bounty on me.

"So, it was the mark that made you want me?" I asked as he slid closer to the line, his face wistful as his gaze shifted from me to the surroundings behind me.

"Open the window," he demanded of Harrison. The command lurched Harrison into action and he quickly opened them all. It wasn't just the forestry, the scenic blue sky, the alluring melon color of the setting moon—it was freedom.

"You seem quite a tasty little morsel, but if you are elven-marked, then you have a link to them and a gateway to their magic. It's been so long since I've seen one." Sorrow swept over Dareus's face and I dropped my eyes to the floor. I wouldn't feel sorry for a demon and I damn sure wasn't going to feel sorry for one who'd put a bounty on me. And the "tasty little morsel" comment definitely wasn't ingratiating him to me, either.

"I won't be able to put you in contact with any elves. The mark has been with me since birth." Although I had taken some liberties, it was the truth. I wished I could get in contact with elves, Nolan in particular.

His hypnotic snake-slitted eyes held mine. Mine slipped from his just in case he had the ability to compel me, like vampires, or force me into truth.

Elven-protected. It meant something to him. Crossing my

arms, I stepped closer.

"Let's make a deal," I said.

A slow, easy smile curved his lips. "Of course. What's the deal?"

"You take the bounty off me."

That was it. I didn't provide a threat or a bargaining chip. It was an outlandish request. Enough so that Cory scoffed and quickly masked it with a choke and pulled a stick of gum out of his pocket and put it in his mouth. It was gumption without anything to back it up. But I'd learned from working with the arrogant, entitled, wealthy, and people who loved their gray areas of morality, that brazen audacity sometimes worked. Either they believed you had something up your sleeve, perceived you as an entertaining maverick, or the absurd request left them dumbfounded. Either way, it worked or it didn't.

But never had anyone thrown their head back in an explosion of laughter.

"Pretty *and* hilarious. Aren't you the package?"

I shrugged. It was worth the try. "You take the bounty off my head and you get to live."

"You're welcome to buy the bounty from me, and in the process"—his finger curved, forming an iridescent gust of blue light before revealing a weathered leatherbound book —"you'll get the Black Crest grimoire."

"How do we buy the bounty?" Cory asked.

Dareus's smile widened and he looked straight at Harrison. "Kill him." The color drained from Harrison's face; his hand turned outward before he assumed a defensive stance.

Damn. How ruthless a monster must you be to look someone straight in the face while trying to convince someone else to kill that person?

"I will find a way to repay my debt to you," Harrison promised.

Dareus dismissed his pledge with a wave of his hand. "I

no longer have use for you. I prefer your debt to be paid with your blood."

"Does it have to be a specific way?" Cory asked.

My head snapped in Cory's direction, my eyes wide with shock. *What the hell! Why are you asking questions? There's no reason for a Q&A.*

"Is it okay for me to hack him into bite-size pieces, or do you want the body whole?" Cory inquired.

Dareus glared at Cory. "I'd prefer the body whole and it to be here in front of me. People want this book because the spells in it arc powerful, the knowledge surpassed by no other books. It will make the magic that you have seem simplistic and ineffectual. You want to control shifters? There's a spell for that. Raise shades? It will show you how." Then his eyes moved to me. "Perform an elven Mirra? This is the book you need. Bypass Klipsen wards or compel other supernaturals? This book will give you access to magic no one else has. And all you have to do is get rid of him."

"But if we kill him, we're not just satisfying his debt, are we?" I asked, taking my line of questioning from Cory. Dareus's face was unperturbed, but the irritation in his eyes was easily read.

"We kill him, the circle that contains you is broken and you'll have a body. A body that you once hosted and with which established a life link." I watched the ire move from his eyes to his face. "That's the thing about being a demon host. Each time the link gets stronger and stronger and eventually you won't have to adhere to the agreement. You can take the body. People who deal in demon magic know this, which is why you aren't allowed to host often. Now, isn't it?"

His chin lifted in a show of defiance and he fixed me with a glare.

"Is it my fault the human body is so fragile that we can't perform magic through it?"

"You're not using human bodies," I pointed out.

He waved his hand in dismissal. "Witch, mage, fae, with the exception of their magical ability, their bodies are as fragile as humans."

They weren't fragile, just not able to easily contain demon magic.

"You were here for a reason: to remove your mark"—he leaned in, giving me a contemplative look—"but you don't need to anymore, do you?" he guessed. I didn't give him any fuel for his speculation, but I was sure by the way his eyes pulsed with intrigue that he knew I had magic, or at the very least, something about me had changed.

In his magical cage, he paced, flipping through the pages of the grimoire. He turned the book toward us. "*Requiro*, an archaic spell, mimics an elven Mirra and can be performed by anyone: fae, mage, witch, perhaps even strong-willed humans."

That was what lured humans to the magical world. The hope that they were the exception, that somewhere in their family history, someone had an illicit dalliance with a witch or mage and they possessed dormant magic. Magic that was waiting to be activated by the right spell, being in contact with the right person, or drinking the right herbs. I was yet to see it. Even the "healing" charms that witches sold did nothing more than give humans the opportunity to fall for a placebo effect.

When I stepped closer, he moved the book so I couldn't memorize any of it.

"Hmm. What else is here?" Dareus mused. "Unbinding spells, love spells, *Aeter*, which is an alternative way of Wynding. It's archaic, but sometimes the old spells are the best ones."

His eyes glinted with a self-satisfaction that confirmed my expression had betrayed me. My interest and curiosity were apparent. Cory was salivating at the possibility of different spells. When we were alone, I'd have to remind him that an old powerful spell had unleashed a fae and put him at odds with the shifters.

"Unbind what?" I asked, making sure to sound indifferent.

He pressed his face against the nearly translucent barrier, his eyes mischievous and his face far too appealing for such a malcontent being. His eyes dropped to the knife sheathed at my hip. "It's full of so many spells, I'm sure there's one that will appeal to you. Just keep the body intact. The circle will be removed and you'll have the grimoire." He didn't even have the good manners to lower his voice. Just "hey, do some murdering for me. Yeah, that guy. The one right behind you."

Harrison took a sharp intake of breath. Then words spilled from him, a curse rather than an invocation. Dareus shuddered, fading in and out of sight as he struggled to stay corporeal.

"I'm not as weak as you seem to believe, nor will I be as easily killed." Harrison spoke more spells and diablerie swept through the room. Its signature dark, dank, pungent odor smothered it. The cloak of it felt like soot. I could still smell magic and suspected it was one of my gifts. But since I had my own magic now, that gift had been tempered. Nothing could tamp down the smell of dark magic. And although it still had earthy notes with hints of cinnamon, like most witches' magic, it was distinctive. This had nuances that weren't quite right. A lightly rancid undertone. Never to be mistaken for regular magic.

Magic laced around Harrison's fingers when we turned to face him.

"If you touch me, I will kill you," he announced. His focus was on Cory, who had asked too many questions about killing him. Cory's lips simply lifted into a mockery of a smile.

"Do you think he can?"

A daily dose of jocular taunts and ego-shaming hadn't

diminished Cory's arrogance a smidge. On an arrogance scale of one, being barely perceptible, to ten, where the person may only be able to love themselves, he was a solid seven plus. Confidence meter on magic, he was a solid ten. He knew where his weaknesses lay and compensated for it. He recognized that he was one of the best witches in the world. With his better understanding of dark magic, he was still confident in his ability to win when challenged by someone wielding it. It showed in his posture, his unnerving calm, and the easiness of his smile. I saw it and Harrison tensed under it.

"Get. Out. Don't come back here again."

Cory seemed content to keep Harrison in a state of high alert, with erratic magic wrapping his fingers and tension and fear marring his face.

When I headed out the door, Cory eventually followed. I jabbed him in the stomach with my elbow. "What the hell was that 'can we hack him up in bite-size pieces'? And I did not enjoy that 'whose magical rod is bigger' contest you pulled with Harrison, either."

"It wasn't even a contest. Mine was definitely bigger. He's terrified of me, which shows that dark magic isn't the power-house people think it is."

He had a point. Dark magic seemed easier, didn't take as much out of the user, but had consequences. Harrison wasn't using dark magic to fend off Cory, but now that his regular magic had been tainted, it all had the feel and smell of dark magic. He'd gone to the well too often and it had changed his magic. It was a warning I wanted to give Stacey and Wendy, although I wasn't sure they'd listen.

"You're one to talk, your negotiation included…let me see…nothing! Seriously, you're sporting some serious gall. Hey, Mr. Demon, give me your grimoire. Nah, I'm going to forgo the negotiation part of negotiating because that's how I roll." He said the latter part in a poor imitation of my voice, with far too much neck rolling and gesticulating. "Classic Erin." He pulled me into a side hug and pressed his cheek to my head.

"I want the Black Crest grimoire," I admitted, getting into the car.

"Do you think it's better than the Mystic Souls?"

"Yes, because from what I saw, it was in Latin and English. We wouldn't have to rely on interpretation and assumptions. And I think it might be one of the few books that has elven alternative magic, maybe even counterspells. I might be able to use it to unbind me from Malific."

"Then what?"

"I don't know."

I could feel his gaze on me as I started driving.

"You don't know, Erin?" he pressed.

It was the truth; I had no idea. There was still that reluctant piece of me, maybe some primitive state of my being that clung to the belief that family members do for family for no other reason than the familial link. An unfounded and unreasonable feeling of obligation that a person wouldn't otherwise have. And that primitive niggling made it hard for me to whole-heartedly commit to killing my mother, despite believing she wouldn't share the same reservations.

CHAPTER 15

ith a bounty on my head, I hesitated before answering my door the day after meeting with Dareus. Although appreciative of the wards the Huntsmen had placed to prevent anyone from Wynding in or using my door as a Veil exit point, I still kept hold of my karambit.

The unsettling feeling had me with a knife in one hand and checking my push dagger necklace as I approached the door. I prepared for the worst. And yet, I still wasn't ready for it to be Malific.

"Hello, daughter," she greeted through the door when I refused to open it. The notes of disdain that marked her words seemed to linger. "Open the door for your mother."

"Go away."

"Shall I make you come out?" There wasn't a hint of a threat in her voice. Just a simple statement of intent, and I knew she'd do anything to make me do just that. I debated whether to force her hand.

Her head eased to the right and my heart felt like it had stopped beating. I couldn't inhale enough breath. I snatched open the door when Malific made her way toward Ms. Harp, who, true to form, had peeked out her door to get a look at the visitor.

When she was just a foot or so from her, I pushed magic into my chest so hard I smacked into the wall. My back ached and pain ran through my ribs. The sudden jolt made my heart beat erratically. Determination made the pain easier to accept, because whatever was happening to me was also happening to Malific.

"Go into the apartment, lock the door, and don't come out until I tell you," I ordered Ms. Harp through gritted teeth. Wide-eyed, Ms. Harp looked at me, then Malific, and slammed shut the door. Magic tugged at mine as Malific tried to release herself. Before she could break free, I released us. I dashed to Ms. Harp's door and erected a ward. It was a simple one that wouldn't withstand a lot, but it provided an obstacle.

Whipping around, I ripped the push blade from my necklace and held it to my throat. Her emotionless eyes trained on it. I wanted to see fear; she denied me that.

"You won't be able to save everyone," she said. "And I have nothing but time."

"If you're thinking about terrorizing or killing my friends and family, it won't work in your favor. Because living in constant fear that you will take them from me isn't a life. Not one worth living. Remember, if I die, so do you." I tensed my body and pressed the blade into my neck, letting her feel the bite of the blade.

I watched her carefully as she settled into the new knowledge that I'd end it for us both in order to save my friends and family.

If it frightened her or gave her any pause, she didn't show it.

"You're right, what type of life is this?" she said in a low voice, wistful. A moment of ennui that I wasn't expecting. For seconds, I thought we were sharing an existential moment. "I have no army, my power is limited, and I have to deal with an ungrateful daughter. This is not a life I would have chosen for myself and definitely not one fitting for me."

Did this woman just usurp my freaking speech and make it about her? A narcissist and a sociopath. You can't be all the horrible things.

My breath hitched but I stood steady while she eased closer to me and studied my face. It wasn't in the manner a mother did, with an appreciation of shared similarities and stalwart affection. There was something more that she searched for. Weakness to exploit? Nolan's features? A way to ease her contempt for me?

"You had to die so that I could escape. A wondrous feat and one that has proven your worth to me."

"Oh thanks. It's nice to know that I, your daughter, have some semblance of value to you."

Ignoring my response, she said, "Perhaps you can do the same again. For a period, give me the ability to create another army, and I promise to leave and no longer be a threat to you and yours."

Even if I believed her and was able to recreate my death to give her power for a short period of time, it wouldn't be enough. The Immortalis were still restricted from returning to the Veil, and she'd do anything to break the curse that constrained them.

Malific's piercing chestnut-colored eyes regarded me, seemingly taking my silence for consideration. Her eyes traveled along the angular lines of my face; the similarity of our features didn't evoke anything remotely maternal. Just the opposite. Antipathy. And not just because I'd diminished her power.

"Will you?" she asked.

"No."

She didn't know that it was impossible to recreate, and I

took some satisfaction in her belief that I had the ability to deny her restoring her power.

"Don't look at it as a compromise of ethics or supplication but rather you satisfying your debts to me."

"Debts?" I scoffed out. Was she high?

"Yes, debts. The one created when I gave you life, and the one you incurred when the Huntsmen killed my army. Either way, I am owed."

What the hell? Despite what I knew of her, I still wasn't prepared for this level of malignant narcissism, delusions of grandeur, and entitlement.

"What about the debt you incurred? After all, I'm the reason you're free," I reminded her, taking a different approach.

"You can't be rewarded for unintentional assistance nor can you use it as currency. You were just a tool. A hammer doesn't get the accolades when the carpenter does the work. My Immortalis performed the labor, while you only did what you were born to do. Die."

We stood eye to eye, glaring at each other as time ticked past. When she spoke again, some of the coarseness was gone. "I'm extending an olive branch that I won't offer again. I'm giving you a chance to survive in a situation you otherwise would not. I suggest you take it."

"I reject it."

My response was met with a flash of anger and she bared her teeth to me as if she had fangs.

"Do you know why you will not be the victor in this?"

"Because I'm not a crazy bitch," I offered.

That insult brought a smile to her lips. She looked at Ms. Harp's door and I tensed, prepared to zap myself with magic to stop her. "Because you have weaknesses I will exploit. I have none."

"I don't consider being human and caring about people a weakness."

"You are my child. Part Arch-deity, and despite being tainted by elven blood, you come from the strongest and purest bloodline. The gods of god and yet you live like this. A servant to others."

"That's an odd assertion to make, seeing that the only reason I'm able to stand in front of you without you attempting to kill me is because we're bound together by elven magic. Magic the almighty Malific can't seem to break. *So*, am I tainted or empowered by their blood? Right now, with all my so-called glorious Arch-deity blood, we're at the mercy of elven magic. You can calm down with touting your own greatness."

Her eyes darkened with the promise of violence. "*I* can create living beings who have magical ability, warriors who exist to serve me. I exiled gods. It took an army to stop me. I conquered those who are immune to magic, forcing them to live in fear of me."

I flinched at her reference to the shifters.

"You didn't conquer them. You murdered them while they were answering the call of the moon. You violated all rules of engagement. You're a cheat. And you didn't do it for your survival. You just had a murderous temper tantrum because they dared to reject your request. That doesn't make you a noble god, it makes you a cheating coward," I ground out, my anger mirroring hers.

"I'm no coward, child. I use weaknesses to my advantage. I call that strategy. I will outlive most, I can only be killed by one thing, and my magic exceeds almost everyone's. No one should ever reject my requests."

"Oh, I'm sorry, do you really believe your magic abilities make you immune to dealing with the very things everyone has to?"

"Yes." The anger had melted from her voice, and her response was a confident whisper of breath. "This foolish, perverse belief of equality is ignorant. I'm an Arch-deity. My blood is strong, my magic nearly boundless. No, I don't feel I should be treated like everyone else, because I'm not like everyone else. I make sure no one believes otherwise. I will rule the Veil. Perhaps here, too. My army will be other gods and my servants the witches, mages, and shifters." She bared her teeth again. "I will entertain myself by getting rid of the elves. Once we are no longer bound, my half-breed child, you will be the first."

I scoffed. Her audacity was astounding. "Half-breed? I'm here because of you!"

"Exactly, but that wasn't my wish for you. My plan was to give you the gift of death, to free me. Giving you a purpose far more fitting than what you are."

I punched her with all the force I could muster, accepting the pain in my face, weathering it because of the satisfaction that it hurt her just as bad. The cool breeze of her healing magic didn't allow either of us to feel the pain for long. But it felt good knowing that strike hurt, even if for only a second.

Her laughter was mirthless, dark, and ominous. "What a pitiful last gasp for a person destined for death. You rejected my offer of kindness. Unbind us, or I'll kill your friends. One by one, in front of you." Her eyes slid to Ms. Harp's door.

My adoptive mother never allowed me to use the word *hate*. She despised it. In her idealistic view of the world, even with me as a daughter who toed that gray line and had an addiction for magic, she believed people "strongly disliked" but never hated. She was wrong. I hated Malific. I hated her for her callousness for life, her cruelty, her insolence, her entitlement. And I hated her most of all for forcing me to become the person I needed to be to best her.

The fire of my hate must have shown on my face because she stood taller, her face sparking with the joy of a warrior who was about to be given a good fight. And instead of cowering, she welcomed it.

I hated her.

"Elizabeth was right about me," I said. "I am quite clever, and it will be to your detriment."

As much as I willed it, I wasn't sure I could become the person I needed to be to best her.

It was as if she'd seen my contemplation. She gave another glance at Ms. Harp's door. "I will kill her first."

"Remember what I said. If you hurt anyone I care about, you won't have to worry about us being unbound. I will end us both."

A slow smile came to her lips, leaving me wondering if it was a tacit agreement or a challenge. She simply turned away and left as if I were inconsequential.

I despised her with a loathsome rage that could no longer be contained in my body.

I marched to my apartment, closed the door, and let the magic spill from me, and when I was done, my apartment looked as if a tornado had been through it.

CHAPTER 16

*T*hat *wasn't helpful,* I thought as I surveyed the wreckage of my apartment. I needed to do something more constructive. My throat got tight and my heart pounded erratically. Ms. Harp could have been injured, or worse. My hands were clammy as I found my phone.

"What's wrong?" Asher asked.

"I need you to get Ms. Harp out of here. Put her somewhere safe." I couldn't tamp down the panic in my voice.

"Okay. What happened?"

Recalling the encounter with my mother made all the feelings of fear, anger, dread, and loathing resurface.

"She's not going to come with me willingly," he said.

"Then do whatever's necessary to get her out of here. She can't stay here."

"Are you sanctioning an abduction?" he asked, amusement and shock in his voice. When I heard a car door close and the change of external noise, my clenched fist relaxed. My nails had left crescent-shape marks in my palm.

"No…well…um, maybe an extraordinary rendition? *But* only if necessary. I'd prefer if she goes willingly. Coax her. Use that alleged charm you keep rambling on about."

"I assure you, there's nothing alleged about it," he said in a low, deep, silky voice. "I'll be there in about fifteen minutes."

If he was at home, he was over twenty miles away. "Great. The fleet of policemen trailing you for speeding might come in handy. Maybe they can help convince her to leave."

His deep chuckle was all I heard before the call ended.

"Evelyn." I cracked the door to better hear Asher trying to coax Ms. Harp. "Open the door," he managed in a tone that was both gentle and commanding.

"Are you going to try to make me leave?" she barked back through the door.

"We discussed this when I called. Evelyn, let me in."

"Not if I have to leave."

"Evelyn, you have to come with me."

"No, I'm fine and I refuse to let someone run me from my home."

"It's not about running. It's about making sure you're safe. We're not having this debate again. It's a non-issue. You will be coming with me."

"And if I don't? What exactly do you plan to do? Break the door down, like a barbarian or something?"

Was this how I sounded when I dared him? I suspected I wasn't very far off.

"Yes, Evelyn, that's exactly what I will do. Neither one of us wants that, but if you don't open the door, you're not leaving me a lot of choices."

I hazarded a peek out of my door just in time to see her open it. "Sometimes you can be so bossy," she chided, and then her eyes flew in my direction. The cold accusation in them had me quickly closing the door and pressing my back to it.

What the hell? I'm seriously hiding from an irritated septua-genarian.

I pushed off from the door and headed to her apartment. I figured Asher would probably need some help convincing her to leave without force. At the very least, her getting the chance to scold me might make her more amenable.

Lightly knocking on the ajar door before entering, I found Ms. Harp with her hands on her hips and her jaw locked in defiance. Her eyes swept from me to the cane leaning in the corner. I was more confident than I wanted to be that either Asher or I, maybe both, were about to be caned.

"Evelyn, this isn't up for debate. Pack a bag."

It was the command in his voice. It spoke to something so innate that it took everything in a person not to submit. Shifters didn't possess any magic other than what was needed to shift. Asher's command, and the force of it, something I was sure was reserved for the people in his pack, had me locking my knees so I didn't find myself walking to my apartment and packing my own bag. Was it compulsion, like the vampires? The indomitable nature of it felt like subtle coercion. It demanded compliance, evoked surrender.

Ms. Harp didn't want to surrender without a fight, but it wouldn't be with Asher. She'd conceded. His face was inscrutable but his posturing was domineering. She was going to pack her bags and leave with him. No questions.

"Minding one's own business seems to be a lost art," she told me with a glower.

You would know.

I wasn't sure if she was blissfully unaware of the hypocrisy of her statement or brazenly accepting of it. Whichever it was, I was left wide-eyed.

"I'm sorry, what?" I sputtered out, wanting her to repeat her comment, hoping she'd notice the hypocrisy, too.

"You should be. It wasn't your business to tell." As she

turned around, she threw a parting shot. "Maybe it was yours to tell. After all, the woman was here for you, not me."

She walked away, a little sashay in her step because she was truly aware of what she'd done.

"You should go pack your things as well, so we won't have to wait," Asher said matter-of-factly, turning to me. It wasn't a command or even a request. A simple order, as if I didn't have a say. I found myself standing taller, arms crossed over my chest, jaw clenched in defiance. *Dammit, I'm Ms. Harp-lite.* But without the decades to perfect it.

"Asher, I appreciate—"

"Save the speech, Erin. You were scared as hell when you called. I heard it. Standing next to you, I can feel it. Why make it easy for her to come back here and hurt you."

"I'm not at risk of her killing me. She hurts me, she hurts herself."

He moved closer, studying me with a perceptive intensity that made me feel as though I'd bared all my secrets.

"But she has, without any regard for that, right?"

I shifted my gaze from him and decided not to answer. He'd know the truth. Why put another one unnecessarily in the lie bank?

I nodded. "I think she and I have an understanding."

"Hmm. And that is?"

"A ceasefire." I was taking a liberty with what Malific's parting smile meant. I decided to interpret it as a tacit agreement of a truce.

"Nothing that you told me leads me to believe there is a ceasefire. If you really felt that way, you wouldn't have called me to get Evelyn." He'd inched closer and placed his hand on my waist; warmth radiated from his touch. "Be truthful with me."

"I can't be holed up anywhere or hiding, Asher. I have to be in a place where Nolan or Elizabeth can get in touch with me." I was hopeful that they would. "If that doesn't happen, I need to be proactive about finding a way to unbind us. I don't want this any more than she does," I admitted.

After several minutes of consideration, he offered a reluctant nod. "Will you keep me informed? I want to know the moment you are unbound." This wasn't just sheer Asher confidence; this was the assertion of a person with a hidden agenda.

"Why?"

"I suspect you plan to just end things, correct?"

I realized I didn't have a lot of options. I would have to end things between me and Malific. And there was only one way it could end.

"If you're not successful, I'll make sure that it's not a complete failure."

Can I get a third of that level of confidence?

"It's not that easy—"

"Because she's a god, like Mephisto and the others he keeps around?" His smirk was accompanied by a brow arch.

Chewing my bottom lip, I realized that denial was pointless. He'd get more information from any attempts to lie. "Malific isn't easily killed."

"She can be, with an Obitus blade, which is praseodymium and some silver. I suspect it can be mixed with any metal to make a weapon. The symbols on the blade aren't magical. They just denote them as being such weapons."

My mouth formed a small O as I scrambled to cover it. There was no way to prevent showing my surprise.

He moved back a few feet and I became aware of the coolness of the room. I missed the warmth of his body.

"You have one, don't you?"

"A sword." His smirk eased into a wolfish grin. "Erin, must you continue to underestimate me? I am a resourceful man."

Resourceful he might be, but it wouldn't override the

spell that covered the people of the Veil. He'd lose his magic if he killed her. His ability to change. I had to make sure I was the one to stop Malific. Before I could remind him of that, he turned around at Ms. Harp's approach. She was in a huff as she rolled out her packed luggage and parked it in front of Asher, accompanied by a petulant glare. Then she marched back into her room and came out with another cane beautifully decorated with colorful flowers—fancier than the one she usually carried—and a garment bag that she gave to Asher, mumbling under her breath the entire time.

Since she didn't need one cane, I had no idea why she had two. She would be safe and that was my only concern.

"I have plans on Friday and just because she"—she pointed at me like we didn't know who was the target of her indignation—"can't manage to walk to her car without finding trouble doesn't mean I have to cancel my plans. I'm sure the trouble has everything to do with those men who visited the other day."

"We'll see," Asher said. I rolled my eyes and groaned at Asher giving the worst possible answer. Was this an Alpha-flex? Her petulance making him assert his dominance?

"We'll see?" Ms. Harp snapped back.

Someone's in trouble.

She'd stalked right up to him. "No, I'm going. I bought a new dress and I plan to enjoy the evening," she told him.

The balm of his calm confidence seemed to drop the temperature by several degrees. The confidence that controlled a room and that subtle warning not to screw with him. It was on full display during interviews, especially when some ambitious and surly interviewer decided to say something rude or demeaning about shifters. A look that spoke volumes, silenced them, and made them quickly reword their comment.

Even Ms. Harp, who didn't seem to ascribe to any social norms I was aware of, faltered under the frosty disposition.

"I'm sure I'll be safe. Erin?" She left room for me to plead her case.

"She has a date," I told him. "You won't have to worry about her safety."

"A date? With whom?"

This is a really good moment for me. Absolutely delicious.

"Landon."

The shock settled on his face and as much as he tried to usher it away, it was fixed there. Rigid.

He was flummoxed. Mr. Alpha. Mr. I-have-everything-under-control. Mr. Listen-to-me-or else, was actually flummoxed. My life was a dumpster fire, but I took a moment to drink in his response.

"She has a date with Landon," I repeated. I'd never been giddy before. It was a strange feeling.

"Wha... What?"

I stood directly in front of him. "Ms. Evelyn Harp has a date with Landon Mikaelson, the acting vampire Master." I spoke slowly for his enjoyment, or probably mine. No, definitely mine because his shock moved to confusion and returned quickly to shock. "It's the epitome of a May/December romance and he's the winter fox in it."

I wasn't sure if nosy, craggy older ladies just made Landon's heart patter, or if he was accepting my challenge, or just being nice, but Ms. Harp was his date on Friday and she appeared excited about it.

Asher ran his hands through his hair several times, disheveling the russet waves.

"I feel like I should have more information, but I don't want any," he admitted.

"She'll be fine with him," I assured him. When I started to back toward the door, he moved closer to me and closed his hand around my wrist.

"Are you sure you don't want to come with me?" he asked.

"I'm sure. But I'd like to ask a favor."

"Of course."

"Once you have Ms. Harp settled, can you come back? I have some spells to try on you."

"Spells don't work on me," he reminded me, looking confused.

"No, they're spells that I perform on me, but I want to make sure shifters can't see through them."

I was sure he wanted further explanation, but despite not getting it then, he agreed.

CHAPTER 17

When Asher returned, I explained the spells I'd learned but left out the part about trying them on the Huntsmen. As I gave him an overview, his head tilted ever so slightly before his eyes narrowed on me.

"What are you *not* telling me?" he asked.

"I'm not sure. I know I told you to stop smelling me, stop listening to any changes in my body, including my voice, and stop calling me out when I tell a small fib."

"You mean lie. Don't make it sound innocuous." His lips quirked into a smile. "You're leaving out something. What?"

"Nothing."

He moved closer, just inches from me. I could feel the heat of his body, the light warm breeze of breath that brushed against my lips. "Tell me," he whispered.

"There's nothing to tell."

"Ah, then it has something to do with Mephisto and perhaps the men who were here a few days ago."

"Men? Surely Ms. Harp gave you names. She's getting sloppy," I teased.

"Kai. Simeon. Clayton." At my silence, he said, "Is it that you're trying not to confirm what they are that has you so tense? Things are really off with you." He kept an assessing eye on me. "The moment I told you I suspected they were gods, your response confirmed it. Or is there something else you're not telling me?"

I kept a blank expression on my face. "Will you help me? I just need you to let me know if you can detect me during a cloaking spell."

I slipped off my shoes and whispered the words for the spell. Being mindful of Kai's criticism, I tiptoed to the other side of the room, to a position outside the second bedroom that I'd converted to a meditation room. Far enough away that he'd have to search, but where I was able to watch him. It was a good sign that his eyes didn't track me as I moved. He closed his eyes, inhaled the air, slowly circled the room, and then moved toward me. I sucked in a breath and stilled. Leaning forward, he kissed the tip of my nose. Then his hand found my waist and rested lightly on it.

"Found you," he whispered.

"But you couldn't see me, right? When I moved, you didn't see me?"

He shook his head. I disabled the spell.

"I found you by scent. If a shifter isn't involved, you'll be fine. If one is—"

He broke off and there were a few beats of contemplative silence before he excused himself. I thought he'd had a phone call or heard a noise. He was gone for nearly ten minutes, which gave me enough time to set up for the *adligatura*.

Asher returned and pulled a small bag from his pocket and placed it in my hand. "Menaden. It's a hybrid plant. You won't be able to find ingredients to replicate it, and I only know of one witch who can make it."

I opened the bag and studied the sage-colored powder, inhaling it.

"Don't ask the name of the witch, and if you ever find out who she is, she'll deny being able to make it. That is the agreement I have with her. Use it and no shifter will find you by scent. A little goes a long way. Rub it over your body. Even if you don't get every part, it will diminish your scent enough that tracking you will be nearly impossible, even for the best of hunters."

I smiled. "I'll never speak of it," I promised. I gave his hand a squeeze before taking the bag to my bedroom. Asher was studying my *adligatura*.

"It's for neutralizing magic," I explained. Running my fingers through my flyaway hair, I explained what it did and that I'd successfully tested it on Cory and Madison. I still felt obligated to leave Mephisto out, not wanting to further substantiate Asher's speculations. And that's all they were at the moment, despite his belief that my responses had given him confirmation. I hesitated before asking. "I know...You've done so much..." My fingers nervously fiddled with my ponytail and then with my blade necklace.

Concern filled his eyes. "What is it?"

"I feel like I'm asking a lot of you these days."

He grunted an amused sound. "Erin, I'd like to think we're in a different place now. You did something exceptional for me and my pack. I owe you. What do you need?"

"I don't want this to be about debts. I made something right that I had a hand in creating." Technically I hadn't, it was Cory, but I was responsible by association and I'd wanted to correct it. And after seeing the anguish and hopelessness in Asher's face, I had to do whatever I could.

"Okay, no debts. I want to help because I like helping you," he said with a faint smile.

"I'd like to see if the *adligatura* can work against shifters. I'd never use it against yours. Ever. That's my promise to you, but Malific used shifters from the Veil and—"

"No need for further explanation," he cut in, shrugging off his suit jacket. He laid it across the arm of the sofa and started to unbutton the cuffs of his sleeves. Once he'd partially removed his shirt, I averted my eyes from his abs and resolutely kept them on his face.

No matter how many times I was presented with the shifters' comfort level with nudity and them indiscriminately undressing, it was still shocking. Responding with snarkiness or admonishments was met with a blank stare or even an upturned nose of judgment, as though you were the one making the faux pas or violating some rules of decorum. As if they weren't the ones standing in front of you with their jiggly bits exposed. I once asked Asher about it and he simply responded that everyone is born naked and it's only a big deal because of humans' prudish beliefs. "The body isn't sexual until you decide it is. Why should we be burdened by what others have done?"

Even with that knowledge, I couldn't help myself. "What are you doing?"

His brow hitched and amusement touched the corners of his lips. "You want to see if your circle can prevent me from changing to a wolf, which entails me actually trying to change, right? You know our clothes rip when we do. Are you suggesting that I rip through a Brioni suit because you don't want to see my bare ass? Besides, it's a nice suit. Midnight blue really is a good look on me." He winked, then shrugged off his shirt to reveal a sculpted chest and defined abs and arms. His smirk seemed to say "you're welcome." His laughter filled the room when I turned my back to him.

I repeated Asher's assertion: *The body isn't sexual until you make it into more. It's just a body.* But everything about his body screamed raw, unfettered, primal sex. So it was difficult to see it as just a body. My struggle didn't go unnoticed.

"Once you're done, just get in the circle." Still turned from him, I said the spell and waited. Several minutes had passed when a massive wolf nudged me. Stroking a shifter like they were dogs never went over well, but out of habit, I brushed my hand over his soft coat. Out of reflex he growled a baleful sound. I sank to the floor.

"Well, at least I have the cloaking spell." It wasn't my limited arsenal of magic that concerned me, it was that I didn't know the extent of Malific's magic or her followers, if she still had any.

The wolf moved closer and dropped his head into my lap, where we stayed in a companionable silence. It was hard to establish a strategy when there were so many unknowns. Not only was Malific's magic a mystery, so were her allies.

Asher shifted back to his human form. "You should come with me and I'll find Nolan or a way to get in contact with him. I don't trust that she won't hurt you," he suggested as he dressed.

"I'm sure she'll try again. But she can't inflict on me what she can't bear herself," I admitted with faux confidence. Malific was a sadist and would endure the pain if she could cause more to others. But I couldn't focus on that.

The level of bravado and self-assurance I showed didn't ease Asher's look of concern.

"If you're even considering some form of extraordinary rendition with me, get it out of your head. Now. I'm not as easily handled as Ms. Harp. I bite." I flashed him a grin.

He bent down until our eyes were level. "So do I," he said in a low drawl. He nipped playfully at my earlobe, moving out of reach when I swatted at him. He wouldn't be Asher if he didn't strike a stance that allowed me to take him in.

"Be careful, Erin." He gave my arm a squeeze before leaving but hesitated at the door. He was reconsidering the rendition scenario; I just knew it.

"You don't want to take me against my will," I warned. "I have no reservations when it comes to rules of engagement. I'll crotch kick men, punch women in their lady pillows, claw eyes, pull hair, and yank out extensions. Getting me in your car would not be an easy task. And I'm immune to your alleged charm."

He quelled the feral impulse that sparked in his eyes and set his jaw at my inadvertent challenge. "I'm just a call away," he reminded me.

CHAPTER 18

*a*fter I awoke the next morning and washed my face and brushed my teeth, I headed for the kitchen for a much-needed cup of coffee. I knew it was going to be a large, strong coffee type of day, so I pulled out my best dark roast and brewed a cup.

I took a long indulgent sip and went to my front door and opened it, prepared for what might meet me there. And I wasn't wrong. The horse-sized wolf that Asher had sent before was sprawled outside my door.

"Good morning. Do you want some coffee?" I asked, raising my mug.

The massive animal nodded, stretching out before grabbing a small drawstring bag between his teeth and trotting into my apartment. He dropped the bag and changed in a smooth movement that left me baffled no matter how many times I saw it. One moment I was looking at a wolf, the next a man. A tall, slender, *naked* man who didn't have the common courtesy to cover his man goodies or at least turn away from me before stretching and settling into his human form.

"Bathroom?" His voice was raspy and a surprisingly deep baritone.

Averting my eyes, I pointed straight ahead. He stretched again, moving his neck and shoulders to work out the kinks.

It's just a naked body and jiggly bits. This isn't weird. No, screw it. Asher is wrong. There should be shame. Shame is good. Cover your jiggly bits.

Before I could instruct him to do so, he moved with the lithe agility of a predator and vanished.

Ten minutes later, he reemerged in sweatpants and a white t-shirt. His auburn hair was ruffled, his skin a light fawn color with a slight blush along his stone-carved cheeks. His golden-brown eyes changed to different hues of brown depending on how the light hit them. He gave me an appreciative nod when I handed him a cup of coffee.

"Sugar? Cream?"

"No, this is fine," he said, taking a seat at the kitchen counter. "It's delicious," he said after a long sip.

"Do you want breakfast?" I asked, going to the fridge.

"What?" he sputtered after quickly swallowing his mouthful of coffee.

"Breakfast? Do you want any?"

He blinked several times as if he didn't understand me. Asher had touted this shifter's ability to speak four languages, which was impressive, but I was starting to think I'd made the wrong assumption that English was his primary language.

"I can speak French?"

"O-kay," he said slowly. "I speak it, too, but why do you want to switch to French? To practice?"

We were standing inches from each other, our faces blank in what I assumed was a mutual effort not to make the other person feel uncomfortable. But after several more awkward moments, I explained. "Asher said you spoke four languages. I know a little Spanish and Latin, but most people don't speak Latin. It just seemed like you were having a problem with English. Did I miss something?"

Daniel's loud rumble of hearty laughter filled the room. His cheeks became ruddier and amusement gleamed in his emotive eyes.

"I speak English as my primary and French, Spanish, and German."

"Then what's with the look?"

"Your hospitality surprised me," he admitted. "After all, you commanded me to move when we first met."

"How should I have responded when faced with an uninvited wolf at my door?"

"Was I invited this time?" he asked, smirking between sips of coffee.

"No, but I was expecting you. I'm learning Asher's ways."

"Hmmm," was Daniel's response, but there was so much more to it. That much was clear from the sharpness of his eyes and the curl of his lips.

"What?" I asked, pulling bacon, bagels, and eggs from the fridge and placing them on the counter.

After several moments of consideration, he shrugged. "Based on the things I've heard about you and your antics with Asher, I think you know quite a bit about our Alpha. You seem to enjoy challenging him and I suspect he enjoys being challenged by you."

Did I want to know what he'd heard about me? I was sure it wasn't any different than what I'd heard about myself. And which antics was he speaking of? I didn't take Asher poaching the Salem Stone from me well, and admittedly I had retaliated in some creative ways.

"You are the Erin who left a caltrop in the middle of his driveway, right?" he asked, relieving me of the trouble of making that decision. "And I'm quite curious to know where you purchased the 'You're a jackass' balloons you sent to his home and office."

Flushing, I turned toward the food. "How do you like your eggs?"

"I'll make the eggs." He hopped up from the chair and grabbed the carton from my reach. With suspicion, I watched him navigate my modest kitchen, getting the salt and pepper out of the cabinets and cheese and milk from the fridge.

I scrutinized him as he worked, my eyes narrowing.

"Wow, you really like to cook eggs," I said.

Putting the butter in the pan, he gripped his bottom lip with his teeth as if he was afraid that whatever he was keeping in would slip out.

"Daniel, why are you so enthusiastic about making eggs?"

Rose brushed over his high cheekbones. "Asher said that while watching you, if I smelled smoke or anything burning, not to be alarmed, it's the way you cook," he admitted quietly.

"You've never heard of blackened food," I shot back in defense.

"Sure I have. It's done intentionally." He glanced at me before returning his attention to the eggs he was beating. "I hear that yours isn't and anyway, there's no such thing as blackened eggs. That's overcooked or burned, and I don't like my eggs either way."

I was too irritated to have the decency to be embarrassed. That's how rumors get started. I cooked well enough to survive and that was all that mattered.

After breakfast was prepared, Daniel and I stood at the kitchen counter, eating. I watched in awe as he scarfed down three-quarters of the nine eggs he'd scrambled. Curiosity got the best of me.

"What else do you know about me?" I asked.

He shrugged, his body moving in fluid sweeps of motion, stretching more. Based on his sinewy frame, I suspected he was used to moving—a lot—and playing sentry wasn't ideal for him. "You seem to be under the misguided impression that you possess a form of adjunct authority or something over the pack." He beamed, making me recall commanding two shifters to stop following me. "Don't be embarrassed, we think it's amusing."

Being *amusing* to shifters wasn't something I wanted, and pointing out my role in their magic immunity seemed obnoxious and a little smug.

"It was worth a try," I said.

"'On the authority of your Alpha, I command you to move.'" Daniel howled out a laugh as he took his empty plate to the sink. "That one gave me a little chuckle for days."

Keep it up, Daniel. That balloon company will make any custom balloons I ask for.

He leaned against the sink. "So, what're your plans for today?"

"Are you my detail for today?"

He shook his head. "I'm your watch at night. The size of the wolf does all hard work for me." A wolf the size of a small horse had its advantages. It definitely served as a deterrent.

After my run-in with Malific, I wanted to see my parents. And it would be nice to see a mother who didn't want me dead.

CHAPTER 19

I knocked on the door of my parents' home. I'd texted them, expecting their typical response telling me they didn't respond to texts and that I needed to call. I couldn't stop the panic that hitched in my chest when they didn't answer. First the text and now the phone. I convinced myself they were safe. I'd made my stance about the importance of my family's safety clear to Malific, but I didn't know if she had taken my threat seriously.

My second knock held a lot more urgency. When no one answered, and despite not wanting a repeat viewing of my parents' naked bodies entwined, glimpses of my father's shockingly pale ass and my mother's girls smooshed on the island, I used my key and let myself in.

"Mom? Dad? I'm coming in." I waited, to give them time to get dressed if needed. "Are you in the kitchen? I'm coming that way."

They weren't. Panic raced through me. After searching the house, I closed the front door and started toward Madison's parents' house. Before I could knock on their front door, I saw Keegan's shock of ginger hair poke out from the back of the house.

"We're back here, hon," he said in the same gentle paternal tone he used with Madison. Maddie and I were raised as if we had two sets of parents, and Keegan considered me his second daughter. Since originally I was supposed to be raised by them, I guessed I actually was.

In the backyard, Keegan was at the grill, Sophie and my mother were sitting next to each other, and Madison was across from them.

After what I'd told Madison about Malific's visit, like me, she must have felt the need to check on her parents.

My dad greeted me with one of his backbreaking hugs. He looked slight compared to Keegan's broad build and height of six-seven. I always teased Keegan that with his size, along with his thick brush of beard and ginger waves, he looked like a lumberjack caricature. Aware of his size, Keegan's hugs were gentle. Little squeezes, as if everyone was fragile glass.

Our impromptu visits gave our parents the perfect excuse for a cookout. Keegan placed chicken and steak on the grill. Sophie and my mother prepared the sides: salad, Pikliz, Haitian cabbage, fruit salad, and desserts and chips that they cobbled together from the two households. I wished our mothers were the ones grilling, because despite their best efforts, our dads hadn't mastered it. But them busy at the grill gave Madison and me time to chat with our mothers. And between their hugs and waving away our offers of help, they found the time to guilt us for not visiting more.

"We live in the same city, it's such a shame we see you two only once a month," Sophie commented.

"Cue the guilt," Madison mumbled. The two women made sure we knew that we were relegated to mere guest status because of our infrequent visits. They handled setting up the table, frequently stopping by to smile or touch our cheeks or say something to us, while Madison and I quietly and furtively debated how much to tell them about Malific.

Eventually we had to resort to texting because of Keegan's increasing number of interruptions as he ruffled Madison's hair or pulled at an errant wavy strand. Each time, his lips pursed into a tight line, but he resisted the urge to comment on her shorter darkened tresses. As a person who took pride in being a ginger and his barely discernible curls, he seemed more displeased with her new look than Sophie, whose tightly coiled ringlets were directly responsible for Madison's waterfall of curls. Madison's sienna-colored hair was definitely Keegan's contribution. Neither parent liked her decision to cut and dye it.

She'd had to defend her decision on many occasions: "Looking like a copper-skinned Merida doesn't really lend to me looking commanding. I don't need people thinking of the song 'Touch the Sky' while I'm giving orders." Her youthful appearance and being the youngest to head a department had its challenges. It caused her to constantly look for ways to appear older and command authority with a simple look.

While passing with a pile of plates, Sophie paused. "It's so wonderful to see you. How are things with... Oh, I forget his name?" Sophie asked innocently.

Madison's lips twisted in wry amusement. It was a tried and failed tactic, but one our mothers dusted off occasionally and trotted out to see if it'd work.

"I'm not seeing anyone."

"Hmm," my mother harrumphed. "I thought there was someone named Dakota, but maybe that was you, Erin, and we're getting things confused."

Nice try, Mom.

Madison and I shared an exasperated eye roll.

"Neither one of us is seeing anyone," Madison told them, a knowing flicker sparking in her eyes. Sophie gave us a coy smile, while my mother maintained her look of innocence.

"Sometimes we get things wrong. If you all visited or called more often..." My mother let her blow land. It did. If it

139

weren't for our parents possibly being in danger, it would have been a little longer before we visited.

I wondered if my expression mirrored Madison's. Despite the scenic-routed guilt trip they were taking us on, they weren't wrong. We had to do better.

After our mothers felt they had sufficiently made their point and had wrangled a promise from us that we would meet for lunch at least once a month, the conversation slipped into our natural flow, discussing books, TV shows, us culling through the dullest parts of our life and work and offering them up. Madison ended with showing them pictures of her new bookcase that apparently was nice enough to become a group share between our parents. Leading me to realize there was always something new to learn about them. Who would have thought a bookcase would have been a ten-minute conversation?

Once our parents had retreated and were huddled at the grill, Madison glanced over her shoulder. "I think we should tell them. You can't protect yourself if you aren't aware of the risks," she challenged in a whisper.

The words got stuck in my throat and the thought made my chest tighten. Could they protect themselves? That was the problem. Madison's parents were earth fae, with her same ability to perform magic and draw from the earth, but it paled in comparison to the magic of gods.

My nod of agreement was cut short as I shot to my feet, my heart thudding, when Malific walked around the corner of the house.

She waved, displaying a bright smile that gave no hint of the violence of which she was capable, her disarming demeanor matching the gentle lilt of her voice as she called a greeting. This wasn't the woman who believed in unfettered violence, violated rules of engagement, and reveled in despotism. This was a cruel deception.

The voluminous waves of her hair softened the sharp

lines of her face, and the hints of red and light hues of brown complemented her olive skin. There was something alluring about her and I could see, if only for a moment, how Nolan could have ignored his hatred of her in order to execute his plan.

She'd traded her form-fitted clothes for a pair of pants and a lilac patterned wraparound shirt that played right into her harmless-suburbanite performance. Our parents' focus moved from her to us and what looked like our alarmed overreaction to a friendly stranger. Her appearance may have been docile, and the hate-filled way she usually looked at me squelched, but nothing could suppress the calculated way she appraised us all.

"Oh." She looked at our parents and then returned her attention to me. "I believe I have the wrong house." A gentle smile fanned over her lips.

I moved quickly to put myself between her and my family.

"I was looking for Kaitlyn Sanders," she said. Menace flicked in her eyes, and where my family might have missed it, Madison didn't. Magic pulsed from her as she moved next to me, placing another barrier between Malific and our parents.

"She's across the street, two doors down. Let me show you," I pushed out through clenched teeth. She waited for me to take the lead, but I wouldn't until she'd moved first. Knowing that she could move like Mephisto, I wouldn't give her that advantage. Looking pleasantly content, she started toward the entrance of the house. She had accomplished what she intended: letting me know that she knew where my parents lived and how easily she could get to them.

"They aren't part of this," I snapped once we were at the front of the house and out of earshot. "If you go near them—"

Before I could issue my threat, she was in my face, her eyes scorching with hostility.

"What? What will you do, daughter? Kill me?" She moved back, a slow deviant smile inching over her lips. "Is that how we will end this? Of course not. You're a fighter and foolishly optimistic that you will prevail. I've not decided if I find such idiotic tenacity endearing or annoying."

"I hope you decide that before I kill you," I shot back.

Amusement glinted in her eyes and for a brief moment there appeared to be a shred of admiration, maybe even pride. It was as if she was trying to chip away at my humanity until the person left resembled her.

My eyes went to the car across from where I was parked and the shifter in it. He was homed in on her. Malific's face lit with the anticipation of violence. When he got out of the car, I shook my head and he slipped back in.

"The shifters listen to your commands. Impressive." She looked pleased and covetous. I debated correcting her but decided against it, on the off chance that it would work in my favor.

She stepped away from me and then took another look at the house before returning her attention to me.

"I considered what you said, and I believe there was some truth to it. It will not benefit me to hurt your family. They will be spared. This is between us."

She didn't exactly have a history of keeping her word. "Will you take an oath to that?" I requested.

"No. If I must make an example of someone, I'll leave them for last. That's the best I can offer. It's too early to break you now." Tilting her head, she studied me. "Elizabeth has gone and has taken Nolan with her. I can't find them. Even if I could, I'm not in a position to force them into compliance."

Her flash of movement had her in front of me so fast, I sent magic thrashing into her chest, pushing me back in the process and putting even more distance between us. Anger and disgust flared in her eyes.

It wasn't just my existence she despised but also what I represented to her. Her weakness. Nolan's treachery. And the limitations of her power.

"Nolan has a fondness for you, and Elizabeth for him." Unable to disguise her antipathy for emotional weakness, she looked as if she'd swallowed bile. She squared her shoulders. "Find him and use those feelings to your advantage. Unbind us. Daughter, don't force my hand. I can only tolerate such insolence for so long. Your family will be the ones who pay for it," she vowed.

She was gone. Wynded away, leaving me staring at the empty space.

I gave my shifter detail a tight-lipped, joyless smile before heading back to the patio.

Madison met me midway with concerned eyes.

"We have to tell them," she urged.

Revealing everything wasn't a good idea, but how much of the abridged version should I give them?

"That woman wasn't lost, was she?" my mother surmised once we had taken our seats near the firepit.

Madison and I gave each other meaningful looks. I shook my head. The distress and concern from both of my families made giving them the edited version impossible. So, I told them everything. Relief and affirmation coursed over their faces when I told them of Nolan's role in the *incident* and that I hadn't killed anyone. The realization that they never thought I had done it lifted a burden I hadn't been aware I was carrying.

They now knew of gods but not the Huntsmen. The Veil. Malific. Nolan. Elizabeth. How me ending up with Sophie was an orchestrated plan after Nolan had seen her with Madison. Sophie didn't seem to find it as disturbingly creepy as Keegan did; his glower became a fixture at the mention of Nolan.

They now knew about the Mirra that revealed my identity as The Raven, and the reason Malific wanted me dead. I performed some editing when relating Malific's horrific deeds, including killing her brother. They knew of the binding, Elizabeth's feelings about me, and the magic I had to protect myself. After they insisted on seeing the Veil, I used the spell I'd used with Mephisto, but as I suspected, like Madison and Cory, they couldn't see it.

It took nearly three hours for the questioning to stop, most of the questions just variations of the same inquiries. It became painfully obvious that our parents were using their interrogation to stall us, unwilling to have us leave their sight. It was difficult telling them that me being at the house put them at greater risk.

I left out my dealings with the demon and the bounty on me, trying to deliver as much detail as I could to inform them of the seriousness of things but without giving them needless worry. But was that even possible? How could they not worry? Their lives had been irreparably changed, just like mine. The network of indiscretions, lies, and incidents had given them a life that wasn't just false, it was manipulated.

"That was Malific, your birth mother?" Sophie seemed to have been struggling with the question and had made several attempts to speak before the words finally came. It was like she was trying to reconcile Malific's innocuous look with the threat she actually posed.

"You're not in danger," I assured her.

"We'll have wards put up to prevent people from Wynding into the houses," Madison said. She glanced at me and I knew Mephisto needed to put the same wards around our parents' homes that the Huntsmen had placed on mine. Then she let me know she'd have Claire, one of the strongest witches in the STF, put a Klipsen ward on their houses as well.

The preparations didn't take nearly as long as it took us to reassure our parents of our safety. In fact, short of agreeing to return home and remain under their constant supervision, nothing we could say would give them the assurance they needed.

I stood up. "It won't be long," I said. "Once we're no longer bound, I'll handle Malific."

"You mean you'll kill her," my mother corrected, blinking hard to prevent her tears from spilling. Wrapping his arms around her shoulders, Dad squeezed her into him. My heart ached at the look they gave me. The same look as after the *incident*. And for days after that. It was the same expression they had when I was struggling to control my magical urges; they couldn't fix it, no matter how desperately they wanted to. I hated being responsible for them feeling or looking that way.

"I'll get in contact with Nolan and they'll remove the bond," I said, leaving my mother's question unanswered. It was implicit.

"Nolan? Your father?" my dad asked.

"You're my father," I corrected. "He's…" I couldn't find the right title for him. Despite the distasteful measures he took to exact his revenge on Malific, and the turmoil that he inflicted on me in his misguided way of doing so, in the end he'd tried to make things better for me. Protect me from his mistake. Make sure I had the spells he thought could protect me. He wasn't my father, but he wasn't an enemy, either.

I shook my head. "Don't worry, it'll be handled soon."

As I started to leave, my mother took hold of my arm. Her eyes were soft and pleading, expressing something that she seemed reluctant to ask aloud.

"I won't kill her," I whispered. It must have rung true because she squeezed me to her and sighed in relief. I didn't

145

want to kill Malific. Despite how I felt about her and how much she deserved death, I didn't think it could be at my hands. Matricide had to do something to a person, something I didn't want, although I was absolutely positive Malific didn't have a problem with filicide.

Madison's and my parents were huddled on the opposite side of the room, their heads lifting occasionally like meerkats to scrutinize Mephisto and the Huntsmen. After a few moments of hushed consultation, they moved in a unified parental unit, our mothers in the lead. Clay's lips curled into an amused smile, Kai's eyes flickered with laughter, Simeon fought to restrain his grin, and Mephisto just smirked at the herdlike approach.

Accustomed to our family dynamics, I often forgot how peculiar it must have seemed to others. Four sets of cautious eyes regarded the Huntsmen, cataloguing their faces and tracking their slightest movement. It wasn't apparent if my parents could feel the thrum of magic that accompanied them, but Sophie and Keegan definitely did.

After their quiet scrutiny of the men, I made the introductions, starting with Kai, Simeon, and Clayton, leaving Mephisto for last because I knew that was going to be a conversation.

"Mephisto? Like Mephistopheles, as in Faust?" my mother clarified, taking in his granite-colored slacks, black shirt, dark hair, and obsidian eyes. Being swathed in mystery and a vision of darkness wasn't doing him any favors; a vision of darkness who went by a name associated with the devil.

Giving her a slow smile, he nodded. "It's not my given name. I chose it."

What are you doing! You're not helping your case or making the situation better.

Sophie's and my mom's gaze slid from him to me as they gave me their none-too-subtle look of "what the hell?"

Shrugging, I said, "It's a long story, but right now we need to get the wards up. We'll discuss it later."

Plastering forced smiles on their faces, they nodded and once again moved in an awkward unit back to their original location. I was fully aware of their attention when Mephisto sidled up close to me, leaning down to whisper in my ear.

"Are you really okay?"

No, my mother just threatened to hurt me.

With a tight, mirthless smile, I nodded.

Mephisto's name might have given my family pause, but there were open-mouthed looks of awe on their faces at the elaborate light show created by the Huntsmen's magic as they erected the wards. The magic of gods. It chased away their fear, which I hoped wouldn't return once they realized that the woman hunting me was an Arch-god, and even more powerful than the Huntsmen.

CHAPTER 20

*D*riving up to Mephisto's home, I tried to hide my disappointment. Elizabeth's home had been locked and there were signs of her permanent departure. Checking throughout the house, I'd found just two basic spell books remaining on the bookshelf and next to them a pen-like object that revealed scribing chalk. Hints of magic lingered in the air. I suspected it was used to remove her imprint from the home. With the exception of the three items left behind, it was as if the WIB had never existed, leaving me feeling abject about the possibility of Elizabeth or Nolan returning.

Despite my uncertainty, I left a note where Nolan had left the spells, with my number and asking if he could convince Elizabeth to remove the binding. It was doubtful he'd receive it. Nothing about the place led me to believe they intended to return.

The only option I had now was to find an alternative.

After my call to Mephisto earlier, asking if I could see him, I wasn't surprised to find that his door was left open so I could let myself in. Benton seemed to have decided that being the answerer of doors was no longer one of his duties.

We were in do-it-yourself territory. I was even less surprised to find Benton in his spot, book in one hand and a cup of coffee in the other. With all his leisure activity, when did he do his druid-ing?

"Benton," I greeted, stopping at the door.

"Erin." His voice was light with amusement. He took a sip from his coffee, eyeing me as he typically did, awaiting a snide comment or snarky remark.

"It's always a pleasure to see you enjoying the day," I said in a saccharine-sweet voice.

"There aren't enough words to express how delighted I am that it pleases you." He took another sip before putting the mug down and returning to his book.

"Are you researching spells?" I asked, fully aware that he had a newly released bestseller mystery book in his hands.

"I wasn't aware that you were nearsighted. My apologies, that explains so much." He made a show of leaning forward so that I could see the cover, his smile widening at the glower I directed at him.

Touché. You win this round.

"I'm going to look at Mephisto's collection," I said. "I'm sure you're aware of my situation."

"Yes," he answered, lifting his eyes from the book. The amusement leached from his expression, revealing a look I couldn't quite make out. Concern? No, it was regret and the powerlessness of seeing a person in trouble and not having the ability to help.

"Elven magic is nebulous. I do wish I could do more to help you, Erin," he admitted. It explained the sound in Mephisto's voice when I asked if I could see the Mystic Souls, because he knew there wasn't anything in it that could help. Wanting to review it was just a grasp at hope.

"Enjoy your book." I said it without sarcasm. The uneasy silence was harder to deal with, the portentous feeling unable to be shrugged off.

I found Mephisto in his office and he escorted me to the room that held his collection. Seeing it again, I felt a renewed sense of awe at the many objects he had collected over the years. Our predicament was quite similar. I had elven magic but not the ability to remove the elven binding between me and Malific. Mephisto had a collection of magical objects, the Mystic Souls, and god magic but was unable to undo the spell cast by Malific that left him exiled from the Veil.

As I walked the length of the room, reading the Mystic Souls, I could feel the warm intensity of Mephisto's eyes on me.

"My demi," he whispered with a hot possessiveness that made me stop abruptly. His eyes darkened to obsidian stones as he looked at me. At his approach, I didn't move away as I should. Even his gentlest of touches sent heat lacing up my arm. "What are you looking for?" he asked.

My shoulders sagged. I had been through all the spells in the Mystic Souls that I could interpret, dissected every item in Mephisto's collection, reviewing their purposes and alternative purposes if combined with another object or spell, but I'd found nothing that would do what I needed it to: unbind me from Malific.

"I don't know," I admitted with a frown. Despite all the ideas rampaging through my head, when he was close, I was painfully aware of him. His closeness. And his hand on my hip.

"Okay. What spells are you thinking about using?"

"I can try to use a ward and trap her and then use the neutralizing spell."

"Only the Omni ward can trap her in, and you saw what happened when you put one around me. I simply walked out of it. With you two linked, wouldn't your magic be neutralized, too?"

I'd wondered the same thing but hoped he'd be able to offer a workaround.

"A ward won't do anything but enrage her. She stabbed her own hand to make a point. Don't for one moment think she wouldn't do worse in reprisal. We need a permanent solution and I think it will have to involve elven magic."

"Elizabeth was able to trap you all in the house," I reminded him. "If she was able to do that, I should be able to do something similar. Trap her." I sighed. "But it wouldn't change anything." I needed to do more than just trap her. I had to disable her ability to physically hurt me.

He glowered. "Elven magic. Although I suspect that her hybrid magic, like yours, is allowing her to do unique magic as well."

Yeah, unique. I wondered how many times she'd tried to Wynd and turned into a feline instead. The most useless trick ever. Mephisto had confirmed what I suspected. There wasn't going to be a workaround. If there was, it would be magic that mimicked elven magic.

"What do you know of the Black Crest grimoire?" I asked.

"The demon book?"

"I was told it was just a book of spells."

"Told by whom?"

"A witch."

"A witch who practices dark magic?"

What is this, a cross-examination?

"She claimed not to, but I got a peek at it and saw a spell comparable to a Mirra. Maybe it has other spells that are comparable to elven magic. Maybe even one that could unbind me."

Mephisto's hand dropped from my waist and he took several steps back.

"How did you see this book?" The edge in his voice possessed the same tinge of disapproval as it had when I thought I'd summoned a demon. Under the inquiring intensity of his dark eyes, I told him: about the bounty on me, the demon circle, Harrison summoning Dareus, and Dareus's request that we kill Harrison in exchange for the book. Mephisto listened quietly, anger and frustration flaring intermittently as I revealed the entire sordid deal.

His teeth were gripping his bottom lip. Slowly, he released it, as if having to coax his body to relax. He shoved his hands into his pockets and with his disarming swift movement, he was against the wall, studying me from afar.

"Why don't you have the book?" he asked.

"Because he would only give it to me if I *murdered* Harrison."

His expression should have changed to horror. It needed to change to horror. But it didn't change at all.

"I am aware of Dareus's terms for acquiring the book," he said with casual indifference. "Isn't Harrison the person who tried to give you to a demon?" It wasn't really a question but rather a defense of his stance. Justification for the indefensible.

I nodded.

"Then why don't you have the book?" he asked again. It was like a replay of Clayton reminding me that I wasn't dealing with harmless garden snakes but venomous vipers. Mephisto, urbane in his bespoke suits, impeccably tailored shirts, and refined good looks, made it easy to forget.

He'd closed the distance between us. The pad of his thumb traced my hand while his dark eyes held mine. Malific's comment, "Same beast, different label," played in my head.

"Do you miss fulfilling your duties in the Veil?" I asked.

Surprise replaced the baleful intensity and he looked at me with renewed interest. The way he looked at me before the Mirra and the raven marked my arm. An unsettling intrigue.

"Yes."

I waited for him to elaborate but he didn't. We were both on a fishing expedition. He was trying to figure out the

152

reason behind my question, and I wanted to know more about the Huntsmen, especially the one who seemed to be the leader.

"What do you miss about it?" I asked.

His lips furled and roguish mischief filled his obsidian eyes. He leaned into me, lightly brushing his lips over mine. Warmth breezed over them. Determined to get my answer, I refused to respond.

He stepped back, his arms crossed over his chest as he fixed me with a hard look. "That's not the question you really want to ask, now is it?"

I shook my head.

"Then ask your question, *my* demigoddess."

He always said the latter part with hints of emotions that were difficult to pin down: reverence, appreciation, allure, seduction, and sometimes unease.

I studied him. "Malific said you were good at your job."

"And you're good at yours. The point?"

"She said you excelled at it, not because you valued justice but because you enjoyed the domination. That you reveled in the thrill of the hunt and the glory of the kill. She claimed that you're the same as her."

He nodded slowly, taking in the question. "And you're good at the many jobs you've done for me because you're a thief?"

Technically, I was a thief. It was often the last course of action. I preferred to negotiate for an item, or find another and tack on a surcharge for the trouble. But sometimes I was a thief because I needed to be, in order to fulfill the job.

"I'm not a thief but I have stolen. But you know that."

"You fight when you need to, right? And if I'm not mistaken, you pride yourself on doing whatever it takes to win, correct?"

I fought dirty. Period. If it was a matter of either saving my life or putting on a tournament-quality presentation of my technique, the presentation was going out the door, because no one cared how pretty the fight was if they had to attend your funeral. And as far as the assailant went, I gave no fucks what they thought of me.

"I fight to survive."

"Ah, in a world of the magically elite, the truly strong and powerful, do you expect me *not* to do what is necessary to survive?"

"Yes, but do you enjoy it?"

"Oh, that is my sin? The mere fact that I have no desire to be killed and that I do whatever it takes to not be killed?" He smirked. He was purposely being obtuse.

"No, do you enjoy all that it entails to do your job? You have to be cruel, violent, morally ambiguous, unyielding. Do you enjoy that part?"

Magic bloomed from him, making me recall how it used to ignite in me a need for his magic. Even with the distance between us, I could appreciate his magic and how vastly different it was from mine, the nuances and simplicity of it compared to my mixed magic.

I appreciated that he took some time before answering my questions.

"I enjoy not dying and apprehending people who deserve it. People like your mother—"

"Malific."

"Like Malific." He gave me a faint smile. "Am I to believe that if I answered my question differently, things would have changed between us?"

"Yes, if you enjoy killing, that's disturbing."

"Very few people enjoy such a thing. But yes, I enjoy the pursuit. You're not the only one who enjoys the rush of adrenaline."

Recent life events may have cured me of that.

"So," he whispered, "we both seem to have needs that aren't being met. What could we do to distract us?"

Before I could answer he was in front of me. His lips covered mine in a hard kiss. He cupped my butt as he lifted me, then walked me to the wall and pressed me to it.

"The shifters?" I panted, pulling from the kiss.

Yeah, moment ruined. I wasn't disappointed. Me being linked to Malific may not have bothered Mephisto, but it did me. I was probably being overly cautious, but I didn't care. It was better than the off chance that she'd be connected to us kissing, or more.

"What?" he breathed out.

"The shifters from the Veil, they didn't like you. At. All. Why?" That had been nagging me since the encounter.

He chuckled. "They seem to believe their dislike for me is justified. And perhaps it is. The shifters here are subdued. I might even go as far as saying that them being susceptible to magic gave them a sense of humility."

"You've met Asher and Sherrie, right?" Humility was not among the words I'd use to describe them.

"Yes, he's much humbler than the Alphas in the Veil. With the exception of my interactions with Asher when it pertains to you, I'd go as far as to say they are docile."

"Docile and shifter can never *ever* be used in the same sentence." And no one in their right mind would even suggest something so absurd.

"In the Veil, shifters have always been immune to magic. They are warriors in their own right and, unlike here, the position of Alpha is acquired through true domination. The idea of domination fights being to surrender, as they are here, would be considered absurd." He let my feet drop to the floor then moved to the shelves, closing the doors that I'd left open, locking cabinets and straightening magical objects.

Until the shifters came out, fighting only to the point of surrender had been considered absurd as well. But under the scrutiny of the world, they had to settle on more palatable ways of determining leadership. Initially, they balked at the

155

interference of others in pack business, but I suspected there had to be some shifters pleased to see the end of such a barbaric custom.

"That doesn't explain why they dislike you," I pointed out.

"Ah," he said. "Then let me get you your answer." He may have sounded unconcerned, but I could hear the heaviness in his voice. I took his extended hand. The steady rhythm of his thumb stroking my hand seemed to be from his unease. What was I about to learn?

I expected us to go to the living room, his office, or the unnecessary "conversation" room. Instead, he led me to Benton, who was still enjoying his mystery.

"You should learn about the shifters in the Veil, more specifically, the Canzin shifters," he said, loud enough for Benton to hear. Benton's eyes flicked from his book to us. Then they roved over me and down to our clasped hands, which prompted a grimace.

Mephisto led me into the center of the room. I'd only seen glimpses from my position outside it while I tried to out-petty the king of pettiness. Despite knowing that Benton was a druid, I wasn't expecting such an extensive collection of information. The back wall was a built-in bookcase, filled with books, some with weathered spines and unfamiliar titles and languages. Next to the bookcase were oversized comfy-looking chairs placed opposite each other, separated by a table with more books stacked on it. On the far side of the room, on a large round wooden table that looked like it was from the Kai collection, was a small cauldron and apothecary equipment: jars filled with ingredients, oils, mortar and pestle, and a yellow notepad with scribbling on it. The remainder of the wall that was visible was textured oyster and limestone.

The room had a warm, studious ambiance. In another corner was a kitchenette. A gooseneck kettle was on the stove and a Chemex coffeemaker sat on the counter. Right next to the counter was a tall, slender bookcase filled with a collection of contemporary fiction.

"Would you tell her about the Canzin shifters?" Mephisto asked.

Benton, who was mid-drink, froze. His brows inched together and his expression grew severe as they exchanged a look.

"Everything?" he asked.

Mephisto responded with a small nod before leaving the room.

"Would you like some coffee?" Benton asked as he stood. I got the impression he wanted to offer me something stronger, which only heightened my curiosity about the shifters from the Veil and what he was about to reveal.

I shook my head and took the proffered oversized chair, near the built-in bookcase. Benton took the seat across from it.

"Tell me what you know of the shifters," he requested, his expression changing from his typical playful mocking look of smugness to intense and speculative.

I told him everything I knew of them. That until recently, only the shifters in the Veil were immune to magic and that because of my intervention, the shifters here now were, too. I was positive he already knew that tidbit. I disclosed what I knew of their ability to shift voluntarily but that they were still required to answer the call of the full moon. That they possessed enhanced strength and healing. That silver affected their healing and wolfsbane temporarily hindered their senses. That their magic overrode all other magic, which meant that procreation with a shifter guaranteed the offspring would be a shifter. I left out the undocumented anomaly, Ms. Harp, and the Menaden that Asher had given me.

He nodded and leaned back in his chair and steepled his hands. "That is all true. The Veil's shifters are immune to magic." He shot me a knowing look. "And *now* the same is true of the shifters on this side of the Veil. The Canzin shifters were an exception. They were an exception to *all* the rules. They could perform magic in human form and were immune to all magic, with the exception of their own. It gave them the ability to attain half-form and perform magic with the benefit of immunity to all magic. They were considered gods among shifters and they believed in their own invincibility."

His voice dropped and his eyes softened. Mephisto had said that all parts of the Veil weren't beautiful, and I got the impression I was about to get examples.

Benton went to the bookshelf and pulled several books from it. Flipping through the pages, he stopped and then handed me the book. "This is them in full animal form."

The gasp slipped from me before I could stop it. Shifters were larger than their natural counterpart, sometimes nearly twice as large. If the odd glint and the intelligent eyes didn't reveal they were a shifter, their size would. Shifters wouldn't be able to easily live among natural animals because their size would make them obvious. But Canzin shifters were massive freaks of nature. Daniel, the horse-wolf, seemed petite compared to the enormous canidae and felidae of these animals. They were larger than the dire wolf and the American cheetah, their extinct ancestors.

"They're massive," I said, looking at the pictures from multiple angles, imagining them walking among us. What would my impression of the Veil be if I'd run into these creatures and they were hostile, as opposed to the shifters I had encountered?

"Yes, they *were*. They're extinct, that bloodline ended," he offered in a tight, low voice. When he sucked in a ragged breath and exhaled slowly, I figured it was to delay telling the story of their demise, in which I was sure Mephisto had played a major role. "As with many," Benton went on, "like

Malific, they believed in despotic rule. Although shifters aren't prone to subjugating others, they are opportunistic. That small group wreaked havoc, caused wars—if you can call it that. Witches, mages, and fae, although powerful, aren't fighters."

Giving me time to absorb that information, he returned to his initial spot to get his coffee—which had to be cold—and took a long drink then brought it back with him to his seat.

"If they had encountered your mother, I'm sure they would have formed an alliance, because they shared a common goal. Oedeus attempted to reason with them, without success. After all, they were a group of a hundred and thirteen, causing the level of destruction of a massive army. It wasn't long before they were sentenced to Abyssus, just eight years. If you had seen their destruction firsthand, you would have thought that quite a lenient punishment for their crimes. But they didn't see it that way, and anyone sent to apprehend them never came back."

He gave me time to read the documented accounts in the book he'd handed me. They were supported by scenes so graphic and morbid, I set it aside.

"They were able to kill gods!"

"Immortality only means you don't age out of life. It doesn't mean you're indestructible and unable to die. Gods are difficult to kill."

I looked back at the pictures of the creatures, flipped to them in half-form, which I'd thought would be like a centaur —half human, half creature—but actually was more like a minotaur with incongruities of human arms, ears, noses on a felidae or canidae. I couldn't imagine how horrifying it had to be to be met with that and be aware that it wielded magic.

"Eventually the Huntsmen were called in."

"Four men to apprehend a little over a hundred shifters?"

I'd seen the four in battle, their stealth, precision, and

spring-coiled violence on display. The muted ruthlessness that accompanied them was easily ignored until you knew what they were.

The pieces fell into place.

"There are more. But for the past three centuries, it has been these Huntsmen. They've held the position the longest, exhibiting the greatest success. I guess they would be equivalent to what you all consider special forces. They're usually called in when everyone else has failed. Which is why your mother—"

"Malific."

"Malific wanted them expelled from the Veil. If anyone could have captured her, they could."

An uncomfortable silence followed. I nodded, urging him to continue. Retrieving another book from the shelf, he placed it on the table in front of me. "This is a chronicle of their transgressions. I have no desire to go into detail, but know that they were deserving of the consequences. Over three hundred deaths and the annihilation of two witch bloodlines and a mage can be attributed to them."

I skimmed it. The stories were gruesome. I didn't want to read about any more violence and destruction. I didn't need more confirmation of the cruel capabilities of others. For years, I'd considered my actions firmly in the gray area of morality and ethics, but the more I was exposed to the atrocities in the Veil, the lighter my gray became.

"I take it their extinction was externally motivated and the Huntsmen were responsible?"

Benton nodded, his expression stoic, his eyes hollow.

I debated whether I wanted to know more. This explained the immediate disdain the Veil shifters had for Mephisto. He had essentially murdered their version of a god, ended a powerful and revered bloodline. Shifters had an unwavering alliance to each other, so their hate for the

Huntsmen would become so entwined it would be a fiber of their existence.

"It's been so long and the story told a hundred times over. The hero of the story always depends on the storyteller's side. Perhaps if a shifter were to tell the story, Mephisto would be the villain."

Benton was right. If this story was told by a shifter, Mephisto, Kai, Simeon, and Clay would be portrayed as villainous fiends who had ended a bloodline of shifters because their magical and fighting abilities surpassed theirs.

Closing the books, Benton sat in silence while I took everything in.

"What were the other shifters doing? Did they just accept the destruction of the Canzin shifters?"

"The Canzins' power and abilities were envied, even revered by some. Some shifters participated, but without the comparable abilities they weren't good allies. But it didn't stop their admiration." No matter how I tried, my scowl wouldn't relax as I listened. "There is a delicate and compli-cated balance in the Veil. Indomitable magic, power-lust, and the need for subjugation exist in a tenuous and volatile state. It exists here as well but on such a small scale it is easily missed or overlooked. Things are different there."

My throat dried and warmth leached from my fingers as I pondered the time I'd gone there searching for shifters. What else I might have encountered. How people might have responded to me, if they knew who I really was.

"Why are you telling me this, not Mephisto?"

Benton's lips pulled into a thin, tight line. Emotion drained from his face and his eyes were impassive. His voice was level, tepid. "For the very reason we are still here, when one strike and Malific would be no more." His eyes dropped to the floor.

If Malific had been bound to anyone else, the Huntsmen would be back in the Veil. They'd have sacrificed that person's life in order to return to the Veil and rid the world of Malific.

He continued avoiding eye contact when he spoke again. "The Laes spell could possibly be lifted if we tried these." He collected the tablet from across the room and held it out to me. It displayed the same scribblings I'd seen Cory do and that I had done most recently when spell weaving. "We could try this on you. But Mephisto won't allow any of them to be performed, despite the minimal danger to you."

The confusion must have shown on my face because he hadn't answered my question. Why hadn't Mephisto told me about the Canzin shifters?

With a mirthless laugh, Benton explained. "I do believe his fondness for you is deeper than even we imagined and he realized." I hated the look Benton gave me, then the scrutinizing and assessing look melted away. "I don't believe he wanted to see your judgment of him for the things he's done."

Benton's lips beveled into a frown, and he looked back down at the woven spells. It wasn't just the Huntsmen who would be able to leave; he would as well. But druids were human, scholars and magical resources. Being magically linked to the Huntsmen probably provided Benton longevity. Unsuccessfully trying to break the Laes spell was probably not as exciting as the life he'd had back in the Veil. I looked at the spells again.

"May I?"

He handed them to me, and I examined them more closely. If I wanted to determine the risk, I needed time to study them.

"I'd like to take them with me, or at least get a copy."

He considered it for so long I thought maybe I was mistaken and he wasn't unhappy here. Drinking coffee and reading books and occasionally opening a door wasn't a bad deal. Maybe he was satisfied with this existence.

"Ah, the double-edge of the sword of Mephisto's affections. I will leave it up to him to determine if they will be shared with you." And with that he went back to his chair and his books, essentially dismissing me.

Up to him? Why was he making decisions when it affected them all? More importantly, why was he making decisions for me?

CHAPTER 21

*S*torming into a room and demanding that Mephisto not prevent me from participating in magic that could possibly kill me was several layers of absurdity and easily the stupidest thing ever. I recognized it for what it was but was unable to rein in my pride and staunch my sense of autonomy. My life was spiraling out of control and I was clinging hard to anything that made me feel like I had a hold of it. Despite how ludicrous it was. And that was where I was. Grasping for some semblance of control over my decisions, my memories, my past, my magical ability, my identity in the supernatural world, and even how I chose to protect myself.

Mephisto was in his office, looking through the floor-to-ceiling window. Slowly and deliberately, he turned to face me. After giving me a long look, he chuckled and moved slowly toward me. "I often wonder if you are just needlessly defiant and uniquely rambunctious," he mused aloud.

Neither. They don't sound like compliments?

"Woven spells, no matter how talented the weaver, are never precise. Those that deal in death are even more unstable. Risky. I don't wish to return to the Veil at the sacrifice of your life," he explained.

He was right and I knew it. I nodded, feeling foolish for thinking for even one minute that this was a battle to take on when there were far more important things I needed to address. He continued to study me, seemingly looking for something. Unsated curiosity lingered in his eyes and expression. I knew he was wondering how I took the information about the shifters. I wasn't sure, either.

When he leaned down, pressing a warm kiss to my lips, I returned it and the tension in the kiss melted away.

"I need to speak to Dareus about the Black Crest grimoire," I said.

"Erin."

I closed my eyes, not ready for the debate.

"You already know the requirement."

"I'm not killing Harrison for it"—I pulled my head back and looked at the determination in his eyes—"and nor will you."

I wasn't going to kill for it, so I'd have to outsmart the demon. Demons were known for their trickery. The question was, how did I out-trick a trickster?

Maybe I wouldn't have to.

Tricking a demon became Plan B or maybe C. It would be better to strike a bargain with him. Between the items in Mephisto's collection and my connections, we had to be able to exchange the grimoire for something Dareus wanted other than me or Harrison's death.

I felt a small sense of relief seeing how difficult it was to summon him. It wasn't calling him that was difficult but rather getting him to respond. Standing in the middle of Mephisto's office, we both studied the demon circle that hadn't been answered in the hour Mephisto had been summoning Dareus. It proved what I had long speculated: Demons didn't have to answer, and to get a demon to respond regularly required an initial introduction. Only then were you given the means to contact them directly.

I glanced at Mephisto. His appearance bordered on petulant and I recognized the look on his face: the same look that appeared whenever powerful people were rendered powerless. He'd taken umbrage at the demon rejecting his summoning.

"Maybe I should try."

"No," Mephisto responded quickly. Summoning was linked to the magic, and demons knew who they were answering. Was it that Mephisto's magic was unknown so Dareus refused to answer it, or the opposite? Maybe he knew and was reluctant to deal with it. If that was the case, he would respond to elven magic. It was the reason he'd put a bounty on me. After several moments of deliberation, it was obvious we needed someone whose magic he'd recognize and respond to. Which led to Mephisto calling Wendy.

Benton escorted Wendy and Stacey into Mephisto's office. Her arrival was preceded by a flourish of theatrics. Wendy's black wizard robe was fluttering like a cape, and since we were inside and there wasn't any wind in the house, it was being done magically. Stacey's robe wasn't making such a spectacle. I should have been given an award for controlling my response. And when I saw Wendy's wand holstered at her waist like a gun, my eyes flew to the ceiling and I clenched my jaw fighting the laughter.

Stacey had her wand in hand with a quiet confidence that didn't ease me the way it should have. Something about her was more unsettling than Wendy, but I couldn't place what it was. Was she a dark horse? Whereas Wendy was bold, intrusive, wearing her confidence like a crown, Stacey was understated with a quiet power and knowledge. I couldn't stop thinking she was the one to really watch. Stacey advanced toward Mephisto, extending her hand to shake his.

"We hope that we can be of assistance," she said, a light flush creeping up her neck and cheek when he took hold of her hand and covered it with his other hand. He held it for an extended time as he gave her a disarming smile. I knew that look she'd given him. Cory, in all his immodesty, called it "hot-struck." It wasn't a thing. I refused to accept it.

Cory had been given that look often and was quick to point out to me and Madison that we'd known him for so long we weren't fazed by his Adonis-like good looks. We simply took turns pointing out we might have if it came with a modicum of humility. A dab of modesty goes a long way. Had I become immune to Mephisto and his alluring mystique? Or were the witches drawn to the otherness of his magic? Whether he muted it or not, there was something undeniably intriguing about it.

"You know Erin," Mephisto said, moving to where I was seated in the chair near the desk. He leaned against it, positioned close enough to rest his hand on my shoulder, making it blindingly obvious to Wendy and Stacy that whatever existed between us was more than professional.

"Of course." Wendy's eyes were drawn to his hand on my shoulder, although her expression didn't change. It seemed like Stacey was remembering the double-cross they'd attempted between him and Landon with the Amber Crocus. Or perhaps she was embarrassed by a double-cross they were planning. Were they in play for the grimoire? I wouldn't get anything from Wendy; she was calculating and opportunistic. Stacey may have been as well, although there might have been a sliver of integrity left in her. But I wouldn't underestimate her.

"You'd like us to summon Dareus, correct?" Wendy asked.

"Yes, we'd like to talk to him."

She examined the circle in the middle of the room. "He's not responding?"

Mephisto's jaw clenched and a glint of annoyance flickered. The look of the powerful rendered powerless. "It is as I told you when I called."

"Then you are aware of the consulting fee."

"Yes." He pushed the words through gritted teeth. I recognized the undercurrent in his voice. Restrained annoyance. I'd been on the receiving end of it during our negotiations. Taking out his phone, Mephisto tapped a few keys to make the payment.

Wendy and Stacey examined the circle. It was probably thicker than they were used to, but we weren't taking any chances. With wands in hand, they slipped off their robes in a flourish of movement, said a spell, and the fabric made sweeping movements around the circle, leaving golden sigils behind.

"It's best to handle demons with caution," Wendy said.

Stacey's robe returned and draped over her extended arm. She slipped it back on. Because Wendy was going to do Wendy and never miss an opportunity to make an ostentatious display, she raised her arms to the ceiling in a theatrical wave of movement, and her robe made balletic twirls and danced overhead before sliding down her arms. She straightened the robe once it was on.

Wendy hadn't gotten the last word of the spell out before Dareus appeared, his brows raised. His face brightened at the sight of me standing next to her.

"Wendy." He addressed her but his eyes kept flicking to me, a slow easy smile spreading his lips. Mephisto, arms linked around my waist, pulled me back, pressing my back into him. He kept a hold on my shirt.

"Wendy, how may I be of service to you?" Dareus asked. And despite her assertion, there was a familiarity to their interaction that refuted her claims of not having a lot of dealings with demon magic.

"She did it for me. I wanted to talk to you," I said.

"How may I be of service to you, elven-protected?"

"I want the Black Crest grimoire. What will you take in exchange for it?"

"I told you already. That's not negotiable, and based on the circumstances in which we met, not an unreasonable request." He directed his attention to Wendy and Stacey. "And *you* know what I want in order for you to have it."

If nothing else, Dareus was direct and rude as hell.

"How will an elf benefit you? It's the magic you want, correct?" Mephisto asked.

Interested, Dareus inched close to the barrier that divided us, considering Mephisto for a long time. He pressed even closer into the magical divider then lurched back, like it had shocked him. His intrigue unsated, he moved to the center of the circle.

"You're not one," he said. It didn't seem like a question, and even if it were, Mephisto appeared unwilling to answer. "Their magic. It is rumored that they can make us corporeal outside the circle."

He wouldn't need a body.

"Does it have to be Harrison, or will any body do?"

I swiveled in Mephisto's arms and glared up at him. Why were we even entertaining this? Did he just have bodies lying around that he could use to barter?

"A body that I've inhabited before. I can give you a list."

"We don't need it," I said. His smile returned as if my response was a tacit commitment to giving him Harrison. "There has to be something else. Name it," I urged.

His eyes glinted as he moved closer to the edge of the circle, his slitted eyes focused on me. "Bring me Harrison or

169

an elf," he said. His head turned toward the witches, and when he spoke, his voice was dagger sharp. "Unless you are summoning me to satisfy the bounty, do not call me again."

Then he was gone. I took the witches not being able to look at me as a bad sign. Would their faces betray them and show them scheming or filled with power-lust?

They removed their wards in silence and departed with just a simple wave. If we had any more questions or requests, they didn't give us an opportunity to ask.

"I don't trust them," I acknowledged once they were gone.

"With the exception of Cory, I wouldn't trust any witch or mage," Mephisto suggested. "Erin," he said softly, in the same disarming tone he'd used earlier.

"I'm not trading Harrison's life for the grimoire," I stated firmly, not leaving any room for argument.

He pressed a chaste kiss to my cheek. The weight of the situation was heavy in the air and our discord was filling the room with tension.

"I can control this situation," I said.

"Can you? Because he's not going to remove the bounty on you. If not Wendy or Stacey, other witches will value the power the grimoire will offer more than your life. Take that choice from them, and in the process, help yourself."

The uncomfortable silence lingered.

"I might have to kill my mother," I admitted. A pang shot through me at that thought. "I don't want to leave a line of bodies in my wake. How would that make me any better than her?"

Mephisto's forehead rested against mine, his warm breath wisping against my skin. The otherness of his magic seemed to envelop me as his fingers interlocked with mine. "Being the better person isn't the objective. Survival is."

I forced myself to move away from him because I wasn't convinced that we didn't share the same vulnerabilities when it came to each other. It felt like I was being ensnared, and giving Dareus what he wanted didn't seem so unappealing.

Taking several breaths, I looked back at the spot where Dareus had stood. It was sobering. "I *will* figure something out, and it won't involve killing Harrison."

With a weak smile, Mephisto shrugged. "If anyone can do it, it'll be you." He sounded wistful but not confident. Then he stepped out of my path as I headed out the door.

I pulled my phone from my bag and called Dr. Sumner.

CHAPTER 22

$\mathcal{T}$he next day, before heading to Dr. Sumner's office, I waved at my shifter detail, a deceptively harmless-looking woman. A platinum pixie-cut drew attention to her round, parchment-colored face. Deep-set, warm, honey-colored eyes made her look unassuming, docile. But there wasn't anything docile, unassuming, or harmless about the stealthy way she moved, coming up behind me, only the cast of her shadow giving away her position. Startled, I unsheathed the knife at my waist and spun to defend myself. She blocked the strike just inches from her throat. Her other hand struck out, gripping me by the throat. Anger passed over her face quickly before she controlled it.

"Dammit, overreact much?" she hissed through clenched teeth.

"You startled me."

"And trying to stab me in the throat seemed like an appropriate response?"

"You were supposed to stay in the car," I snapped, trying to look down at the offending hand clenched around my neck. *This does look bad.*

She released me with a sharp exhale of breath. "I decided to escort you in," she explained.

"Everyone else just stays in the car."

"I would have but I need to stretch my legs. You've been driving around for over an hour."

I had, hoping it would clear my head and maybe spark some ideas. Instead, the long drive just heightened my feelings of desperation and hopelessness. I was really looking forward to talking to Dr. Sumner.

"I don't need an escort. I'm just going to see my therapist." I gave her a sidelong look when she sidled up next to me as I started toward the door.

She huffed in annoyance. "I'm sure you don't, but I could use the break and can assure Asher that you made it to your destination without suffering so much as a hangnail."

I could imagine how peculiar this had to be for the shifters, protecting someone who wasn't part of their pack. My role in making them immune to magic might not have been met with the same level of appreciation as it had from Asher. And I was fairly sure some believed I'd crossed the lines of respect and decorum when dealing with an Alpha. I wondered if she was one of those people.

Once at the door, I turned to her. I started to address her when she realized I didn't have a name.

"Scarlett, Scarlett Sullivan." She waited, amused, for the name to register. *Sullivan.*

"You're Asher's sister?" There wasn't any resemblance, with the exception of the slender build and height. But that could be said of most shifters. Asher was defined angles and striking features with eyes that sparked with implacable confidence, defiance, mischief, and hints of wolfish arrogance.

Harboring that many emotions in a look seemed like more effort than Scarlett was willing to make. The sly smile was similar, and I was getting the full display.

"Cousin." She shrugged. "I asked for the detail. Curiosity got the best of me. I needed to see what had activated full-on Asher the Alpha—or rather Alphahole."

I snorted and planned to use the title forever.

"And you did *not* disappoint. A woman who tries to stab you just for walking close to her, sends Asher vulgar hate balloons, and who's defiant for no other reason than it's Tuesday or whatever is pretty much on brand for him." She rolled her eyes. Her voice still maintained a casual neutrality that made figuring out her opinions of me difficult. But I was a total fan of hers.

Once we were at the door, I turned to her. "You can't sit in." I was always unclear about the boundaries set for people who were indifferent about showing the world their goodies, so I wanted to make mine clear.

Her brow rose and her smirk deepened. "I have no desire to lift the hood and see what makes *you* tick," she said, backing away. *Maybe I don't like her.* She flashed a smile. "The sausage is always better if you don't see how it's made." *Team Scarlett, maybe?* If nothing else, she was an enigma and that was refreshing. She seemed to need more than a walk across the street, and she headed in the opposite direction when I entered the building.

Dr. Sumner met me with a faint smile. As I'd predicted, the after-five shadow was now a low-cut beard a few shades darker than his hair. His hipster accoutrements consisted of large circular black glasses with an old-school elan. My lips quirked. He ignored my long, assessing look and pushed his new glasses up his nose. I wondered if, when he purchased the monstrosities, he'd been aware that they'd draw attention to his eyes, which were crystal clear, light blue, and emotive. As I continued to scrutinize him, he ran his hands through his hair, which was now longer and shaggy. The beard just added to the look. During our last visit, I learned that he taught at the college part time. If his new look was to serve as a deterrent and prevent him from being a distraction to the students, he'd failed.

Should I tell him none of this is subverting the indifferent-about-his-appearance-hot-professor cliché? Nah, the way he lifted his chin and rested back in his chair gave me the impression he was proud of his new appearance and felt like it was working.

"Nice vest," I commented, eyeing the dark brown garment.

"Thanks." It was the brightest he'd ever sounded. So proud. I thought to myself: *Look class, ignore my face and divert your attention to my very smart vest, super-sized glasses, and the beard that I think looks straggly and unappealing.*

I'd give him this. He really seemed to need it.

"It's really working for you."

He looked at me suspiciously. Well, I tried.

"And I see you decided to do Atticus Finch cosplay today," I teased.

"Atticus Finch?"

"From *To Kill a Mockingbird*."

"I know who he is, but during the many times you attempted to avoid therapy, you vented about your dislike of most classic films," he explained, despite the comment lifting his mood. *Weird look to be going for, but okay.*

I shrugged before dropping down on the sofa. "There are some I like," I admitted. "How is teaching going so far?"

"Great. I believe because of my work with supernaturals, the students are interested in my class. So, mine filled up pretty fast and I've been asked to teach next semester."

"Because of your knowledge of supernaturals?"

He missed the sarcasm.

"We don't discuss it. After all, it's psychology one-oh-one, the basics. I just think I'm popular because of that. Humans are fascinated by the world, and the fact that I have a history treating supernaturals appeals to them."

Sure, it's the supernaturals that they can see everywhere and not the professor teaching the class? Okay, let's go with that.

"You think your class fills up because of your link to the supernatural world? The world you *don't* discuss in class?"

"I'm a good instructor," he shot back.

"I'm sure you are. But as you pointed out, it's an entry level course. You don't think it's the professor that's the draw?" My smile was insinuating.

Should I be trusting my mental health to someone so obviously clueless?

After a few moments of him thinking about what I said, rose coloring crept along his cheeks and jawline.

"Maybe we should start discussing boundaries, Ms. Jensen." His eyes were stern but his voice lacked the same severity.

While I rustled through my bag, I thanked him for seeing me.

He bowed slightly, in a show of faux reverence. "My door is always open for you, god." The humor hit his eyes although he didn't smile.

"I thought I was a demi-elf?"

"Yes. I stand by it because it is apropos to me, but to others, your god status has meaning. How do you feel about that?"

Any other time, I might have made a joke about his clichéd question, but it was an inquiry I wanted to explore.

I pulled out my flask and the two shot glasses and set the glasses on the table. Dr. Sumner's lips twisted in disapproval and he gave me a chastising look.

"Aren't we past pretending these sessions are remotely normal or proper? I'm a demi-whatever who will probably have to kill my mother," I said, pouring tequila into each glass. "After I finish telling you everything that's transpired over the past few days, I think you're going to want this."

I tossed back my shot, relaxed against the sofa, and

started talking, without an iota of a filter, in a manner I couldn't with anyone else, sharing my fears, vulnerabilities, and true feelings without tempering anything for fear of worrying others. Surprising myself, I even told him about Mephisto and me stopping the sex we definitely were about to have.

"Mephisto?" I heard him move through his notes. "The god?"

I nodded.

"A Huntsman," he added.

I confirmed with another quick nod.

"What about the…" More rustling of papers. "…the shifter. The one you helped with his magic."

"Shifters don't really have magic," I reminded him.

"I know, but you helped him by making sure magic won't affect him. To stop a fae from using magic against them, correct?"

Dr. Sumner was doing an excellent job remaining impassive and objective under the onslaught of so much new and possibly unsettling information.

"Yeah."

He urged me to continue. He was blanched when it was all done. Removing his glasses, he placed them on the table and scrubbed his hand over his beard, the warring of emotions clear on his face. His eyes had softened and were full of sympathy, sadness, and pity. I had to avert my gaze and look at the floor. It was the pity part that hit the hardest. But I'd needed to purge it all.

"There's this naïve, ridiculously optimistic part of me that wants to believe that I'm not a disposable tool that can be discarded on a whim to give her more power. It's hard to believe I'm nothing more than a roadblock to her achieving her despotic dream." The tears welled and spilled down my cheeks. I was slow to wipe them away. "She's still my mother, no matter how I try to separate it. I remember the pain my adoptive mother felt when I struggled with not having magic. The sorrow on her face at not being able to make things better and the unconditional love she and my father have for me. And they had nothing to do with me being here. Malific is why I'm here. It just seems like there should be more. Like some type of remorse or hesitation, but there isn't. She'd kill me at the first opportunity."

Dr. Sumner moved from his seat and grabbed a box of tissues from the table. He moved the flask and the shot glasses aside and sat on the table, directly in front of me. He handed me the box of tissues. He'd managed a look of impassivity, which I appreciated more than pity as I wiped away the tears.

"You feel uncomfortable," he acknowledged.

I nodded. "I just broke down like an idiot."

His lips lifted to a small half smile and he poured a little tequila into each shot glass and then handed me one. He took a small sip, made a face, and leaned in closer. Speaking quietly, he said, "What makes you feel that way?"

"I should be able to handle this?"

"Handle finding out that your mother is a violent god who only had you as a means to get out of prison? Has every intention of committing filicide? And you feel foolish for not being hurt by this?" He reached out for me but changed his mind. Covering my hand with his, he gave me a small reassuring smile and my hand a gentle squeeze. "I've worked with supernaturals before, and your situation is unique. Give yourself some leniency."

"I'm going to have to kill my mother. How do you come back from that?"

It was a statement of intent and also a desperate plea for an answer that I knew he couldn't give. It left me feeling empty: a husk. Dr. Sumner remained expressionless, but during his moments of quiet contemplation I knew he was grappling with the morality of advocating murder. No matter the rationale, I had just confessed to premeditated murder. It was hard to put a poetic spin on it.

"She's your mother. And everything we've been taught about parents indicates that they should love us unconditionally, but that's not the case here. And it has nothing to do with you and everything to do with her."

"She's a sociopath," I offered.

He gave me a tight smile. "I can't make that diagnosis. I've never met her or spoken to her."

"I know. Take my word for it. She's a narcissistic, amoral, heartless sociopath."

"What happens next?" Dr. Sumner asked. "How do you reconcile the way your mother should feel about you and the actual way that she does?"

"I don't think I ever will. When I kill her, I won't be proud about doing it, because I think that might be the best I can hope for. I can't think of her as my mother but as someone intent on killing me."

Oddly, admitting that I would kill her was freeing, in a distorted way. I felt unburdened by the "what if." It no longer existed. It wasn't a leap to no longer think of Malific as my mother but as an assassin.

In need of a subject change, I said, "I learned to do this."

I whispered the spell, pulling my hand from him. The cool breeze of the magic and its confining presence enveloped me. I was cloaked, and Dr. Sumner stared at me, his expression blank. Reaching out, he touched my face, or rather, smashed his palm into my nose trying to find it. I jerked back, blurting an "ow."

Instead of being impressed, he looked disturbed. I knew it wasn't because of me disappearing but because of my introducing new facets of the supernatural world. Because of me, he'd seen me attacked by the Immortalis when they Wynded into one of our sessions, and he knew about deals with demons, elves, gods, and the Veil. Despite his attempts to make a name for himself as the foremost therapist for supernaturals, branding himself as the person to consult about out-of-control vampires and rogue shifters required very little skill on his part, because if they drew enough attention from the media, then it wouldn't be Dr. Sumner who straightened them out but Landon or the shifters' Alpha. He'd take credit for something that wasn't entirely his doing. Right now, though, he was getting the unvarnished version of the world, which I was sure had just lost much of its charm.

Dropping the cloak, I lay back on the sofa and he returned to his chair.

After several moments of awkward silence, I closed my eyes.

"How do you feel?" he asked, sincerity in his voice.

"Tired," I admitted. Living on a knife's edge left for a lot of restless nights. I gave in to the palliative easiness that Dr. Sumner's office seemed to create.

I jumped up, throwing off the blanket and looking around, panting. Dr. Sumner was at his desk, typing away on his laptop. His glasses were gone, his hair was mussed, and a jacket was tossed over the chair where he normally sat.

"I fell asleep," I acknowledged. "Sorry."

"No worries. I put a blanket over you, taught my class, and caught up on some notes. I do have another client in two hours, though, and I need to get something to eat."

"How long have I been asleep?"

He glanced at his watch. "About three hours."

Standing, I stretched. I could imagine what Scarlett would have to say about a person who needed a four-hour therapy session.

"Same time next week?" I asked.

Dr. Sumner shrugged on his jacket, leaving his glasses on the desk as he followed me out his office door.

"Do we have a set time?" he asked. He was right; our therapist/patient relationship was anything but typical. But I wasn't a typical patient. "If this time is good, then I'll see you next week this time."

I only had a glimpse of Malific's taunting smile before an explosion of magic hit Dr. Sumner, sending him airborne and smashing him into the wall across the room. He crumpled to the floor. In a strike of movement, she was next to him. Her lips furled into a cruel smile and my scream was drowned out by his wail when the blade in her hand slid into his chest. She yanked it out and was about to plunge it into him again when I blasted a sphere of magic into her, sending us both careening into the wall. I pressed my hand into my chest, magic battering against it as I kept us both on the ground. I'd had the advantage of surprise. I could feel her powerful countermagic working to release herself and steeled myself against the onslaught, trying to figure out how to tap into only my elven magic, to keep her from breaking my magical hold. I said the words of the spells that Nolan had given me, hoping it would keep me anchored to the magic somehow, but Malific chipping away at the magical hold was weakening it with each passing moment.

Before she could do it completely, I released it and ran to Dr. Sumner, whose mouth gaped open, each breath ragged as his face grew increasingly pallid.

"You'll be fine," I assured him, but my voice was thready and light, quivering as I fought back tears. Holding him to me, I put a protective ward around us, blocking Malific from advancing. No ward formed around her. It seemed that the binding only affected offensive magic and not defensive, which was why her Wynding hadn't affected me. Malific walked toward us, knife still in hand, glaring at the protective field I had erected.

Her unmerciful gaze slid from me to Dr. Sumner. Her smile widened, revealing a depravity that lacked reason. "He's the first of many," she sang. "Find a way to unbind us or I'll go through your friends and anyone who has ever spoken to you until—"

"Until what? You've broken me? You try and I'll take you with me," I promised. Whatever showed in my face made her swallow. The smile wavered. Did I look like a person who had been pushed too far? The final tendril of humanity snapping? A person whose cruelty and bloodlust could rival hers?

"You promised you wouldn't hurt anyone."

"I said I wouldn't hurt your family, but, daughter, I feel that unbinding us isn't a priority for you. I must make it one."

Hate-fueled anger rampaged through me, making my heart race. I wanted to drop the field and grab her throat. Jab my push knife into her. Throttle her. But none of it could be done without inflicting the same on me. I didn't know who I despised more: Elizabeth or Malific.

Malific crouched, examining Dr. Sumner through the ward. "He's not going to make it. The first casualty of war is on your side. How many more will there be?"

Then she was gone. Wynded away. It was only then that I allowed the tears brimming in my eyes to fall.

I unbuttoned Dr. Sumner's shirt, pressed my hand over him, and performed a healing spell. The wound knitted closed but his breathing continued to be ragged and he was so pale. Pressing my fingers to his neck, I found only a weak and intermittent pulse.

Cursing, panic-stricken, I pulled out my phone and called Cory.

"Cory!"

"Erin, what's going on?"

"The spell's not working. I think he's dying. Why isn't it working?"

"Erin," he said, keeping his voice low and calm. "Who's dying?"

I sucked in a shuddery breath and exhaled slowly. "Dr. Sumner. Malific stabbed him and I used magic to heal the wound, but it's not working."

"Where did she stab him?" he asked, his soothing voice acting like a balm against my fiery panic.

"Chest. He's pale, short of breath, weak pulse."

"It could have punctured a lung or cut a major blood vessel."

"I did a healing spell."

"Magic heals superficial wounds. We can mitigate injuries like torn tendons and broken bones, but we can't heal vascular problems." He was losing his ability to keep calm. I could hear the deep breaths he was taking to keep the urgency out of his voice. "Call an ambulance." He paused. "Or…"

He didn't have to finish; I knew what he was going to recommend. Call a vampire. For a few beats, I debated whether to call Mephisto instead of Landon. They had brought me back from the dead, but I'd survived because it was a magical death. This wasn't. Vampire blood would heal him. Vampires didn't readily give up their blood, protecting it like the priceless resource it was. The debt incurred for requesting it ensured that a person never asked again. And asking wasn't a guarantee. If it wasn't as simple as opening a vein, they'd often decline.

My hand shook as I made the call. It wasn't the request that made me nervous, it was the rejection. Especially since the last time I'd interacted with Landon, I gave him the finger.

"Erin." He didn't greet me with his customary seductive airiness and hauteur. This was cold and unmistakable hostility.

"L-Landon, I really n-need your help," I stammered out

183

between tremulous sobs. "My friend's going to die if you don't. Will you please help me?" I tried to steady my breathing, calm the feeling of helplessness as I watched the rise and fall of Dr. Sumner's chest become shallower and more infrequent. His coloring blanched. The silence on the other end of the phone was unbearable. I used the time to review my CPR, sure I was going to have to perform it.

More silence.

Please say something.

"Where are you?" His voice was still curt and frosty.

I gave him the address.

"Are there any wards to keep me from Wynding in?"

"I don't think so, but he's not in a position to answer."

"Very well, I will be there in a few minutes."

Having access to a century-old vampire who could Wynd had its benefits, so I waited.

CHAPTER 23

$\mathcal{M}$y attention was pulled to the sound of the door opening. Afraid to move Dr. Sumner, I placed one of the pillows from the sofa under his head and the blanket he'd placed over me, over him.

His body was losing heat and I was starting to wonder if the knife had a spell on it.

"What is the situation?" Landon asked, his tone clinically cool as he closed the door. It made me lose some hope. It had the sound of a person who would say no without a lot of consideration. Could I force him? Drawing blood would be easy but it wouldn't be enough to heal Dr. Sumner.

"You're going to be fine," I assured Dr. Sumner in his ear, adding to the many platitudes and promises I had made without a lot of options to make it happen.

"He was stabbed." I choked on the words, unable to bring myself to say that my mother had done it.

Landon casually lifted the shirt. "There's no stab wound."

"It was healed," I told him, intentionally vague.

"By whom?"

"Me," I admitted.

He shifted and looked around the room, probably for

185

whoever had loaned me magic. After all, Landon was only aware of me being a death mage.

"And that failed?" he asked dispassionately as he stood. I'd even describe it as callous.

"Yeah."

"He's human. Call their healers."

He started toward the door and I called out, tears streaming down my face. He might die because of me. I couldn't let that happen.

"They *might* save him. I know you will."

I was brushing the tears away as quickly as they fell, trying to shore up the steeliness needed to negotiate.

Landon moved quickly to me. He canted his head and looked at me with a wary interest. He lifted my chin until our eyes met. He regarded me for a long time, his thumb sweeping over my cheek, brushing away the tears.

"Well, this won't do," he whispered. "I don't wish to see you like this."

His gaze slid to Dr. Sumner and then back to me. His onyx eyes held mine with dark intensity that reaffirmed why he was the Master of the city's liaison and that he found humans and some supernaturals "entertaining."

"My help comes at a cost, Erin. Do you understand?"

I closed my eyes and let it sink in that I was about to be indebted to Landon. An open-ended debt.

He leaned in even closer. "Payment is not negotiable. Are we clear?"

I took a shaky breath before I answered with a nod. The hate for Elizabeth and Malific was so rampant and uncontrollable that it was a forest fire burning through me.

Landon's lips pressed into a tight line.

"If you call now, the human healers can probably save him," he said. It should have given me a moment of unease that he was so adamant about giving me an out.

"They might, but you'll definitely leave him whole, as if he'd never been injured. He'll be left with scars if they do it."

"Very well, then, we have an agreement."

He kept his eyes on me as he took out his phone. I only heard light mumbling as Landon placed an order for people in the same manner one does when ordering wings with differing sauces. Male Asian, age thirty to forty-five, no ink, domestic. Black female, age eighteen to twenty-five, no ink, international. Caucasian female, natural redhead, over forty, no ink, international. The specificity left me debating if it was -ist: classist, racist, sexist, jingoist. But no, it wasn't -ist, just... *Ick.*

Was one of them the appetizer, another the meal, and the other the dessert?

As if he could read the inquiry on my face, he said, "People taste diverse. Tattoos distort the taste of the blood. I'd like to be adequately sated after this." He shrugged.

Double ick.

After his order, Landon lowered himself next to Dr. Sumner. He eased Dr. Sumner into his lap before biting into his own arm. Blood welled and ran down it. When Landon put his arm to Dr. Sumner's lips, Dr. Sumner looked away.

"It will heal you. I know it's not appetizing"—*or probably anything you ever wanted to have happen*—"but it will ensure your survival," I assured him. Barely conscious, his head dropped and Landon had to reposition him to cradle him in his arm.

The arrogance was gone, the aura of affluence discarded. In that moment, Landon seemed almost human. Kind. Nurturing. Stroking Dr. Sumner in comfort and reassuring him that he'd be okay. When Dr. Sumner shivered from Landon's cool body next to him, Landon carefully wrapped him tighter in the blanket and positioned him more comfortably.

It took longer than I expected. The way the rumors

depicted vampire healing, it seemed like the wounded person was just seconds from crossing over and after only a drop of vampire blood was up and doing a dance number in the street. But actually, it was a long and arduous procedure, requiring Landon to stop periodically to evaluate the extent of the healing before continuing.

When the office door opened with a powerful swing, I was immediately in front of it with my weapon drawn. I relaxed when Scarlett burst into the room. Her knuckles were stained crimson, her shirt ripped, her hair disheveled. Primal ferocity was alight in her eyes as if she was preparing for another fight. She scanned the area and calmed slightly. Her head tilted as she seemed to do an auditory assessment as well.

"Are you okay?" she asked.

"I'm fine." It didn't sound that way. I sounded weary. "What happened?"

"When I returned to my car, something seemed off. I couldn't quite put my finger on it. Strange magic, maybe…an unease in the environment. When I tried to get out of my car, I couldn't. The doors were stuck. I broke the window. The moment I did, I was attacked by two men. Magic, but not witches or mages. Definitely not fae." The nuances of magic, to me, always had a smell. Since the shifters' immunity, magic no longer affected them, but now they detected it differently.

"Were they using their hands?" I demonstrated some of the movements I'd seen the Immortalis do when performing magic. The Huntsmen had killed all the Immortalis they could find, but Malific still had two.

She nodded. "When magic didn't work on me, they attacked and then just left."

They were the distraction.

She glanced into Dr. Sumner's office and cursed under her breath.

"I'm sorry I didn't get here in time," she said, frowning at the sight of Landon and Dr. Sumner.

"What? You shouldn't have been here at all," I admitted. "I need you to leave. All the shifters. I don't want anyone to come to my home. No more details." Before she could argue, I added, "I'm serious. This isn't Asher's decision to make; it's mine. The person responsible for this attack won't hurt me, but she will hurt you all to make a point. I can't give her that opportunity. Please."

I thought she was going to decline with the stock response of "I follow the Alpha's rules." She didn't. Instead, she said, "If someone's after you, accept the help. We're a pack of hundreds. We can help you."

"I know, and I appreciate that. But you being around just gives her more ammunition to use against me. You'll become pawns and she'll sacrifice you to hurt me."

The internal debate showed on her face.

"If Asher takes issue with you leaving, just have him call me," I told her with a sigh. I didn't have it in me to fight with Asher, but I didn't want Scarlett to have to deal with the repercussions of my decision.

She scoffed, and her laughter eased some of my tension. Perhaps you don't get to be the big bad wolf when the person has probably seen your mother wipe your nose and change your diaper, which was probably the case since Scarlett appeared to be older than Asher. She agreed and left with assured defiance that made me confident she wouldn't have any harsh dealings with Asher.

An hour later, after he'd canceled his appointments for the day, a red-lipped Dr. Sumner was standing and preparing himself a cup of coffee. Moving with the unfamiliarity of a toddler discovering the capabilities of their limbs, he seemed stunned by how fluid, fast, and graceful his movements were. And shocked when a light tug of the drawer pulled it to the floor.

"It will be like that for just an hour or so. Then you will be back to normal," Landon's faint voice informed him. His head was resting back on the sofa where he'd retreated once Dr. Sumner was completely healed.

Landon looked exhausted. Vampires refusing to use their blood for healing wasn't just about them hoarding the resource but also how it affected them. He was vulnerable. I went to him and placed my hand near his mouth.

"No, I have people on the way."

Yep, a three-course meal.

As if summoned, there was a knock on the office door and a woman in her mid to late fifties led in three people.

"Your requests," she said, in the cadence of someone placing a bottle of wine on the table. I checked the arrivals' eyes. Compelled people had a glassy look. It was illegal for vampires to compel, but not all vampires followed the laws. There were consequences if it were ever discovered. If I hadn't seen firsthand what a compelled person looked like, there were plenty of books about vampires that provided a description. The older the vampire, the harder it was to determine if a person was compelled by them.

Landon gathered enough energy to examine his meals and pointed to one. "You will be first." The appetizer, I guessed.

"I will need an hour," Landon informed us in dismissal. He didn't have to tell us twice; we were rushing out the door before he could sink his fangs into his first meal.

"Same time next week," Dr. Sumner said at his car, which was parked close to the front door. I had stayed with him while he packed up his things and locked his office after Landon left.

I shook my head. "No, I won't be coming back. Not until this is over."

"Why?"

"Why? Are you kidding me! You almost died."

Lips pulled into a tight line, he touched my shoulder and gave it a squeeze. "But you didn't let me."

"I can't," I admitted. It felt like defeat, but risking his life again would be reckless.

"You can and should." Where this optimism and feeling of invincibility coming from? Was it the remnants of getting vampire blood? He knew enough about vampires to know he wasn't immortal now. "Same time next week?" He beamed and I wanted so badly for his optimism to be contagious, but it wasn't.

I gave him a reluctant nod and a bold-faced lie of a commitment. I had no intention of returning.

CHAPTER 24

I need your help, Dad. I didn't care if the note sounded like I was pandering. Desperation had taken away any ego and I did need him. Cory was right: If Nolan didn't care, he wouldn't have left the spells for me. I placed this note in front of the note I'd left for him previously, clinging to the shoestring hope that he and Elizabeth would return for the two spell books and the scribing chalk. But if they were of any use or special, would they have left them behind? The skeptic in me questioned whether Nolan was even in a position to help me. Elizabeth was stronger and definitely more skilled than he was. Perhaps it was her that I needed, but I could only get to her through him.

For the third time, I went through the house, hoping I'd missed something and would find something of Nolan's that would allow me to do a locating spell. Without blood or hair, the success rate was minute. Less than one percent.

Hope wasn't a great plan. I needed to be proactive and think of something else. But what?

I decided to stay at Madison's instead of going home. Malific had struck once. I was nearly certain she wouldn't strike again. She wanted to make her point—and she had.

And Madison was safe; she had to have been granted the same clemency as my parents. It was Cory I wasn't sure about.

Messaging was how Madison and I usually communicated, so I expected her to sound concerned when I called. My voice, unrecognizably hoarse and raw, caused her to pepper me with questions when I asked to stay, but she eventually relented when I told her that we'd talk in person.

It took less time than the estimated twenty minutes to get to her home. With my overnight bag in hand, I headed up her driveway to find Clayton leaving. He stopped. His eyes immediately dropped to my bloodstained shirt, then rose to study my face. Then he changed direction, following me into Madison's house. I opened the door and was met with the enticing aromas of roasting garlic, onions, and chicken, reminding me I hadn't eaten. A bakery box was on the kitchen counter.

"I have dinner for us," Madison said, turning with a laden plate. Her lips pressed into a tight smile when she saw me standing next to Clayton. Her gaze followed mine to the decanter of wine on the table.

Really, Maddy? That's how you're going to play it? I'm supposed to believe you roasted a chicken for me in twenty minutes? I didn't say it, but I gave her the look and she knew exactly what it meant.

"I guess we can have dinner after all," Clayton said, going into the kitchen and grabbing another plate, wine glass, and silverware. He was very comfortable in Madison's home and was overly familiar with the layout.

Yes, we will be discussing this.

A light glow settled along Madison's cheeks and the bridge of her nose. The tight smile turned to concern as she took in my appearance. She poured half a glass of wine and brought it to me.

"What happened?" she asked.

I'd only planned to take a sip, but the glass was empty by the time I pulled it away.

"I need a shower first, then I'll tell you everything."

———

Showered and wrapped in a towel, it felt good not to look down at my shirt to see a reminder of the day I'd had, although the shower hadn't been as relaxing as I thought it would be. It just allowed my mind to relive Dr. Sumner's near-death, ruminate over the open debt I now owed Landon, and fixate on Malific's need to "motivate" me into finding a way to undo the binding. She had been successful. No longer did I cling to the sentimentality of a mother/daughter unspoken obligation.

I dressed, towel-dried my hair, and gathered it into a presentable topknot before heading downstairs. I groaned at my ringing phone. After my shower, I'd checked my phone and had a missed video call, a phone call, and two texts from Asher. I'd wanted to eat before speaking with him, but it didn't seem like that was going to happen.

"Erin," he greeted when I returned his call.

"Hi, what's up?" The halfhearted attempt I made to sound livelier was met with silence. Uncomfortable silence that stretched for nearly a minute.

"Are you okay?" Asher finally asked stiffly.

"Yeah," I croaked. The conversation was stilted. "How's Ms. Harp?"

He sighed heavily. "Ms. Harp is Ms. Harp. But she's adjusting to not being in her apartment. She's safer where I have her. As you will be."

His assertion was slipped in so smoothly, I was stunned into inaction.

"What?"

"As you will be. You're at Madison's, right? I assume you

have an overnight bag with you. If necessary, we can get more from your apartment. I'll pick you up in the morning."

I see what you're doing, you wily wolf.

"Asher," I said in gentle warning or perhaps to calm him. He was in full-on Alpha-mode, his tone implacable. A reminder that the Asher-verse was an autocracy.

"No, Erin. We tried it your way and someone nearly died."

It wasn't difficult to surmise that although Scarlett had respected my wishes and left, she'd reported everything to him.

"Me being holed up in one of your homes isn't going to stop it. In fact, it will put other people in danger," I pointed out. "No, I'm not going anywhere with you. Okay? And I need you to honor my wishes about your shifters staying away, too."

The complete silence on his end was worse than us debating the matter. I didn't want to debate, but it would have allowed me to gauge the situation. His silence left me in the dark. What was going through his mind?

"Asher?"

There was more silence.

"She can't kill me. But she will kill your shifters and anyone else just to make her point. If one of them dies because of me, I'll carry that burden."

"No, I will. It's not yours to carry. Do you have a plan?"

"Not yet. But I will have something by the end of the night." I was taking liberties with the truth and there was a lot more certainty in my voice than I felt. It was convincing. Which led to another sweep of contemplative silence.

"Asher?"

"I'm still here."

It was the stiff response of a person in deep deliberation. Everything fell on the Alpha. That was the disadvantages of the position. There was unwavering fealty to Alphas, but in exchange, there was the expectation that the pack would be safe. Everything from financial security to protection from physical harm. Which made me think it would be good for him not to take on more responsibility.

"I have this," I assured him.

He scoffed. "Do you forget that I can tell when you aren't telling me the truth?"

"No, but it would be pretty cool if you didn't call me out on it. Every. Time," I teased, hoping to relieve the tension. It was met with more silence.

"Enjoy your evening with Madison," he said. Hearing the finality, I said his name before he could disconnect.

"Will you honor my wishes?"

He sighed. "I like having you around, Erin. And I'm a selfish enough bastard to do what is necessary to *keep* you around."

"I don't know what that means," I admitted.

"Erin, you have proven yourself on more than one occasion. I've underestimated you often. But I'm not sure you're going to be able to do this alone."

"You didn't answer my question."

"I know, because I don't have an answer." He disconnected the call before I could say anything else.

Great. The unexpected was always worse. How was I going to counter that?

By the time I got to the table, the day had caught up with me. I took a few bites of food while they waited patiently for me to tell them everything.

Neither Madison nor Clayton touched their meal, giving me their undivided attention as I retold the day's events.

"And Landon came at your request?" Madison asked, her mouth slightly open and the fork laden with the potato that was the first bite of her meal hovering in front of it.

"To be honest, I didn't think he would," I admitted, then finished telling them about the blood exchange and everything else, with the exception of my recent conversation with Asher.

Madison's dismayed appearance warped into something indecipherable. She stared at me for a long time. "Vampires have let people die. I've seen them do it. They have no legal obligation, which they're quick to point out, and trying to press them as it being a moral obligation has never worked. Landon, the acting Master of the City, saved Dr. Sumner?" She seemed to waver between incredulity and admiration. She finally managed to get the potato into her mouth and chewed thoughtfully.

"Do elves have compulsion magic?" she asked Clayton after a minute.

"Not that I'm aware. I suspect that if Elizabeth had it, she would have compelled us to kill Erin."

We lapsed into silence, eating. I considered my options. How did I stop Malific while we were still bound to each other?

"Maybe I could do a sleeper spell or something. Keep me in a stasis while you all find Elizabeth," I suggested.

"Those only last for eight hours," Madison said.

"Will it work on you? Because they don't work on us," Clayton pointed out. "We've established what magic you're able to perform, but we've yet to figure out what magic will work on you."

"I'm not sure, but it's not like you all are immune to spells," I reminded him, and the unintentional blow landed: a reminder of the Laes that was keeping them out of the Veil.

"If you were able to bring me back to life, there has to be a way to…well, not let me be alive."

"There's the *Medul* in the Mystic Souls, where you're in a deathlike state. I've never done it. Never saw the point of such a spell. A magical coma seems impractical."

"Doesn't seem so impractical now," I said. "It's radical but possibly the best option."

"No," Madison interjected softly.

But I persisted. "If that can be done, then you'll have to find Elizabeth, get her to break the binding."

Madison rejected the suggestion again. I didn't want her to discourage Clayton from sharing, so I asked.

"Do you see any obstacles to doing it? Will the Immortalis be able to break it? Or anyone loyal to Malific?"

Madison stood. "Are you two fucking kidding me! We aren't having this conversation." Her voice reverberated with anger and her eyes were glistening, I wasn't sure whether from anger or sadness. She looked directly at me. "Seriously?" Grabbing her glass, she turned her back to us and took a long drink from it. "Clayton, I need to talk with my sister. Will you excuse us for the night?"

He nodded and stood, his eyes darting between the two of us. His gaze remained on Madison for a long time as if he wanted to say something, but he decided against it.

Take me with you, I thought as he departed. I didn't want to have the "sister" talk. I'd rather her take out a shank and try to gut me. I could parry that. But the sister talk? You couldn't parry the emotions, distress, sadness, and concern that came with it. As much as I wanted to go full throttle, ignoring all the external noise until I succeeded, I realized I was doing it at the expense of the people who cared about me.

"What are you doing?" she asked, now standing in front of me. I dropped my gaze, unable to look at her pained expression.

"You didn't see Dr. Sumner, or the look of satisfaction on her face. I'm out of my league." That realization hit me hard, dousing any hope I had. "What type of person will I have to become to best her? On my way here I even considered fulfilling Dareus's request to get the grimoire. And there's no guarantee it could even help. Do you understand that? I considered *killing* someone to get a book that has no guarantees of helping at all. That's how desperate I am."

Madison inhaled a shuddering breath and then released it.

"I get it. But trying the *Medul* seems reckless. Cory released a dangerous fae by using the Mystic Souls, and you're considering trying an untested spell from it? Don't do that. Please."

I had no defense against her fear and sorrow. Even if I did, I couldn't do that to her.

I didn't have a lot of other options. We could try to imprison Malific, but she could still hurt me. I'd live in a constant state of fear, wondering in what sadistic way she'd exact her revenge.

There weren't a lot of options.

The realization that Nolan was my only hope made sleeping nearly impossible, and I'd been tossing and turning since I got into bed. There was a light knock on the door before Maddie crept in with a bag of Jelly Belly. In our childhood, whenever I'd had a particularly bad day managing my need for magic, she'd crawl into bed with me and we'd eat the bag. Which led to us being unable to sleep because of the sugar and us staying up all night talking. She opened the bag and I grabbed a handful of jellies that managed to simultaneously enrage me and bring me joy. Who was the brainchild behind buttered popcorn flavored Jelly Belly?

Picking through the beans, I said, "So, dinner with Clayton?"

Madison shoved a mouthful of candy into her mouth then shrugged.

I smirked. "Go ahead, I can wait for you to finish those because there's no way we're not discussing it."

"It was just dinner," she said, feigning indifference. And doing a poor job at pretending she wasn't infatuated by the charismatic god.

"First date?"

"We had lunch yesterday and I met him before work for coffee once or twice."

"So...not the first date?" I teased. "You're dating."

She chewed on the bottom of her lip, then after relaxing her hold on it, popped a few more jellies into her mouth. "What's the deal with Asher and Mephisto?" she inquired in a transparent attempt at a topic change.

Well played, sis.

My shoulders dropped with the sigh. "I don't know." When it came to this topic, I felt clueless, but that wasn't really the case. It was complicated. From a cursory assessment they were so similar, but when I looked deeper than good looks, money, power, and how they made me feel, they couldn't be any more different.

Taking my silence for contemplation, she said, "You do realize there's more to Asher wanting to protect you than mere obligation. I think he's always had a thing for you."

"I don't know if that's true. With Asher, things are unclear. And I was drawn to Mephisto's magic, but now that I have my own, my attraction to him goes deeper than his magic."

Madison laughed. "That hasn't gone unnoticed by anyone."

I scrunched my nose at her. "Asher is intense but in a different way. He commands hundreds who follow him blindly. Whether it's intentional or not, he seems to expect that from everyone—even me."

"You realize in a pack it's not as blind as it appears. They follow him because they trust him. If they don't, he's challenged. I don't believe he's ever been challenged since becoming the Alpha. That says a lot about him."

"He's dominant," I pointed out. "Why are you defending him? You don't even like him." Madison always had choice words to describe him, and the choice was always between expletives that ended with -er.

She shrugged. "I don't dislike Asher the person. He's charming, confident, funny, stylish, and let's admit it, as arrogant as he is, he does have cause."

That was debatable.

"It's Asher the Alpha who'll do anything for his pack. The Alpha who flouts our laws, circumvents policies and restrictions without so much as a fine, and who has a vault full of illegal magical objects but has avoided being caught with any of it." Registering my surprise at her knowing about the vault, she gave me a half smile. I knew he had the vault, but I'd never told her. "I just want to smoosh that smarmy bastard and his attorney in the face."

"Madison, it's just us. No need to be coy, tell me how you really feel," I teased. "Why smoosh? Why not punch?"

"Smooshing is ten times more insulting. You're pretty much saying you can't stand to look at their face any longer. It's the perfect offense, and can you imagine doing it publicly?" She did a chef's kiss. And when she was done with her ardent explanation of the merits of the smoosh, I was laughing. Whether it was the moment of being unburdened or the laughter, it seemed to give me some clarity about Asher.

"I feel like I'll get lost in him," I confessed. My attraction for him couldn't be ignored. There wasn't anything overpowering or dominating about his touch. It was just a gentle intensity that he managed the measure of based on the need.

Madison's smile fell and she studied me for a moment. "Lost?"

I knew I hadn't explained it well, because I didn't quite understand it myself. "Asher is, well…Asher. This bigger than life individual, the Alpha, with meetings with congress, corporations, teams of lawyers." I chuckled at the snarl that the mere mention of his attorneys brought to her face. "And a pack, and a world that revolves around him. I wouldn't be Erin with him. I'd be Asher's girlfriend or the woman he's seeing. Even today, after asking him to pull his pack back, I have no idea if he'll do it. Because it's Asher's will that matters. And then it's his pack. His loyalty will always be to them. I get it, but I suspect that would lead to problems. And typically, shifters tend to want to mate with other shifters. Could we have a future? If it got serious, would he expect me to change to a shifter?"

Madison was now just nibbling on a jellybean.

"I don't think things would be any better with Mephisto," I went on. "He's duty bound to the Veil. The moment he's able to return to it, will he want to come back here?" That was a question that lingered about Clayton as well. "Sometimes, with him, it may be just physical." I sighed, leaving out the part that the craving I used to have for his magic was now directed solely at him.

I sagged back against the headboard and closed my eyes, feeling a tinge of guilt about the conversation. Like we'd devolved to our teenage years where discussing my struggle with my urges quickly moved to hormonal-driven conversations about boys. Now it was about men.

"I don't think who you end up with will be decided by a list of pros and cons. You'll know because it will feel right."

I opened one eye to look at her. Did she attend Dr. Sumner's masterclass of clichés and platitudes? My thoughts must have shown on my face because she said, "I know it's a cliché but sometimes there's wisdom to clichés."

Giving her a half smile, I slid down into the bed and so did she. I was right about one thing: It didn't seem like I was going to find an answer to the pressing things in my life, including how to handle Malific.

CHAPTER 25

*C*ith the need for an early start the next day, I headed home before daybreak and was surprised not to see anyone tailing me as I drove into my apartment complex. Despite his parting remarks, Asher seemed to be honoring my wish. A request that I now regretted at the sight of an unknown person moving from the entryway of my apartment and getting into a car parked a few feet away. I was willing to bet they'd just left a demon-summoning circle at my door.

I couldn't decide which was more offensive: the bounty on me, the lack of sophistication or ingenuity of the so-called *bounty hunters*, or the quality of them. This wasn't even B-team quality hunting. Clearly the D-squad was deployed and were using lazy and uninventive tactics.

Despite it being amateur hour, it needed to stop.

My car went unnoticed by D-squad-bounty-hunter. I wasn't under any illusion that they were just being stealthy. They just weren't paying attention. I parked in the second row, at an angle to give me a better vantage point. Even after getting out of my car, retrieving my iridium manacles, placing them in my back pocket for easy access, and donning an ankle sheath, the person still hadn't looked up.

Damn, this isn't even D-level.

When I approached my apartment, I got a better look at the amateur hunter. His head jerked up at my approach, making it obvious he was unaware that I hadn't been at home.

This level of incompetence was insulting. Mr. Amateur waited to give me some space before getting out of his car to follow me. His version of being inconspicuous included dropping to a kneel, pretending to tie his shoe when I looked over my shoulder at him. *Really?* His novice tailing skills gave me the perfect opportunity to cloak myself.

After losing his visual on me, he hurried past the outer entryway, a few feet from my front door, and looked around. His gaze darted around the area before he shoved his hand through his shaggy, dark copper-colored hair, exposing a network of ink on his arm. He stood back, eyed my door, checked his circle. Once he'd checked it, he slipped a stun gun from his pocket. Not as amateurish as I thought.

He knocked on my door.

The nerve!

Clearly, his plan was to knock on my door and stun me when I opened it. Settling my anger before I moved, I eased toward him quietly, the heavy cloaking spell causing me to lose some of my normal grace and ease of movement. To maintain the secret of my magical ability so I could continue to use it as a tactical advantage, I quickly dropped the cloak and shoved him into the door. His face smashed into the doorframe. Wrenching the arm with the stun gun behind him, I snatched the gun from his hold and gave him a taste of the treatment he'd intended for me. I stepped back when his body convulsed. He was still standing, so I swiped his leg. His hands flew up to defend himself when I stunned him again.

He struggled, hitting out frantically at the sight of the

iridium manacles. The threat of not having access to magic made his defense more desperate and panicked. A well-placed strike to his forearm prevented him from pelting me with offensive magic. Using my positional advantage, I rolled him to the side and clamped the iridium brace on his right arm. I placed the stun gun next to me and retrieved my knife from its sheath. Jerking him to stand, I put a few inches between us, taking a defensive position with my knife at the ready.

He continued to glance at the entryway leading to the parking lot.

"You'll never make it. I'm close enough to strike without much effort. I don't plan to hurt you, *but* we need to talk."

Surprise and confusion marred his face; he'd underestimated me. Which reinforced my decision to keep my magical abilities a secret as long as I could.

"Talk?"

I jerked my chin to where I wanted him to stand so I could open my front door. He fidgeted.

"You tried to give me to a demon. If you make me chase you down, I'll remember what your intentions were, and I guarantee you won't be running anywhere for a long time." My eyes narrowed on him.

His wide, fearful eyes tracked the knife as the light hit it, making it glint. He nodded, entered my apartment, and took a seat where I directed him. I grabbed the stun gun off the ground and made a show of letting him see it before taking a seat on the table in front of him.

His unruly hair kept blocking his eye and he fidgeted as he scraped it back.

"Your name?"

Lips drawing into a defiant line, he offered a glare in response.

"I'm going to get the information. You either have a wallet with your ID on you or in your car. It's up to you how painless you want this to be. I'll just keep zapping you with this"—I raised the stun gun—"until you give me a name, or I get bored enough to see if you have ID in your car. If it's in your car, I'll break the windows. My last few days have been really crappy. Power-hungry asses have decided the Black Crest grimoire is worth more than my life." I shrugged. "You need to decide if you want to be the recipient of all this pent-up rage."

"Trace," he said.

"Show ID," I demanded. With a glare, he reached into his pocket and showed me his license. I took note of his address as well. "Which coven are you with?"

The muscles of his neck bulged. He jumped to his feet. I clipped his legs before he made it even a foot. He fell sideways. I dropped down next to him and pressed the knife to his throat.

"Tsk. Tsk. You're not here on behalf of the coven, are you?" I didn't wait for him to answer. The knife pressed harder into his skin, blood slid down his neck, fear drenched his eyes. "Your coven doesn't know you practice dark magic, do they?"

Most witches wouldn't willingly admit to it because of the associated stigma, and some covens had zero-tolerance for it and regarded it as grounds for removal. But some called it gray magic, to justify their dabbling. Technically, if there wasn't a death involved, it fell on the other side of dark magic.

"I don't practice dark magic," he objected through gritted teeth.

"You're trying to give me to a demon. Contrary to what you've convinced yourself, you've crossed over to the dark. Do you know what he wants with me?" I asked, letting the blade bite into his skin again. His ivory-colored skin lost even more coloring. "Exactly. You don't know. Your magic might not be dark, but the moment you decided that a book was more important than a life, your intentions became soot dark. I don't care if you're a dark magic practitioner or not. As far as I'm concerned, you're dark as hell."

I took a calming breath and relaxed the pressure I had on the knife, for fear the anger in me would take over. "So, this is what you're going to do. Get the word out. Let anyone who's considering making a play for the Black Crest grimoire know that if they come after me, they won't be returning. This is not a threat, it's a promise."

"How am I supposed to do that?" he ground out through ragged breaths.

"Have a meeting, go door to door, send out a bat signal, I really don't care. You need to make sure they understand it, because I'm holding your life as collateral."

His glare was sharp, his fear palpable as I moved, giving him room to stand. He touched his hand to his neck where the knife had drawn blood. His gaze moved to the blade of my knife and his blood on it.

"You need to clean that off," he commanded.

"If I do, how will I be able to find you?"

I slipped into a fighting stance when his posture became hostile. "You can try, but remember, your magic is inhibited. Do you really think you'll win?"

Not only am I a better fighter, I'm going to take great pleasure in whacking you in your man berries, too, just to drive in my point.

"I'll get the word out, but I can't make any guarantees."

"It's going to be quite unfortunate for you if you don't," I countered. Walking to the door, I kept the knife trained on him while I searched for the keys for the manacle.

I opened the door to Mephisto, who was just about to knock. He regarded me for a moment, the knife, the manacle on the witch, the demon circle at my door, and came to the right conclusion. Anger, raw and unfettered, washed over his face. Trace saw it before Mephisto could mask it. He stood taller in defiance, squared his shoulders, and jutted out his chin.

Giving Mephisto what I hoped was a disarming smile, I waited for the menace to wash away. He looked like death incarnate, in his midnight clothing. His marble-black eyes gleamed with barely concealed fury and violence. He relaxed some, sinking his hand into his pocket as I removed the cuff from Trace's wrist.

"Remember what we discussed," I reminded him. Responding with a short nod, he moved past Mephisto.

Trace wasn't fast enough. The sphere of magic hit the door and not me, the intended target, and the second one missed Mephisto completely. It whizzed past him, out the back entryway. I was unable to follow its path because my focus went to Mephisto, who moved so fast it was nearly impossible to register. He grabbed Trace, yanking him back against his chest. His hand grasped Trace's jaw, positioning it so that one hard jerk would break his neck. And if that wasn't enough, the gird that Mephisto formed around Trace's chest would crush the breath out of him.

I inhaled several slow breaths, trying to make my haphazardly spiraling world slow down. I didn't have it in me to talk Mephisto out of it, despite knowing I should. I met Mephisto's inquiring gaze. He was waiting on me to give the order: release him or finish the job.

Tell Mephisto to release him, I ordered myself. *Say it.*

But I didn't. The words wouldn't form. Trace's hand was clawing at Mephisto's without success. I knew I needed to stop it. I had to. But I could not make the words come out.

Say it.

I never spoke, simply shook my head. Mephisto whispered something in Trace's ear and shoved him away. Trace scrambled backward, putting a great deal of distance between him and Mephisto, his hand positioned to perform offensive magic, unaware that it wouldn't do anything to

Mephisto. Standing before him was a man who had decimated a race of powerful shifters, and everything, from his coiled strength, stealth of movement, and the restrained lethality of a viper waiting to strike was on display. Trace seemed too afraid to turn his back on him, so he backed away, slowly, and once in the parking lot, dashed to his car.

"What did you say to him?" I asked Mephisto, turning to close the door once we were in the apartment. He stopped me, waved his hand at the door, and removed the demon circle. He was less cautious than usual about exhibiting his power and magical abilities. Was it because he expected to leave soon?

"What did you say to him?" I asked again once the door was closed.

"That your presence was the only thing protecting his life."

"Okay, that was straight out of a mafia movie. Why didn't you just give him the kiss of death, like in the *Godfather*?"

Cory would be so proud of that reference.

"Because my kisses are for pleasure only." He moved toward me as if he wanted to show me that and so much more, but he didn't. Despite me tilting my head up in expectation, he simply ran his thumb over my bottom lip, light and unhurried.

He didn't make a move to kiss me. I should have appreciated his restraint. I needed it because the way his eyes were roving over me, mine was dwindling by the second. The distance he put between us when he sat on the sofa was appreciated. Clasping his hands behind his head, he said, "I've been made aware you're considering doing the *Medul*."

Really? You were "made aware." I bet Clayton couldn't contact you fast enough. "Hey, M, you have to hear this ludicrous idea Erin came up with. She wanted to do a Medul but Madison wasn't having none of that foolishness and nipped it right in the bud."

I nodded.

"It's not a safe spell, Erin. You leave yourself vulnerable, and even if you are warded, people can get to you. Your mother—"

"Malific."

"Malific may have her allies, but there are also people who want her dead. The easiest way to do that is through you. And you have to think of other matters. Plans must be in place to keep you well during your time in that state." He sighed, frustration heavy on his face.

"It's not an option anymore," I told him. His rigid frown relaxed. "I'm going to get the Black Crest grimoire, find a way to unbind me from Malific, then kill her."

He might have taken my assertion as bluster, and some of it might have been, but it was a resolution.

His brow raised knowingly and without judgment.

Why aren't you judging me?

"I think this is a good strategic move," he said.

"I'm not killing Harrison. It's not just out of principle. Because of Dareus, I have second-rate, wannabe bounty hunters after me. He will not be rewarded for his bounty. I'm going to make him think he gets me as a temporary host in exchange for the book. I'll convince him that since I'm elven-protected, he'll have a better chance finding an elf out here in my body than waiting for them to come for me."

"How do you plan to do this?" he asked, his voice as neutral and indecipherable as his face.

"Phylaca urn. I'll make one of the conditions of me hosting him that he gives me the book first—or Cory or Madison. Once it's in our possession, instead of getting my body to host, he gets a nice stay in the urn." Despite not getting much feedback from Mephisto, I knew it was a good idea. The grimoire wouldn't be available anymore; it would be in my possession. It would void the bounty he'd put on me. It was a complete win.

"Is that where he will remain for eternity? Because if not,

you will have an enemy, and killing a demon is quite difficult."

"What must the Veil be like, if allowing a person to live or murdering them are the only two options? There are hundreds of other choices."

His austere look was a reminder that he was used to dealing with people far more dangerous and powerful than those on this side of the Veil. Which was probably why it wasn't unreasonable to think that Malific was out of my league. She was able to banish the Huntsmen here, and it took a group of witches and gods to imprison her. I pushed the thought out of my mind, refusing to be debilitated by fear and insecurity.

"I know there are more options than just life and death—there's prison. Which you are doing. Be prepared to keep him there eternally, and for the repercussions if he manages to escape."

He wouldn't be corporeal, so how would he escape? Then I thought of the people who'd hosted him, giving him a link to them. Would he be able to signal them? And if he could, would they find a way to release him? I knew the answer. To secure a debt from a powerful demon, they'd do it without hesitation.

I wasn't going to let that derail my plans. "I have to make sure he doesn't escape and that he can't communicate with anyone who hosted him. So I need a phylaca urn and I need it reinforced to prevent communication. I need to have full control of the situation."

Mephisto smiled. "Excellent, my demigoddess. Where do you start?"

I retrieved my phone and scrolled through the pictures I'd taken from the dragons' hoard I discovered during a job. After the job, I'd established a tenuous, strained relationship with them, more specifically with the witch who was the leader, but nevertheless, they were a resource.

While I scrolled through the pictures, I overheard Mephisto's conversation with Benton, asking for all the information he had on securing a phylaca urn and preventing demon communication with previous hosts. Once I found what I was looking for, I stepped into my bedroom and called the number I had for Maddox, the nicest of the trio of thieves that consisted of two shapeshifting dragons and a cantankerous witch. The witch's dislike of me was reasonable. After all, I did charge through her ward with a mage, shifter, and witch to confiscate items they'd stolen during a poker game.

"What?" barked Lexi, the witch.

I looked at the screen. I had definitely called Maddox and not the number for the burner phone they'd given me after our first business transaction.

"I'd like to speak with Maddox."

"No. He might find you amusing, but I don't." She huffed. "What type of person gets a demon bounty?" There was far too much judgment coming from this common thief.

"Did I miss something? You steal as a hobby. Not even for a reason, just to have things. You're a crook. So, you can drop the attitude, Ms. Judgy."

Maddox had advised me to be polite to Lexi because she could make them sever all ties with me. I wanted to, but the level of hypocrisy was hard to ignore.

"They're dragons. It's their impulse to hoard," she countered. "Why not just ask them not to breathe?"

"Well, I'm an Erin!" I snapped back at her. The silence was expected. My answer was a straight disaster and had no relevance to the conversation, but if she was going to spew nonsense BS, I was going to respond in kind. Dragons hoarded; that was common knowledge. Usually they amassed magical objects, gold, often inexpensive trinkets that piqued their interest. But these thieves' trove consisted of expensive liquor, high-end electronics, and jewelry. They weren't just dragons being dragons; they were thieves, along with their witch partner.

"What?" she blurted.

"You've met me, right? Is it implausible that I provoked a demon and now I have a bounty on me? If they get a pass on their theft for being a dragon, don't I get one?"

She let out an unexpected burst of laughter, but it seemed like it tilted the scale in my favor, so I'd take it. "You're insufferable, but at least you're aware of it."

Look, witchy, I can insult me, you can't. I gritted my teeth and held my response. After a few moments of silence someone else spoke.

"Erin." Maddox's voice was vibrant and welcoming and a direct contrast to Lexi's. I'd gained favor with the younger of the two dragon-shifters after giving him a Glanin's claw instead of activating it and injecting him with silver that would have prevented him from shifting.

"Maddox, it's good to talk to you."

He didn't answer immediately, but I could hear air whipping against the speaker and him moving. "Is it, or are you just happy I'm not Lexi?" he teased.

"Both."

"What can I do for you?"

"I need a phylaca urn."

"So, you really do have a demon problem? There has to be a story behind that."

"Yeah, a very long story."

"I have time. Maybe we can discuss it over dinner at Kelsey's," he suggested, a reminder that I'd invited him there. Before I could answer, Mephisto entered my bedroom, one hand on the doorframe while he waited for me to get off the phone.

"We're definitely going to Kelsey's, but we have to plan it, so I can get reservations." It was a good excuse, although I knew that in order to give the appearance of exclusivity, the restaurant claimed to have less availability than they actually had. "Besides, I have a demon bounty on me. You might want to keep your distance."

He chuckled, a lively deep sound that was diametrically opposed to the ill-tempered person he was when we initially met. "You'll get your urn. I need to discuss the fee with my brother. I'll text it to you."

I started to remind him that I was going to get him reservations at one of the most exclusive restaurants in the city, but he disconnected before I could. They knew I was desperate, so I wasn't looking forward to the text.

"You made a date?" Mephisto's brow inched up and there was a noticeable clenching of his jaw.

"Not a date. Just dinner because I promised to get him reservations at Kelsey's."

"Reservations?" He seemed surprised that they were even needed, which meant he was probably on the privileged short list.

"We mere mortals have to grovel at the feet of the reservation gods to be granted access," I joked. Because of my past dealings with the owner, Victoria, I was given preferential treatment as long as I pretended her pet snow leopard was an adorable kitten and not an apex predator.

"You are not merely a mortal, my demigoddess."

My thoughts turned to what Madison had said about the Huntsmen returning to the Veil, and my mood turned somber.

"You have a good life here. Once you're back in the Veil, will you miss things here?"

A contemplative moment stretched longer than I expected. During the silence, he closed the space between us.

"The comforts that I have here, I enjoyed in the Veil as well. The few things that aren't available, there are substitutions, often better. Except one."

There was no restraint in his kiss. It was hot, ravenous,

and all-consuming, leaving me softly panting when he pulled away. His eyes darkened with desire and as his fingers slipped under my shirt, caressing my skin, the temperature in the room became unbearably hot. In that moment the binding between me and Malific seemed inconsequential. I wanted him.

Saved by the ping of a text notification, I stepped back to retrieve my phone from the dresser. I looked at him.

"What happens when you return to the Veil? Will you come back here to visit?"

His face revealed nothing. I wished it had, so I could prepare myself for hearing it aloud.

"You should see about the text. It's important that you get the urn."

With effort I dragged my eyes from him. His evasion stung.

The text from Maddox with their price for the urn was the splash of cold water I needed.

I frowned at the high four-figure amount. *Well, you just priced yourself out of dinner at Kelsey's. Use this money to bribe them to give you a table.*

Mephisto slipped out of my room before I could question him further, leaving me debating whether it was better that I didn't know.

CHAPTER 26

$\mathcal{L}$ife was much more efficient with a druid in your life. By the time I got the phylaca urn from Maddox, Benton had created a woven spell similar to a neutralizing spell. Twenty minutes after acquiring the urn, it had been bespelled to prevent Dareus from communicating with any former hosts. All I had to do was activate it once he was contained.

Now I just needed Cory to summon Dareus, but instead of demon summoning, he decided it was better to lean against the wall and scowl at me and Madison, who was a reluctant ally.

"I'm summoning a demon?" he finally asked, exasperated.

"For the third time, yes," I answered, massaging the rigid creases in my brow.

"And you plan on offering yourself as a host?" His hand washed over his face before he pushed himself off the wall and started pacing the room.

"Yes, but that's what the urn is for. It's bespelled. Once we have the book secured and release Dareus from the demon circle to inhabit my body, Madison will capture him in the urn." I hit him with a reassuring smile as the muscles in his neck bulged from him clenching his jaw. "When he crosses, he'll be corporeal and he'll have the grimoire. He'll hand the book off to you before becoming incorporeal in order to use me as a host. We have to trap him in the urn before he gets to me." I eyed him. "Once I make my commitment, I'm bound to it. He *has* to be intercepted before getting to me."

Cory turned to stare at Madison. "And you're okay with this madness?"

Seemingly unable to say it aloud, she simply nodded, if you could even call it a nod. Her head barely moved.

Cory walked to me and started checking my pupils. "I'm taking possession of it all. The oxy, your weed, and I'm probably going to take all the liquor, too."

"I'm not on anything and haven't been for weeks."

"What? So, the let's-trick-a-demon-plan was concocted without the influence of drugs or alcohol! This was a sober, lucid decision?"

Love is not delivering a crotch punch to a person truly deserving of it. *This is what personal growth looks like.*

"I have no intention of hosting him. We're going to trap him."

"Yeah, after you make a blood-agreement to host him. And success hinges on us capturing him in the urn before he gets to you. There are so many things that can go wrong with that plan." He gave an exasperated sigh. "I vote for a god and a shifter to be involved. Get your phone."

"We can't. Dareus was wary of Mephisto, wouldn't even answer his summons. Don't you think he's going to be suspicious if a shifter is present? What reason would I give?"

Shrugging, Cory gave me a tight smile. "Tell him he's your court-appointed guardian. After hearing this plan, that seems reasonable."

My glower did nothing to soften the rigid creases of his frown.

"Cory, I need you to do this," I cajoled. "I can't summon

him because he'll be able to sense my magic, maybe even discover I have elven magic." Cory's reluctance was something I hadn't expected. "Come on, I don't have a lot of options. It will work."

"If it doesn't?"

"It will." No matter how confident I sounded, it wouldn't remove his doubt. This was a situation where I had to hide all my uncertainty because Madison and Cory had more than enough.

"Okay, but anytime I feel like things are going south, I terminate it."

I agreed. The sentiment was nice, but if this failed, there wasn't any stopping. Once I made the agreement, I was bound to it, and the only way out was capturing Dareus in the urn.

Cory summoned the demon twice without any response. Madison and Cory looked relieved. I wasn't.

"Try again."

"What, you think he didn't answer before because he was too busy watching *Game of Thrones*?" Cory asked.

"What's that?"

He glared at me. "I. Will. Divorce. You."

"How does a divorce between us work? Will I no longer be obligated to tell you how gorgeous and talented you are, because that's going to free up a lot of my time. Will you hide your Instagram stories of your workouts? My life just won't be the same without those. After all, the highlight of my day is seeing you do what can only be described as kettlebell sex in the gym. I'm sure Alex is quite jealous of them." I snarked back, making a sour face. "*Please* assure me that despite our divorce status, you'll drop by every so often to remind me I'm messy and can't cook. Seriously, those critiques give me life. Without our friendship marriage, who'll commandeer my weekends and force me to be visually accosted by people jumping around and gyrating their hips because of a loose foot or something?"

"It's *Footloose* and it's a classic!"

"Is it, though? It was made in a time before Facebook, Instagram, and Netflix. Could it be that the entertainment bar was pretty low?"

The eye twitch is new. I should probably stop.

His wrinkled nose made him look like a petulant child. "That's enough from you, woman. Let's summon a demon." Some of the tension around his eyes had relaxed, but he still wasn't completely on board. He winked. "Because after this, we're watching *Footloose*."

Yeah, karma just gave me the middle finger.

Perhaps Dareus had been watching *Game of Thrones* because he responded quickly to the third summons. His eyes landed on Cory, giving him a once-over, a wash of surprise on his face, then his eyes cut to me, then Madison, who was strategically positioned in front of the side table where the urn was placed. We needed it out of sight but easily accessible. As soon as Dareus crossed the barrier, it had to be put between the two of us, to intercept him. If any part of his corporeal form came into contact with me, the urn would be of no use. It wouldn't be able to extract him from me.

"This is an interesting turn of events. You summoned me, witch?" he asked, still looking around the room, disappointment on his face making it apparent that he'd expected to find Harrison's body or me sedated or secured and ready to be handed over to him. "You don't have what I requested, so I'm quite curious as to why I'm here."

"He summoned you for me," I said. "I'd like to strike a deal."

"Color me intrigued," he said, inching closer to the edge of the circle and eyeing me with unconcealed longing. "And what is the deal, elven-protected?"

"Me."

A mélange of emotions crossed his face: lascivious intent, wanton intrigue, suspicion, and wary excitement. I averted my eyes from the hypnotic beat of his eyes to the grimoire nestled at his side.

"I get you," he repeated.

I nodded.

"Why?"

"I want the Black Crest grimoire." I kept my voice level, hoping he couldn't hear my desperation.

The wariness remained as he continued to study us. His attention fixed on Madison. He canted his head, looking at her as if she were a conundrum or riddle.

"You wanted me in hopes of finding an elf, correct? You need a host. If they exist, then you will have the opportunity to find one."

I hazarded a look at his eyes to see if some of the suspicion was gone but remained cautious, never looking into the mesmeric slits for too long.

"This appeals to me. But am I to believe that you are okay aiding me in becoming corporeal and existing among you all?"

"Not at all. I hope you don't find an elf," I said truthfully.

Cory's eyes widened at my candor, and Madison gave me a tight smile of disbelief, but Dareus seemed to appreciate my blunt honesty. The harsh truth was necessary. Dareus wasn't naïve enough to believe I had suddenly become his advocate. He had to believe my self-interest came first. A lesson learned from working with my clients was that the more self-serving you were perceived to be, the more you were trusted. They understood greed, power-lust, and self-ishness.

"I want the grimoire and for you to take the bounty off me. I'm not willing to kill Harrison for it. You accept my offer, and this is a win/win for me without having to commit murder."

His mouth beveled into a frown as he regarded me. "You're not nearly as nihilistic as I was led to believe," he eventually said before slipping into silent consideration. He hugged the grimoire to his chest, and I distracted myself from fawning over it by inching a few more feet from him. The farther back I was, the easier it would be to invoke the spell and capture him in the urn.

"You're not threatened by the prospect of me finding a way to live among you all?" Dareus inquired, his brow raised.

"There's only one of you. No matter how powerful you are, you won't be a match for the Supernatural Task Force, or any allies they recruit to apprehend you. If you become a menace, it won't be for long."

"How long will you give me?"

"A day?"

He threw his head back in a peal of laughter. "You amuse me. For the grimoire, I expect nothing less than a month. As you pointed out, finding an elf will be difficult. I need time."

It was worth a try.

"A week?"

"I think I've changed my mind. Your audacity isn't amusing, it's annoying."

A month, year, century, it didn't matter since I had no intention of fulfilling the agreement.

I nodded. "A month."

He stepped closer, pressing the grimoire to his chest, grinning when my focus went to it. My longing pleased him.

"Well, that is an offer I can't reject." His smile broadened. "Once the atropinism is complete, you must open the circle," he instructed Cory. He looked at me. "It is not complete until you agree. You must say *Gavale Bradish* Erin Katherine Jensen."

I wasn't sure which was more disturbing: him knowing my full name or how easy it was to host a demon.

"Closer," Dareus ordered.

I tried to keep enough distance from him to give Madison time to retrieve the urn and me to invoke the spell and capture him. I made a few micro steps toward him. His head suddenly whipped in Madison's direction and fury glowed in his slitted eyes.

I tried to make sense of the sharp change in his mood. Had he seen the urn? Did my reluctance to move hint at betrayal? In an attempt to allay his wariness, I moved closer to the circle.

"Come closer to me, fae," he demanded. When Madison didn't move, he sneered. The full force of his fury was directed at me.

"I reject your offer," he hissed.

He moved around the circle, scanning the room and its contents. Periodically his head would snap in my direction, his eyes pulsing at a steady beat, seething with anger. I rapidly went through options to salvage a situation that was spiraling.

He was fully hostile and suspicious. "I don't see the urn, but I suspect that it is close." Again he looked at Madison, who appeared totally unaffected by his accusation.

"You reject the offer and you'll never get another chance," I warned him.

Yearning emerged that made me hopeful. Scowling, his sibilant sounds matched his snake eyes. "You never have to worry. Your attempt at betrayal will not be forgotten, elven-protected." His form became a diaphanous cloud. I lunged toward the circle, hoping to grab the book before he could disappear, but Cory's arms formed an unbreakable hold around my waist as he yanked me back. Dareus's taunting laughter lingered long after he vanished.

I slumped into Cory's chest.

"What the hell just happened?" Madison asked, planted in her initial spot as if she expected Dareus to return. "He couldn't have seen the urn."

"I don't think he needed to. He was overly cautious. If he knows me, he probably already had his suspicions." My gray past gave me credibility with people who wanted to hire me but left room for doubt. In this situation, it had hurt me.

Once the circle was cleared away, we lapsed into a weighted silence, the unspoken question lingering: *What next?*

CHAPTER 27

*D*esperation and hopelessness made the plans I devised increasingly dangerous and irrational. I'd revisited the idea of doing the *Medul* or finding another demon who might be able to take the grimoire from Dareus. For the past three days, I'd performed locating spells in hopes of tracking down another elf who could remove the binding.

My hatred of Elizabeth's solution grew at the same pace as my desperation. And I had zero patience with anyone, so when I pulled into the driveway to my apartment and found River parked outside my building, I was prepared to tell him to go to hell in no uncertain terms and to give him very specific direction on how to do it. It was on the tip of my tongue as he approached me once I got out of the car. He wore his triumphant smugness like a well-tailored suit as he presented his badge.

"Erin Jensen, you are under arrest for the murder of Harrison Meadows."

"What?" I sputtered as he handcuffed me. Bile crept up my throat. So many thoughts ran through my mind. Harrison was dead. Someone had possession of the Black

Crest grimoire. Were these events related or coincidence? Was Dareus in possession of Harrison's body?

"Erin Jensen, you are being arrested for the murder of Harrison Meadows." There was a note of dark pleasure in his voice as he read me my Miranda rights. When he placed the steel around my wrist, the memories of my first arrest came flooding back. I wasn't responsible for that crime but had been left with the guilt and a blurry memory of that day. This one, I knew I hadn't done. I couldn't have done.

I resisted as he attempted to usher me into the back of his car. "Call Madison," I demanded. "This needs to be handled by the STF."

He scoffed. "I'm sure you would love that. The Axios Act," he rebutted as he tugged me harder to get me to move so he could put me in the back seat.

Had I been so concerned with my own problems that I missed the Axios Act becoming law? Since supernaturals came out of hiding, there had been an ongoing battle over how crimes would be handled. Most police were duty bound to handle a crime, but if supernaturals were involved, most were happy to have the Supernatural Task Force handle it. And the same courtesy was extended to the police when humans were involved. There was an implied protocol, nothing written into law. A small group of people wanted to merge the organizations. It was an issue that had been debated, argued, and litigated for years, with the STF citing that humans weren't equipped to handle the crimes of supernaturals and that pairing an STF officer with a human would put the STF officer at a disadvantage and put them both at risk.

The supernatural community policed themselves: the shifters by their Alpha, vampire families by their Master, the consortiums by the head mage, and covens by their elder. Humans would never be privy to the intricate network or tacit agreements and parts of our world that were purposely hidden from them.

No one really grasped how tenuous the thread was that allowed us to mutually exist with humans. It was a thread that would quickly snap if humans were exposed to the unedited, unvarnished versions of the supernatural world. It was plain hubris for humans to believe they would be better at regulating us. It would end up being a political nightmare of epic proportions, maybe even a civil war, and River, driven by indignation and spite, was unable to see that.

At the police station I sat in the interrogation room and stared at him, refusing to let him see a hint of doubt or uncertainty. I remained silent during his questioning.

"Witnesses put you at Harrison Meadows's home on several occasions. And I have it on good authority that your interactions were hostile."

My lips pressed into a thin line, denying him the ability to use anything I said against me, even if it was to declare my innocence.

He relaxed back in his chair, the rigid frown easing into a placid smile, although his eyes darkened with surly malevolence as they fixed on me.

"Do you think you can get away with it twice? You're a death mage and you give in to your impulses on a whim. What happened? Did he want his magic back and you refused? What did you do with the body?" After several long moments of silence, he leaned forward. "Erin," he said softly, "I know it's hard. I hear it's like an addiction, and if you confess, they'll treat it like one. I can get you the help you need."

"Oh, you're going to play the role of good cop *and* bad cop. That's a pretty lofty task. For the record, you should work on your good cop. You're not even believable as kind-of-okay-cop," I retorted.

His teeth gripped his lips.

I stared at him. "When this is over, I'd like to see about filing a complaint. Do you think you can help me with that?"

"You're so smug, aren't you? Got away with murder once and now you think you're untouchable. Well, you won't get away with it twice."

The accusation in his scowl niggled at me. I wanted to declare that I was unjustly accused of both crimes, but even if I could present him with verifiable evidence, he wouldn't believe me. In his eyes, I was a murderer who'd never paid for my crime. I'd circumvented the law.

Silencing the part of me that wanted him to think I was better than a murderous fiend and was stronger than my magic addiction was increasingly difficult. I wanted to defend myself, tell him that I no longer suffered from the cravings because I had my own magic. It was useless; I'd never change his mind, and River was the last person I wanted to know about my heritage and magical abilities.

"What are you able to do with the magic? I've always been curious." There was more derision than curiosity in his tone.

"The STF provide plenty of classes to learn about 'our lot,'" I shot back. "And Google is your friend. I suggest you use it."

When a spark of amusement flitted across his face, I regretted letting him provoke me.

Just be quiet, Erin.

"I'm not saying anything until I have an attorney present."

It was a good idea to have a lawyer on retainer, especially with the jobs that I'd taken and the people I'd worked for. I got *detained* more than any person would be comfortable admitting. Sometimes I got fined, sometimes just questioned. I felt a rush of guilt thinking of how often Madison had stepped in to make things better. I'd call her instead of a lawyer. Once she found out about this, she'd intervene, even if only to get the right lawyer. I sighed inwardly. An interrogation room definitely wasn't the place to have an existential crisis, and definitely not the optimal moment. Yet here I was having an epiphany and a raging case of regret for being such a burden to her.

There was a light knock at the door. River's eyes narrowed on it and I sat up straighter. Expecting Madison, I was surprised when another officer came in. Her softer features and disarming smile made her seem less combative than River. I was sure that was their intention. I found myself wanting to relax.

She brought in a bottle of water, coffee, and a bag of chips and sat them in front of me. When River left, she sat in his chair. She pulled a few creamers and packets of sugar from her jacket pocket and slid them over to me, offering to loosen the cuffs if they were uncomfortable and explaining her disappointment that, because of protocol, she couldn't remove them.

"You're not hungry," she stated after several moments had passed and the only thing I'd managed to do was put sugar in my coffee and take a sip from the bottle of water. "River's personality can be a little off-putting," she admitted, then she leaned forward. "And he may seem like a jerk sometimes, but it's because of his dedication to justice. I'm not making excuses, just explaining."

This was just offensive. Did she really think I was going to fall for *this* version of good cop? With a great deal of effort, I managed to stave off the smirk that was threatening to emerge, and my eyes stayed firmly forward instead of rolling. Even the indignation was kept at bay. Instead, I simply took another long, slow drink of water.

"I know about the other supernaturals, but death mages are still such an enigma. You're able to borrow magic from others by putting them in a state of death?"

My head barely moved into the nod.

"Interesting." She gave me another warm smile. "Once you return the magic, they come back to life, right?"

I gave her another unenthusiastic nod. "They're not dead, just in a state of in-between."

"I think I recall hearing that if you don't, the person... well, they stay like that, don't they?" She offered a faux shyness, as if she didn't know about the *incident* and wasn't well-versed on death mages.

"Don't sell yourself short. You have a keen knowledge of death mages."

"It's my understanding that some people are drawn to sharing their magic with a death mage for the same reason some people like to feed vampires."

That just earned her a shrug.

"Based on our interviews, it seemed like Harrison had a penchant for cheating death. The euphoria that some get from doing it. Adrenaline rush, perhaps? Or is it more sedate, like a dose of melatonin?"

"I wouldn't know. I'm not able to have magic borrowed from me," I explained. "I don't have magic."

"You have magic now," she slipped in, a gleam of pride in her eyes as if she thought she'd successfully laid a trap.

"Well, I'd hope that if River thought I had magic, he'd have me in more than these handcuffs."

"They're silver."

"That would be adequate if I were a shifter."

Confusion swept over her face. Dear fates, how were they going to police the supernaturals when they couldn't even get the basics?

"Silver affects shifters." The vacuous look of confusion made me feel a little sorry for her.

"You have to use iridium with magic wielders. If you're planning to enforce the Axios Bill, this is just basic information you should know," I chastised.

"Axios Act?"

"Bill, Axios Bill. That's why I'm here and not with the STF."

Irritation coursed over her face before she found something that looked almost impassive, but her previously warm eyes now held a sharp edge.

"Tell me about your relationship with Harrison. What sparked your arguments?"

"Tell me about Axios, why you said it was an act. If it's still a proposal and not a bill, then why haven't I been turned over to the STF?"

She swallowed, ignoring my question. "What type of relationship was it? Business, friendship, intimate?"

"What type of relationship do you and River have with the truth? Tenuous, on and off, tumultuous, or nonexistent?" I made no effort to hide my irritation.

"Ms. Jensen, will you answer my question?" Frustration was pulling her lips into a tight thin line.

"Maybe, but it depends on your relationship with the truth. After all, if you don't have one, then the answer won't matter because you'll just make up whatever story you'd like."

Her face was hard, eyes like daggers as they bored into me, and it was very apparent that if necessary, she could easily play bad cop. She knew the gig was up; her pleasant mask had slipped and the illusion that I could talk freely to her had gone with it. She forced a semi-pleasant look, but it was too rigid to be comforting.

"Let me get you another coffee. I'm sure this one is cold by now." She swept it up and left. River didn't return immediately. I figured she was briefing him.

River's air of confidence when he entered the room concerned me. Was it an act or sincere? And the Cheshire cat smile taunted me with the possibility that he had damning evidence.

"There's a witness who said that you were seen leaving Harrison's trailer. His blood was all over the place and so were your fingerprints. What did you do with him, Erin?"

My jaw clenched.

"Did you take his magic? Did you do it forcefully? That's what happens when a person like you borrows magic and the person dies. You get use of their magic for a while, don't you?"

Before I could consider an answer, someone knocked and a man in an impeccably tailored dark-blue suit, silk tie, and Italian leather shoes, and radiating the assurance that made people cower, came in. His black hair was shorn short and his tawny skin had a glow that I wasn't sure was genetics or tanning.

The smile he flashed seemed pricier than his suit. It was the beam that often followed a high three- or four-figure-an-hour rate. I knew who he was before he introduced himself: Van Hudson of Hudson and Parker LLP. I'd heard Madison say his name and the name of the firm through gritted teeth followed by a slew of four-letter words and variations of her disdain for shifters and their pain-in-the-ass lawyers. I was looking at the top pain-in-the-ass lawyer whose face Madison wanted to smoosh.

River's face had turned a peculiar shade of red. He couldn't seem to relax his sneer, but it didn't appear like he was putting much effort into doing so, either.

"We don't usually see you here," he said. "I just hear of your antics from the people at the Supernatural Task Force."

"I'd like to think I offer much more than just antics. But speaking of antics, what are you trying to pull? She falls under STF. They should be questioning her, not you. I've made a call to Madison Calloway to inform her. While we wait for her response, do you mind if I speak with my client?"

Before River could excuse himself, the lawyer opened the door to reveal another familiar face: Ava. I'd met her during a contract negotiation with Mephisto. She and the petite woman next to her were dressed in similar dark-gray designer pantsuits. Ava's peach-hued shirt complemented

231

her umber-colored skin. The granite-gray blouse the other woman was wearing contrasted with her whey-colored skin that was slightly flushed. Ava's short hair with the swooping asymmetrical bangs was modern, but her mannerisms and appearance were an anachronism; she belonged in the twenties. But the woman next to her with the tight low bun, stern hazel eyes, and austere look that made me sit up a little taller for fear I would be reprimanded, was exactly where she belonged. In a precinct, defending her client.

"Ava Charleston and Mallory Kane from Turner and Brenham."

River's nostrils flared at the names, but I wasn't sure if it was the attorneys or the firm that caused the reaction. Either way, he wasn't pleased.

Whose lawyer should I use: Mephisto's or Asher's? If a decision had to be made, I wanted Mallory: The hunger in her eyes that were fixed on River indicated he was about to be breakfast. From the look he gave her, he knew it, too.

I wasn't given the opportunity to choose. From my vantage point through the half-open door, I saw Madison storm through the precinct like a category 5 hurricane. A frown and icy glare as sharp as a blade had people moving out of her way as she strode toward the interrogation room. Even the attorneys did a double take and made plenty of room for her to enter.

She shoved a paper into River's chest. "Take the cuffs off her." He was too busy reading whatever she'd given him. "The Harrison case is STF. You never should have been on it and don't give me that crap about it being your duty to investigate. One call, that's all, and we would have taken over the matter." The calm timbre of Madison's voice seemed to fluster River even more. Probably from past dealings with her, he was aware that it was the precursor to a reign of terror. The calmer she appeared, the more wrathful she was, because it meant that nothing was being done from emotion and everything was being done from a calculation of her success.

She took a breath, then slowly exhaled. "What did you think was going to happen, River? You don't have a body and you made an arrest, which I must point out was signed by your fraternity brother, on the account of an anonymous source and a report that Harrison's been missing for three days. A report from a friend of his who doesn't talk to him regularly and simply told you that was the last time he'd heard from him. Harrison's not active on social media, so even a cursory review of his interaction wouldn't have given you enough information to declare him missing, let alone dead."

The veins of River's neck were turgid, his face flushed, and he was making an effort to be just as challenging and unyielding as she. He wasn't succeeding, not by a long shot.

"At what point will you put the pursuit of justice over your vendetta against Erin?" Madison asked. "If you'd taken just one moment to use logic and employ your resources, you wouldn't be looking like such an incompetent idiot. You have made us the enemy when we clearly aren't. A witch or mage with necromagic could have told you if a death had taken place in his trailer. Even the use of a necrosi could determine if someone had died. A shifter could have helped with the search." She turned to me. "Why didn't you request that you be turned over to the STF?"

"I was arrested under that Axios Bill," I told her, fully aware that River had taken liberty with the truth. Who was I kidding? He'd lied through his teeth and not only did Madison know that, but also the attorneys who would surely take note of his unscrupulous behavior. It might work in his favor in the police force, but with Madison and the STF, it wouldn't.

Madison didn't even give him the courtesy of refuting it. "Axios Bill," she said coolly with a dismissive smirk. This situation would probably be used as another example of the flaws and drawbacks that would be encountered if it passed.

Once the cuffs were off, I thought she'd at least put me in cuffs as she transferred me from police custody to the STF's. She didn't and looked at River in defiance as she waved me to follow. She gave Van an obligatory smile. It was tight and curled into something that barely qualified as one. He returned it, the two of them displaying their mutual dislike and respect.

As we moved through the precinct, people parted to let us through, confirming that Madison wasn't one many wanted as an enemy. River wasn't far behind and followed us until we were out of the building and away from everyone. His anger was on full display: skin flushed, eyes wild, and fists tightly clenched at his sides. Gone was the charismatic composure that would have catapulted him into his well-known desire for a political career.

"It's only a matter of time before the body is found. Then what? Look at the report. She visited him more than once. It wasn't just an anonymous report that put her at his place. He'd feared for his life and told his friend that. Was it Erin he feared? I'll hedge my bets that it was. At what point will you stop putting your career and reputation on the line for her? When will she be held accountable?"

"It's not my reputation and career you need to worry about. When this is over, I'm pretty confident I'll still have my job." Madison didn't bother finishing. The words lingered ominously, holding not the emptiness of a threat but rather the commitment of an oath.

CHAPTER 28

*I*nstead of taking the bridge that linked the STF and police buildings, Madison escorted me to where Cory was waiting in his car.

"You have evidence to prove I didn't do it?" I asked once we were far away from the buildings and any observers.

"The shifters said your scent was there but faded, proving you hadn't been there in days. There were three detectable scents, but we could only identify Dareus and Harrison." Madison frowned. "I had to enter your apartment without permission, but…" Her look was wry and apologetic for invading my privacy. She had no idea how little I cared. She was probably concerned because the apartment was untidy; something that would lead to sleepless nights for her but that I could not care less about. I didn't have a problem asking people to step over the pile of laundry sprawled on my floor. And I wouldn't apologize for the sink full of dishes or the trail of crumbs or popcorn from the kitchen to my living room. If they commented, I'd kindly show them where I stored the vacuum, point them to the dishwasher, and invite them to wash my laundry.

"Sorry, I needed evidence to challenge River," she

explained. She exhaled audibly. It relaxed her, as if she'd been holding her breath.

"I guess Harrison is dead and the third person fulfilled Dareus's request and now they have the Black Crest grimoire."

She shoved her hands through her hair and relaxed into her sigh. "We had a necromagic mage at the scene and they didn't detect a death. He's the best of the four in the department," she said. "I can't confirm Harrison's dead. I only know that there were three people in the room: Harrison, Dareus, and an unknown." She gave my arm a squeeze and looked behind me. "You go handle your situation and I'll investigate this more."

My situation?

Her lips quirked into a wayward smile. I turned and followed her gaze and groaned.

My situation was Asher, leaning against his car that he had parked behind Cory's.

"Hi," I greeted him, my brows drawn together. It was more a question than a greeting. "What are you doing here?"

"Making sure you get to a safe place," he said. "I have your overnight bag. I'm not sure what you have in it and didn't check. I assumed that since the bag is kept in your car, you have sufficient supplies for a few days. If not, I can send someone to your apartment to get more." He opened the car door.

That level of unwavering confidence and assertiveness needed to be bottled. He had loads to spare and would make a fortune.

When I didn't budge, his hand pressed into the small of my back.

"What?" I managed. "Safe place?"

"Yes, it'll probably be better to stay with me. I have a cabin, apartment, and another home where I know you won't be found. I'll add guards to ensure your safety."

"Asher, no." *Bad wolfie. Bad wolfie.*

He leveled a look at me, and all my mastered steely looks and obstinance wasn't a match for his.

Asher's overbearing and indomitable personality was driven solely by his need to protect, but despite knowing the root cause, his expectation of my compliance made me defiant.

Just as I was about to argue my case, his statement took full form in my mind. My mouth dropped open. *What the hell?* "You have my clothes with you? You broke into my car!"

"Broke into makes it sound so unlawful. I merely retrieved the overnight bag you keep in the trunk of your car."

Closing my eyes, I counted, hoping by the time I'd made it to ten, my rage would have subsided. Kneeing the wolf's Alpha in his Good and Plentys in front of the police department in broad daylight wasn't a good look.

"I'm not your pack. I appreciate all you do, don't ever think that I don't, but I don't work that way. Your wants don't take priority over mine. I'm going home."

He listened, his jaw clenching and relaxing as I spoke. This was asking a fish not to swim, a bird not to fly, a person not to breathe. He moistened his lips, his posture stiffening at the possibility of a concession. It bothered him.

Did he know how to turn it off and just be a regular person who took cues from other people, or was this who he was? It took longer than I expected for him to work out something that should have been a nonissue.

"Are you finished?" His tone was soft but determined.

I shifted my gaze to Cory, who was craning his neck to look at us.

"Asher," I said firmly, "I appreciate you sending your attorney." I didn't even bother asking how he knew. It wouldn't surprise me if he had eyes and ears in the police department and the STF.

"You never would have been arrested if you had been at my home," he pointed out.

Maybe that was true with the STF, where my arrest wouldn't have precipitated a windfall of inquiries and lawsuits. His lawyers made dealing with shifters a collective pain in the ass, so arrests were only made when absolutely necessary. I wasn't sure if the same level of caution would have been extended to the police department.

"Asher."

"Erin."

"What is there to think about? You have to honor my wishes. I'm going home. Give me my bag and we'll talk later." I felt proud of my patience; giblet punching was my first impulse and I had squelched it in lieu of something more diplomatic.

"I don't like this," he finally admitted.

I nodded in understanding. He didn't, and as difficult as it was for him to concede, he had.

He went to his trunk, opened it, retrieved my overnight bag, and handed it to me. I shouldered it, promised to call him later, and started to kiss him on the cheek, but when I leaned in, I gently brushed his lips. He pulled me closer, one warm hand splaying across my back, the other cradling my head and slipping his fingers into my hair. His lips pressing against mine was a heated torrent of pleasure as our tongues caressed.

Every alarm rang, telling me to end it. Ignoring them, my bag slid from my shoulder to the ground and I fisted a handful of his shirt, pulling him even closer. His tongue slid languidly against my bottom lip as we pulled away. My eyes dropped from his and I paid far too much attention to picking up my bag, using it as time to get my thoughts together. When I stood, our eyes reconnected and neither one of us would let our gaze drop. Finally, I looked over at

Cory. Even from that distance, I could see his jaw dropped open and his eyes wide.

"I'll call you later, okay?" I promised Asher, keeping one hand on the strap of my bag and the other clenched at my side to stop me from touching my mouth where I could still feel the taste of his mouth and the heat of his lips.

I tossed my bag onto the back seat of Cory's car and quickly got into the passenger side.

"What the actual hell, Erin!"

"I know." I groaned, pressing my head against the dashboard. The coolness felt good against my flushed face. Not only did I engage in a ravenous kiss with the Alpha of the Northwest Wolf Pack, but I did it in front of the police station for everyone to see, and I hadn't even had the where-withal to look around to get an idea of who had seen us. Did it matter? What could I do, close my eyes and start bumbling around as if I were in a trance or something and pretend my actions weren't my own?

"So," Cory said slowly before pulling out of his parking spot. I could feel Asher's eyes on me but didn't look back. "You're on a roll with bad ideas, so should we stop by the zoo so you can poke a bear?"

"It was supposed to be just a peck on the cheek," I admitted with another groan.

"Hmmm. Kiss on the cheek. You missed! All you had to do was go a little farther to the right or left and you'd have been fine. The cheeks are on the sides of the face. I thought I was going to have to douse you two with my bottle of water."

"Yeah," I breathed out, fully aware that I'd just made things exponentially more complicated. I frowned.

Cory reached over and gave my leg a pat. "Tell me what happened with River."

It was a well-needed opportunity to stop thinking about the kiss. I related everything to Cory, but thoughts of Asher kept popping up as I speculated what a relationship with him would be like.

Cory was chewing on his bottom lip by the time I finished. "I think Harrison's dead."

"Or missing," I offered unconvincingly.

"I'm betting my money on dead. Now we need to find out who did it. Since I'm placing bets, I'm going all in on Wendy."

I looked at him in surprise. "Wendy?"

"I think we've underestimated her. She's power hungry and she's not easily deterred. She blackmailed the vampires, remember? And even after almost being killed during that fiasco, she has every intention of doing something with Willows Dawn. I don't know if she plans to blackmail the shifters, too, or create something on the black market that can be used against them. She's the one to watch."

He wasn't wrong, but I wanted to be sure before I accused her, and I told Cory that. I made a note to message Madison.

"What do we do next?" Cory asked, pulling into the parking lot of my building while I finished off the remainder of the fries from the drive thru.

"Maybe"—I grimaced, preparing for his reaction—"we should summon Dareus."

"Oh, so you did want to go by the zoo and poke that bear. Well, buckle up, buttercup, we're going on a road trip."

"It's not as ridiculous as it sounds. He might respond. We'd at least know that he wasn't able to get anyone to kill Harrison."

"We're just going to pretend like he didn't discover our plan to capture him in the phylaca urn?"

I shrugged. "Desperation makes people more forgiving than you'd expect."

"It's a terrible idea. It would be smarter for us to go to Wendy."

"If we do and she doesn't have it, there'll be chaos, everyone in the community trying to find out who has the grimoire. And if we accuse her and we're wrong, it's doubtful she'll ever have any dealings with us again. What happens if we need her or the Lunar Marked coven in the future?"

Cory considered my argument and agreed with a reluctant sigh. "Why don't we let Madison work on this, okay? At least for a day. She has more resources. I know you don't like to be idle, but I think us intervening might make things worse."

He followed me into my apartment as he typed a text. Based on the smile on his face, I knew it was to Alex.

"You have plans," I said.

"We did, but I'm canceling them so I can stay with you tonight."

I took his phone from him, hoping he hadn't yet sent the text. "You will not. Go. I'm fine. I have wards in my house. Even if Dareus still has a bounty on me, I'm sure no one's willing to risk trying to get it. I have magic and a ton of weapons. I'll be fine. And I don't believe I'll have to worry about River for a while. Madison scared the bejeezus out of him."

"Yeah, she stopped by personally to ask me to follow her to the precinct to get you. She was all take charge and no nonsense. It was sort of hot in a twisted way."

"Ick. In a *really* twisted way. Let's pretend that's not a thing you said," I told him, handing back his phone. "Go on your date, you weirdo."

"Thank you. They're showing *The Room* at the Landmark theater." He stopped on the way to the door in a moment of consideration. "*The Room* is this absurdly campy movie, I think you—"

"Pass!" I said, before he could get out an invitation.

Grinning, he shook his head at me. "You really should explore the boundaries of your comfort zone."

"I do, but it won't be with your campy movies or 'classic' movies." I emphasized the latter with air quotes because I was convinced he used that word rather liberally, along with "cult classic."

"I'm going." He looked down at his phone. "Make sure you text me every hour so I know you're okay, *and* right before you go to bed," he ordered.

"No."

He huffed out a breath. "Erin."

"You're being ridiculous. I'll text you before I go to bed and in the morning. And *do not* come back here with Alex to hang out."

Cory and I knowing each other so well had its disadvantages. I could almost see the thoughts forming from his expression, the set of his mouth, and even the quirk of his lips.

"This is the personality that makes some men swoon?" he speculated in a tease.

"I'm cute," I countered.

"Yeah, and how can we forget that and your sexy kitten face?" His eyes rolled, and his lips twisted in what looked like a flehmen response. I opened the front door and playfully nudged him out, only to find Mephisto just a few inches from it.

"Hi," he greeted as Cory's and my face went blank. By the suppressed look of amusement Mephisto gave me, my face probably wasn't blank but more like a deer caught in the headlights.

I managed a greeting while ignoring the looks Cory sent back over his shoulder as he walked away.

Mephisto brushed past me and remained standing when I sat.

"It is my understanding that you had adequate counsel today," he finally said, his level tone concealing his emotions as much as his expression.

"Yeah, thank you for sending Ava and Mallory. If I'd

needed to make a choice, Mallory would have been it," I admitted.

That seemed to please him, as a glint flickered in his midnight eyes. "Will you tell me what happened?"

After having told the story once already to Cory, retelling it to Mephisto was smoother, since I incorporated answers to all the questions that Cory had asked. Mephisto listened, his gaze dropping occasionally to the floor in thought. When our eyes reconnected, his were as depthless as an abyss.

"Do you regret not doing what was necessary to get the grimoire?" he asked. The question spoke volumes. He believed that Harrison had been killed and the person responsible was now in possession of the grimoire.

I shook my head, finding it difficult to ask what I needed to ask the man who tried to persuade me to fulfill Dareus's request. My mouth felt like the Sahara. My throat felt raw and the question came out in a rough whisper. "Did you kill him?"

He moved until he was directly in front of me, his steely demeanor a reminder of his role in the Veil. I found some solace in knowing that Harrison's death was probably quick. Mephisto sat on the table and leaned in, holding my gaze with his full intensity. His pensive deliberation only took moments, but it seemed to drag on for hours.

"Would it change how you view me if I did something cruel on your behalf?"

I didn't have an answer. I bit my bottom lip, trying to navigate the complexity of the situation. If Harrison was dead and it wasn't at my hands but Mephisto's, should I take the spoils and use the grimoire?

"Did you?" I asked in a tone that was replete with uncertainty. Everything was just speculation until he confirmed. I needed confirmation.

"No, but only because I honored your request. *But* I don't believe it was in your best interest to do so."

Releasing the breath I held, I flopped back on the sofa and closed my eyes. "You might be right," I admitted. But I couldn't be burdened by what-ifs.

My eyes snapped open when I felt his presence just inches from me. His arms caged me in. Then he dropped one arm, using the hand to cup my chin, and let his thumb indolently glide over my bottom lip. "May I ask a question?"

I nodded. His stony expression made me feel guarded.

"Your kiss with the Alpha today, what was its purpose? To send me a message?" His low husky whisper was laden with command and displeasure. His magic, presence, and intensity overpowered the space we shared.

"I need some space," I said. When he'd returned to his seat on the table, the air didn't feel any less thick nor did the feeling of being engaged lessen. His penetrating gaze demanded answers. Answers I didn't have.

I moistened my lips and his eyes dropped to them. "I wasn't trying to make a statement to anyone," I said. "It was an accident."

"Ah, I can't count the times I've accidentally kissed someone." It was supposed to be a joke, the amusement that shone in his eyes was proof of that, but it wasn't in his tone, which was rough and tepid. "I want you in every way possible, and whether you decide to kiss the werewolves' Alpha or someone else, it only delays the inevitable. We will be together."

"But you hate Malific, and rightfully so. How can you want her daughter?" Was this some twisted fetishization?

He took a slow breath. "I want Erin Katherine Jensen." He gave me a crooked smile. "My demigoddess. It has nothing to do with anything other than you being you."

Silence passed in slow ticks as he kept looking for a sign that I'd accepted it or believed him. I finally nodded.

"You've had an interesting day," he said. He grimaced, but I'd had more interesting days than I could count. I was in desperate need of a reprieve from all the "interesting" in my life.

He stood, extended his hand to me. I took it and stood. "Sleep would be good," he said, guiding me to my room. It wasn't quite nine, but I wasn't against sleeping. A good rest, if that was possible, might give me a clearer outlook.

I started for my bedroom, Mephisto for the front door.

"Stay," I said before he could reach it. It took him so long to respond, I figured he'd say no. After seeing me kiss Asher, it would be understandable.

He nodded.

My bedroom could fit into a corner of the guest room I stayed in at his house. The queen-sized bed made the room seem even smaller. After I showered, changed into a tank and shorts, and brushed my teeth, I crawled into bed.

He slowly unbuttoned his shirt before shrugging it off and removing the t-shirt underneath, exposing ripples of defined muscles, corded abs, and definition in his chest and arms. Then he slipped off his pants. I averted my eyes from his arousal, but not before getting a glimpse of his sculpted legs and butt. He slipped into bed with me and I rolled onto my side. Snuggling in close to me, he buried his face in the crook of my neck. Heat licked at my skin when he whispered.

"I'll stay until you fall asleep," he said before turning off my bedside light.

I turned to face him. His eyes blended with the darkness.

"Okay," I acknowledged, holding his midnight gaze, my eyes fluttering to fight off sleep.

His deep chuckle filled the room. "My demigoddess, even sleep you seek to defy." Kissing me lightly on the forehead, he wrapped his arm around me and rested his chin on top of my head. "Undeniably Erin," he whispered with a sigh.

I willed my eyes to stay open, but eventually I gave up the fight.

CHAPTER 29

*T*rue to his word, Mephisto was gone when I awoke to the absence of his warmth and my phone pinging from a text message. Then the vibration of my phone.

"Erin, there's a bear-wolf outside your door," Cory informed me as soon as I answered. With an eyeroll, I got out of the bed.

"That's Daniel. I think he's more of a horse-wolf. Taller and sleek opposed to wider and stout." I wasn't surprised that my detail had returned.

"Really? That's our discussion, which oversized animal he's similar to?"

I laughed before plopping back onto the bed. "Just tell him to move. Let yourself in with your key. I'll be in the shower."

"I told him to move and then he stood up. Damn, Erin, he's a travesty of nature."

"He's a Mackenzie Valley wolf," I explained. "They're huge." Though Daniel was massive by even those standards.

"He won't let me get past him. When I tried, he shoved me back and then he showed me his people eaters. I didn't have fight a bear-wolf on my Erin bingo card. Fight a demon, yes. Prevent an apocalypse? How could I not? Break you out of prison? Of course, I have my plan ready to go. But not fighting a bear-wolf."

"Shifters don't eat people." There wasn't any evidence of it, but it was possible, as with any other carnivorous animal.

"Most don't, but this one could definitely devour a hot man in one sitting."

"It couldn't just be a 'man.' It had to be a 'hot man.'"

"I didn't make the rules, I just play by them. It's not my fault I look like a tasty treat."

"A *modest* tasty treat. Don't you dare forget the most defining quality about you."

I rolled off the bed and headed to the door. "Daniel, let Cory in," I said from a few feet away, aware he'd be able to hear me. Minutes later I heard Cory's knock at the door. I opened it and poked my head out. "Daniel, you're welcome to coffee and food if you want." Then I trudged back to my bedroom and face-planted onto the bed, Cory not too far behind, before the wolf carrying a drawstring sport pack in his teeth decided to change.

"This is your plan for the day. Have a freak of nature shifter loiter in your apartment while you lie face down in bed?"

"I don't know what to do next," I admitted, helplessness inching into my voice.

"You're going to get up, shower, wash your hair, for fates' sake run a brush through your hair once or twice. Okay"—he ruffled it—"maybe ten times, then you're going to figure out your next move, because you are Erin. No matter how reckless, ill-conceived, and probably dangerous your plans are, you do Erin and make it work."

It had to be dark days when Cory was encouraging my behavior. He fit comfortably in the role of naysayer; it was hard seeing him as cheerleader. He slapped my butt.

"Get up and prepare to slay this in a way that only Erin can."

I lumbered out of bed with a groan and headed for the bathroom.

When I returned, showered and dressed, my brushed hair pulled into a functional ponytail, Cory was sitting on my bed, looking at his phone.

"I spoke to Madison this morning and the STF tried to summon Dareus but without success," he said.

How was she going to justify her team doing something so dangerous on my behalf? Although it was in relation to a murder, so it might not hurt her professionally. The rationalization didn't prevent the wave of guilt that moved through me.

"The necromagic is still inconclusive," he added.

"If a demon is using his body, it won't register," I concluded.

I started pacing the length of the room. Cory's gaze followed me, his wistful look making it harder to think. Inhaling the aroma of coffee that was wafting throughout the apartment, I gave in. I needed a break. And caffeine.

"Coffee. I need coffee," I told Cory, heading for the kitchen.

Daniel stood in my kitchen with disheveled hair, a lightly wrinkled t-shirt and loose-fitting jeans hanging low off his hips. He looked like he belonged in a coffee commercial. In his two visits he had become quite comfortable in my kitchen. I took the proffered cup of coffee and took a sip. My uninvited guest made great coffee.

"You don't have a lot of spices, and your apples looked a little suspect, but I tried to make it work." He slid a plate in my direction. Apple compote, toast, and scrambled eggs. The smell of cinnamon drifted from the plate.

"I had cinnamon?"

He laughed. "Yes, in the back of your cabinet, unopened."

Madison had gifted me with a basket of spices in her less-than-subtle way of saying I needed to use them. I still had no idea when to use ginger, paprika, or cumin. I suspected people put a dash of it in things, just to say they'd dashed it.

"Thank you for breakfast," I told Daniel, biting into the toast. "You can just leave the dishes when you go. I'll clean them."

If his amused smirk was any indicator, he knew what I was doing and it wasn't going to work. Being direct was the only thing that was going to work.

"Daniel," I started off, "Asher and I have had this discussion. I can't have any shifters here."

His lips stretched into a tight line, not from defiance but from the inability to take my request over that of his Alpha.

"Do you want me to see if I can track Harrison?"

At least he wasn't pretending as if he hadn't overheard my conversation with Cory.

I declined. There wasn't anything he'd find that the STF hadn't. Heeding Cory's warning, it was prudent that I stay away from the scene and let Madison handle that aspect. I needed to spend my day trying to locate my father.

The notebook. Jumping from my seat, I headed for my bedroom to get the notebook Nolan left for me. His scent might still be on it.

Before I could make it any distance, a knock at the door stopped me midstride.

My heart pounded and my breath caught when Nolan's face appeared in my peephole. Flooded with relief, I yanked open the door and launched at him, pulling him into a hug. Embarrassed, I stumbled back, my hands immediately covering my mouth.

"Sorry," I squeaked through my hands.

He smiled at the unexpected show of affection, although it faltered when he entered the apartment and I moved to keep some distance between us.

"Don't be," he said. "I'm the one who should be sorry. I came here as soon as I got your messages."

Cory looked relieved and Daniel confused. I couldn't have the conversation I needed to have with Daniel present.

I went to him. "Daniel, this isn't debatable, you have to leave. Please."

He regarded me, Nolan, and Cory with a thoughtful expression and then nodded once. He left. His departure cued Elizabeth to appear. Her contempt-hardened expression remained despite the shallow smile I gave her in greeting.

"You got the spells," Nolan whispered softly, for my ears only.

I nodded. With practiced ease, I performed the cloaking spell. Pride brightened his face and remained as I released the spell with the same level of skill.

"She seems protected enough. Why are we here?" Elizabeth challenged.

Pinning her with a sharp look, Nolan snapped, "Because she asked for her father."

"I can't stay bound to Malific," I said, trying to reason with Elizabeth. "She's retaliating and"—I remembered the knife incident—"pain doesn't deter her. She doesn't mind suffering if the result is me suffering, too."

Nolan cringed. "She's exhausted any compassion or restraint I have. If you ever get a chance to kill her, do it. Not prison, not containment. Death."

I nodded.

"Do you have a plan?" he asked.

Nope, other than Find and Eliminate.

"Elizabeth." Nolan called his sister with a note of

command. She was wearing her typical gothic Victorian dress. It was in contrast to the simplicity of Nolan's light-green button-down shirt, khakis, and loafers. Coal black-lidded eyes rolled in my direction. The high-collared dark blue shirt made her chin lift in a look of haughty defiance. The half petticoat wasn't as dramatic as others I'd seen her wear. She trudged farther into my apartment as if every step was an insult to her.

"Contact Malific and have us meet so you can remove the binding," Nolan instructed her. He looked at her with a gentleness that belied the coolness of his command.

"Brother, the well of sympathy and compassion for your foolish endeavors is running dry. At some point you must sever yourself from your past. Accept defeat and move on. I've made Malific vulnerable, doing what I could to mitigate the situation of her being free, while keeping *it*"—she lobbed a dagger-sharp look in my direction—"alive. How much more do I have to give to this fruitless mission?"

"I ask for just one thing. Remove the binding."

"It is the only vulnerability she has. Once that is severed, she'll kill the thing you claim to want to protect."

"Stop talking about me like this. I'm neither an it nor a fucking thing!" I snapped.

She eased closer, her gaze stony cold. "You are Malific's daughter. I think no higher of you than I do of her. Should her creation deserve better? I will not humanize you when you were born from a monster. A product of a monster is nothing more than an extension of it."

"She's mine, too." Nolan pointed out.

"Soot dropped on snow doesn't become whitened but instead tarnishes the snow," she replied.

I was pretty sure she wouldn't be inclined to remove the binding if I kicked her ass, but I was itching to do it. Could she think any worse of me than she already did? So why not get something out of it?

"Enough!" Nolan's voice thundered throughout the apartment. "You can't lay the blame at her feet. You can't make her the target of your hate for Malific. She is no more to blame for her actions than she is for her birth. It was my foolishness." His voice dropped toward the end, his words softer, as if offering an apology. An explanation. He turned to her. "Driven by my need for revenge, I let it harden me. Blind me. Erin is the one really being affected. I'm to blame for this. If you want to lash out at someone, lash out at me." He touched Elizabeth's arm. "I'm making an attempt to atone for you feeling the need to intervene—I'm not sure there's more for me to do."

"What more can you do? Honor your promise to me," she said.

Seeing the pained look on her face made me turn away. It chipped away at my hostility. My hate. It complicated my feelings. I wanted to dislike her for being a villainous fiend who hated me without cause and was undeserving of sympathy. But she was a sister who loved her brother. In her way, she was trying to protect him. Their well-intentioned actions often made them agents of disastrous situations. Where precision was needed, they used blunt force.

"After you told me you bound her to Malific, I went with you." He shook his head. "It is the height of cruelty for you to use her safety as currency."

"Currency?" she fumed. "I used it as leverage. We were supposed to go away and finally live. And you came back." Tears welled in her eyes. "You promised. I held up my end of the bargain. How easy it would be to kill her and end Malific at the same time. But I gave you my word to protect her life and I've done that."

"And it came at a great cost to me, too. You made me stay away from her." He sighed. "I should not have agreed to abandon my daughter for your help."

"Abandon?" she yelled. "You did no such thing. I simply

asked for us to move on, for us to walk away and live our lives." She closed her eyes. "I knew about the spells you left her, yet I left them there for her to find, hoping it would give you the closure you needed. I'm not naïve or foolish enough to believe you wanted to return for books that had no relevance to you, and a scribing stick. You needed to know she had the spells. I wanted you to have that closure, thinking it would be enough to satisfy the irrational need you have to watch over Malific's daughter. If I am as cruel as you have convinced yourself I am, I would have imprisoned you until you came to your senses. I didn't do that."

Unmoved by her words, he countered. "You restricted me from seeing my daughter."

She jabbed her finger at me. "She's not your daughter in the manner you are trying to make her be. She is the result of a strategic maneuver that failed. You could have walked away. She's capable of protecting herself. We are protected from Malific. I've protected Erin." She winced at the use of my name. I guessed she would have preferred to continue referring to me as an "it." Humanizing me made her the monster, not me.

She hadn't protected me, or maybe she didn't realize how truly sadistic Malific was. Willing to hurt herself to hurt me. Power-driven, Elizabeth had blinders on, too.

I touched Nolan's hand, and he looked down at it. "Thank you," I whispered. It wasn't just for the spells he left; Nolan was trying to right an egregious wrong.

Elizabeth studied us with the knowledge that something had passed between us. We had an obscure connection.

"Make arrangements to meet Malific to remove the binding," Nolan commanded in a patient voice.

After moments of consideration, Elizabeth looked at him with the same unyielding coldness she reserved for me.

"No."

"We've discussed this. You will do this for me. For her."

"I owe Malific's daughter nothing."

"What about me?" he whispered. "Do I not deserve your help?"

Her lips tightened, seemingly having difficulty with finding the right words. She shook her head.

He looked despondent and I watched the exchange between them. Unable to understand their words, I had to rely on their nonverbal communication that bounced between anger, sorrow, frustration, and exasperation. Madison and I had had our share of squabbles as children, and a few disagreements as adults, but I couldn't recall us having fights that had so many peaks and valleys of emotion.

Nolan lashed out with something that caused her to flinch as if slapped. Eyes glistening, she blinked several times, pushing back the tears.

"I will do this for you, but know that you will have to live with what you've done. You claim her as one you should care about, so you must own her death that will follow and the destruction and havoc Malific will wreak once at her full strength. Do you not have enough burdens?"

Nolan wiped his hand over his face, making it apparent that they didn't fight often and it had taken a toll on him. He closed his eyes, inhaled several long breaths, and ushered a feeble smile onto his face.

"Just do as I request, please." His turning away from her served as a dismissal.

He pulled something from his pocket, his face brightening as he showed it to me. It was a phone. Something that everyone had delighted him. I didn't think he used them, being a person who relied heavily on magic and seemed quite removed from this world.

"You can always get in touch with me," he said.

I took it from him and entered my number and then added me as a contact. Daughter. He smiled at the entry before returning it to his pocket. Elizabeth didn't leave as I'd expected her to. Was she there as his protector or his warden or a warped combination?

Unburdened by his fight with his sister, Nolan focused on me and asked me to show him my spell work. I quickly obliged.

CHAPTER 30

*P*erhaps it was fitting that Elizabeth had arranged our meeting with Malific in the same shed in the middle of nowhere where she'd bound us. Nolan, Elizabeth, and I entered the shed just minutes before Malific arrived, her sword sheathed at her back and ominous magic rolling off her like a dense fog. The moment we were unbound, she'd be using both against me.

Cruel eyes fell on Nolan. He met them with the same level of hate, but because he was oath-protected, she couldn't act on her feelings.

The sheer loathing of each other made it difficult to believe they had been able to put it aside long enough to have sex. Was their form of cuddling glaring daggers at each other while the mere thought of touching each other made them shudder in disgust? Or had it festered to this level?

"Nolan." She pushed his name through gritted teeth as if it was a curse.

He acknowledged her with a slight nod. I was surprised at how much her eyes had softened when she finally looked at me.

"Daughter." The word didn't hold its usual disdain caused

by me being the embodiment of her diminished power. I'd even go as far as to say it sounded warm and welcoming. I wasn't foolish enough to believe she felt either of those things. I was a means to an end, nothing more. And I knew she had every intention of delivering that end. It was the one thing we had in common.

This would be the location of her demise. If I failed, Mephisto and the other Huntsmen were backup. Abetting in an ambush unsettled me, but I didn't have a lot of alternatives. Malific had to be stopped. Her death would end the spell of the Laes and allow the Huntsmen back into the Veil, and it would allow me to return to my life without worrying about her trying to kill me and how to put a halt to her reign of terror.

"Weapons," Elizabeth demanded, standing in front of Malific, allowing her eyes to reconnect with hers.

"Not yet," Malific said, unsheathing a knife from her waist and marching out of the shed.

We rushed out behind her, my heart pounding at her discovery of my secondary plan.

Her eyes glinted with hubris and assurance, and she gripped the blade firmly.

"Hunters, reveal yourselves. I know you're here."

Hidden in the crowd of trees, lying in wait, they were camouflaged, but nothing could mask the aura of violence in the air.

"She has human fragilities. *We* are cut from the same cloth. You are aware that I can tolerate the pain and that she can't. Reveal yourselves, or I'll make you."

I wasn't sure why having a high tolerance for pain was brag-worthy, but she seemed quite proud of it.

Mephisto was the first to reveal himself. His expression exhibited the virulent anger and contempt he held for her. It was so intense, he briefly lost control of his glamour. It shimmered away, giving us a rare glimpse of his normal appearance. Sword in hand, everything from the tension in his set jaw, his dark arctic gaze, and his fighting stance demonstrated his desire to end her. The air of violence swarmed throughout the area from Mephisto and the others who had come into sight and surrounded her, their rage directed at the woman who had expelled them from the Veil, taking away their life and the job they were committed to.

My body became rigid in an attempt to ward off the pain of Malific pressing the knife to her neck. Mephisto's eyes narrowed. From her profile, I could see her smile widen, comfortable that she was safe from his wrath. She looked over her shoulder at me and returned her attention to Mephisto, whose concern was apparent. Pressing my fingers to my neck, I felt blood. I stood taller, exuding an assurance that I hope comforted him. Malific would hurt me, I was sure of that, but she couldn't kill me. Not yet.

"I'm going to kill you," Mephisto promised. The calmness of it sent a chill through me.

She moved her eyes from his to Simeon, to the right, then to Clayton, then nearly a full circle to Kai, who was just a few feet from her.

Amused rather than rattled by Mephisto's threat, she chuckled. "You seem to forget yourself and think far too fondly of your past. Have you forgotten your enemies? They haven't forgotten you."

Moving with preternatural speed, Mephisto spun around, his sword striking the knife lobbed at him by a man who moved with the same speed. Distracted by the knives thrown at him in rapid succession, Mephisto wasn't able to evade the strike of magic that blasted into his chest, sending him careening into the tree a foot away. Another bolt of magic struck his head and snapped it back against the tree.

A gasp escaped me and I'd started to run toward him when he stopped me with a shake of his head.

"Erin, I do believe you possess false confidence if you

think you would be anything more than a distraction if you intervened."

Would I? Rooted in place, I couldn't leave. When Malific started back toward the shed, I debated whether to follow.

I was still mulling it over when the light was eclipsed by opal-colored wings. Balls of fire were hurled at Kai by a wrathful-looking man with similar seraphic features. He was nearly as pale as the tips of his wings. I thought the glow of his eyes was from the fire he wielded, but it wasn't; there was an orange blaze set in them.

Targeted strikes of fire engulfed Kai for a moment and I held my breath. I tried an elemental spell, calling wind but only assembling an unimpressive breeze. I wasn't convinced it was my doing or from the expansion of Kai's wings emerging from the flames like a phoenix. A cast of darkness moved over us as thrums of magic came from Clayton, clouds crowding the graying sky. Thunder sounded and the rain fell hard, dousing the fire and rendering the fire-thrower powerless.

My hair matted against my scalp and I could barely make out Kai soaring toward the opal-winged man, sending him rushing back. Unable to look away but afraid that I was moments from seeing them plummet to the ground, my attention was pulled away by the clash of steel on steel, the whirring of Simeon fighting a woman wielding a saber. It was complete chaos between the magic and fighting. While Malific watched with rapt appreciation, I yanked the knife from her and started toward the melee, assessing where I would fit in.

Brushing the water from my face, I could just make out bodies clashing, magic being cast, and brutal violence that made me wince.

Malific tugged me to her. "No worries, daughter, they're only a distraction. I give you my word, the Huntsmen will do what they do best. I just needed them to be entertained."

She was a freaking monster. These weren't allies, as I'd thought, or perhaps they were. To her, they were theater. To be sacrificed to keep the Huntsmen busy. I tore away from her.

"Don't touch me."

"Am I to be blamed? Am I responsible for their skill, for their arrogance? I gave them what they wanted: a chance for revenge. I wasn't under any illusions that the Huntsmen's time outside the Veil had dulled their skills or quenched their thirst for violence."

She reveled in my realization that what she said about them was the truth. As the rain slowed, I could see them moving in the fight. The fluid skill of their sword-fighting was nothing like what I'd seen when they fought the Immortalis. This was violent, raw, and superb. As the clank of metal hitting metal resounded and strong magic inundated the air, I understood that the tailored suits, fine foods, and worldly indulgences were cloaks of deception that the Huntsmen had simply shrugged off.

There was no easiness to Clayton as he wielded his blade, warding off two attackers. The genteel kindness of the animal whisperer was just a memory when Simeon sliced into his opponent without the slightest hesitation, and Kai was drilling at the wings of his airborne attacker, forcing him to retreat and descend. It was only a matter of time before he'd hurtle to the ground. I wasn't sure he'd die from the impact, but whatever violence was awaiting him once he landed would kill him.

"Same beast, different label, Erin," said Malific, as if I needed that reminder.

My worry about the Huntsmen being injured faded, but the level of violence on display remained as I followed Malific back into the shed, my attention fixed on the sword sheathed at her back. An Obitus blade. One well-placed strike and I could stop her reign of terror before it began.

But as long as we were bound, I would die, too. I wasn't ready to make that sacrifice.

As if she could read my thoughts, she looked over her shoulder at me and gave me a smile of malicious intent.

We were awfully cordial for two people who knew that in just minutes they would be trying to kill each other.

My life was more abject than a Greek tragedy.

The moment we entered the shed, Elizabeth demanded our weapons again.

I handed her Kai's dagger with the Obitus blade that I had sheathed at my waist and the knife sheathed at my leg. My double-edged was stored in the easy release cross-shoulder bag, where I'd practiced until my retrieval of it took fifteen seconds, but it wasn't visible. Elizabeth glowered at the backpack when I kept it with me. When she remained standing in front of me, waiting, I handed it to her. Instead of making another request, she snatched the push dagger hooked on my chain.

"You are your mother's daughter," she spat before placing the weapons a few feet away, easy to retrieve with a quick lunge.

She made the same request of Malific who, with a tight-lipped scowl, removed the knife from her sheath, a cuff from her wrist where a push dagger was hidden, and another blade from a sheath at her ankle. Her weapons were placed nearly an equal distance away.

Standing back, Elizabeth gave us both an assessing look, her expression revealing her knowledge of our intentions. The moment we were unbound, only one of us would leave. I was sure that in some sordid and twisted moral gymnastics, she was congratulating herself for preventing it from happening in her presence—more importantly in Nolan's. They were protected; she'd achieved her goal.

"You have my weapons, but how do you think this will end, Nolan?" Malific asked. "You spared her life temporarily.

Whether it is today, tomorrow, or days from now, she will serve the purpose for which she was born. You won't win this." Then she directed her attention to Elizabeth. "You are misguided in your impression of my daughter. We share very few things. She might adore violence, but she is restrained." Her expression held the same comfortable malevolence as it had when she drove the knife through her hand and when she stabbed Dr. Sumner. "I don't suffer from such problems."

"Of course you don't," Elizabeth acknowledged icily.

Elizabeth pulled a piece of paper out of her pocket and handed it to me. "Once blood is spilled, you must say the words exactly as they are written. I will complete the spell to unbind you two and then..." She left out the part about the dysfunctional and depraved cage match that would ensue.

First, after a quick, quiet invocation, the serpent coiled around Elizabeth's arm became sentient, unwinding from her and striking Malific, leaving a blood trail. Elizabeth walked to me and the snake did the same. It wasn't the bite that hurt, it was the dragging of its fang across my skin. It felt nothing like a vampire bite. But it served its purpose—simply what a knife could have done—and probably with a lot less pain. I was sure that was the point.

Elizabeth backed away until she was standing right next to Nolan. She clasped his hand. He tugged at her hold and she responded sharply.

"We've discussed this. I unbind them and you come with me. Otherwise, there is no deal, brother."

His expression of helpless desolation made it hard to look at him. Nolan closed his eyes. He sagged. My birth was the result of his revenge blindness. His attempt to protect me had landed me in the Stygian and made me live my life guilt-ridden about a murder I hadn't committed. And now, he was responsible for facilitating the removal of a binding that his sister created, but he wouldn't be around to see if I survived against an incalculably powerful, cruel, and sadistic god.

Squaring my shoulders and drawing up taller, I showed more confidence than I felt and gave him a reassuring look as Elizabeth tightened her grip on him. The network of bindings began to snap, the tension relaxing, until all that existed was the niggle of a barely noticeable link.

Then that snapped and Elizabeth whispered something in Nolan's ear. He collapsed to the ground with a thud. His chest rose and fell in sleep. Elizabeth lowered herself to him, palming a stone in her hand before reciting another spell and vanishing with him. She never looked in my direction.

I lunged to the ground, missing the sphere of magic Malific lobbed at me. It hit the ground like a ball of lead, cracking the floor and sending pieces of it scattering. I rolled, causing two more to miss me and placing me just inches from the blade. I couldn't risk taking my eyes from her.

Offensive magic required a lot of energy, and most wielders couldn't sustain it for a long time. Fifteen minutes of aggressive offensive magic depleted them to the point that usually they couldn't cast even simple spells afterward. When the barrage of spherical magic bombs eased, with a calculated roll, I grabbed Kai's loaned blade, pressed my body into the wall, and invoked the cloaking spell.

Malific backed away, scanning the area. Fear and doubt crossed her face. My magic wasn't just an anomaly to me but to her as well. She could Wynd, but could I? She had no idea that each attempt ended with me shifted into a feline.

"I know you're here, daughter," she sang in a cloyingly saccharine voice.

She didn't.

Her movements were careful and calculated as she backed toward her weapons. Each step she took, I took two stealthy steps, closing the distance between us but careful to navigate around the splinters of plywood from the destroyed floor.

I stopped when she halted and cursed inwardly when she noticed the slight movement of a piece of flooring that rolled when I moved past. The rapid fire of magic clipped my arm, unbalancing me. No longer able to use the element of surprise to my advantage, I released the cloak and fired back, hitting her in the chest and slamming her back into the wall. My magic served as a tactical advantage; hers for destruction. I couldn't give her the upper hand or the distance to perform any more magic.

I lunged, knocking her to the floor. The headbutt to her nose shocked her; tears watered in her eyes. She tolerated pain but wasn't immune to its effects. The blow she slammed into my side sent blinding pain through me. It wasn't a human hit; I'd had those. Magic. It had to be. I inhaled a breath. It was painful, but I didn't think my ribs were broken. She shoved me off, my blade barely missing her. I needed a killing strike.

Moving with the same speed as that of the Huntsmen, she was near her weapons, with her sword in hand. She glanced down at her arm, checking for injuries. Fury blazed in her that she was nearly cut by an Obitus blade that would prevent her from healing.

A knife against a sword left me at a disadvantage. I needed her closer. But a knife could be used with one hand, whereas she'd need magical enhancement to wield her sword with one hand and would be unable to perform magic. A dilemma she'd be aware of. Offense was the best tactic, and I went for it for all it was worth. The first strike of magic I used as a distraction, moving her to the right, the second to her left, then I lunged forward, another near strike but at her arm. I needed more vulnerable areas. She swung her sword. I dropped to the ground as I slashed at her leg, trying to disable her. She had a tactical advantage because she could move so much faster than me. Blurs of movement that made my attacks miss.

She kicked the knife out of my hand. I rolled in time to miss the strikes of magic. Going on the defense, I cloaked myself. Which wasn't enough of a defense. Dirt, debris, and splintered plywood made it too difficult for me to navigate the room under her acute awareness.

But it gave me a slight reprieve, a moment to think. How do you kill a god when they have so few vulnerabilities and too many advantages? Scanning the room, I found where Kai's blade had landed. Should I chance a healing spell, deal with the wounds, and try to make it to the blade? Any weapon would hurt me, not just the Obitus.

I quickly revealed myself and sent a sphere of magic toward the wall, where her attention followed. I darted for the knife, only to get there and find her blade drawn at an angle just inches from where the dagger had fallen. One strike and I was over.

Neither of us moved. That second became an indeterminate time. She paused. And she seemed shocked by the pause. I slammed my fist into her side and landed another into her kidney. She stumbled back.

It wasn't just the blows I inflicted. She had hesitated. That moment of humanity had shocked and perplexed her and it showed on her face. I wasn't sure it would last. I lunged for the blade. She responded faster. Magic struck at the knife, and I jumped back in time. Avoiding the second strike, I backed up to the wall. Magic danced around her fingers before she whipped toward the door, releasing the magic in the opposite direction from me, hitting the door and the person behind it. Mephisto.

He was thrown back with the same force with which she'd blasted away the floor. I swallowed my scream, aware that it was unlikely I'd survive a hit like that but hoping he had.

In her moment of distraction, I lunged for the blade, grabbed it, and started toward her in a blind rage. She was gone, but Mephisto was standing in front of me, his sword drawn, ready for a strike. Standing back-to-back, we scanned the area, waiting for her to return. Hoping she would return.

She didn't.

Despite not having rid myself of Malific, I still marked this as a win. I wasn't bound to her and I was alive.

"Are you hurt?" Mephisto asked, sheathing his sword and looking me over for injuries.

I winced when he touched my side. She hadn't broken my ribs, but now that I wasn't riding on adrenaline, it hurt like hell. I sucked in a sharp breath when he laid his hand over the injury, the coolness of his magic easing the pain until it was gone. Leaning into me, his lips were light and soothing as they brushed against mine.

"You're okay." His voice was laden with relief.

"Where are the others?"

"They're leaving the area as it was," he informed me. No further explanation was needed, and it sounded a lot better than "they're disposing of the bodies."

We remained hyperalert as I gathered my weapons and the ones Malific had left behind, before making our way out of the shed. Mephisto kept a watch from the left, me from the right, and we continued scanning the area as we walked to the car.

"She was expecting you all to be here," I noted.

He nodded. "Our anonymity wasn't just so we could survive here but also to prevent retaliation." He frowned, but not just from displeasure; he clearly missed the Veil.

I was thinking about Malific's hesitation so intently that I didn't respond.

He stopped. "What's wrong, Erin?"

"She hesitated," I blurted, and despite my comment lacking a lot of context, Mephisto's lips tightened. "She had the advantage. She could have killed me, but she hesitated."

There was a long pause before he spoke. His words were chosen carefully. "Perhaps. I urge you, Erin, not to be fooled by her fleeting moment of humanity. Although it might make you hopeful that she values your life, she will use that weakness to her advantage."

His words were the cold splash of reality I needed from a person who knew her better than I ever would. Nodding, I continued to walk but stopped abruptly at the sight of my car. It looked as if it had been in a multicar accident. The front was smashed and the sides were collapsed onto the tires. The rear was flattened. My car had been destroyed in a fit of rage.

Her brief moment of humanity came at a cost and this was it.

"I need a new car."

Banality was all I had. Because anything else would lead to me spiraling out of control and that was the last thing I needed. Dealing with Malific required a level head.

I accepted that whatever happened in that moment of hesitation, this was the result. The totality of everything that existed between me and her. Destruction.

CHAPTER 31

$\mathcal{M}$y morose mood was probably why Mephisto took me to his home and not mine. He was probably thinking what I had: The destruction might not have stopped at my car. The same might have been done to my apartment.

Madison and Cory got an abridged version: *I'm alive and so is Malific.* I appreciated them not pressing for more, because rehashing the day would have only dampened my mood more. And Cory reluctantly agreed to share the abridged version with Asher. I didn't need his tight, strained voice of agreement to know I should not be the one who called. Because it would have led to me explaining to him why Mephisto was there when I met Malific and not him. Cory's reaction was ignored as well as the tight set of Mephisto's jaw and the sidelong look he gave me at the mention of Asher's name.

"I need a shower," I told Mephisto once we were in his house. He pointed me upstairs and followed. When I headed toward the guestroom where I'd stayed before, he took hold of my arm.

"This way," he said, leading me into his room. It wasn't a

bedroom but a refuge. Slate-gray textured walls, tranquil monochromatic art, large picture windows that took up most of one wall, a stone fireplace and a chair large enough to seat two. He adjusted the lights until they gave off a warm glow. I wanted to take my shoes off and sink my feet into the plush-looking rug near his bed.

I cocked my head at the decorative pillows on his bed. For a man who seemed to love modern décor, sleek lines, and minimalism, they seemed out of place.

He shrugged, his eyes cast downward.

"Shower?" I asked.

He led me to the bathroom, passing his closet where I got a peek at just rows of black. Next to each other, the variations in the dark colors were obvious.

Following Mephisto, I couldn't stop thinking about Malific, Mephisto's warning, and everything that had occurred. I desperately needed a reprieve. He opened the door but remained in my path.

"It is neither naïve nor foolish to have wanted more from Malific. There should be more to her than there is," he said softly. He seemed to be searching for the right words as his finger ran slowly along my cheek. "I warned you because I don't want you to suffer Oedeus's fate. Deserving better from her but never getting it."

"I had no expectation of her," I lied. Contrary to what he said, it *was* foolish and naïve to want it. I wasn't willing to pay the cost of such idealistic thinking.

"I need a shower," I told him again, but he remained in my way, scrutinizing me. His eyes were midnight pools.

"Erin," he whispered. Not quite a statement or a question. An entreaty.

"I'm death. My magic was to take it from others and leave them in a state of in-between. A quasi-death. My existence is the result of a revenge plot because of the elves' death at Malific's hands. The sole purpose of my birth was for me to die. My life will go back to somewhat normal—or what can be passed off as normal—once Malific is dead." My shoulders drooped. "I don't know why seeing my car destroyed was the breaking point. But it was."

His palm caressed my cheek and I turned into it, absorbing the warmth. The languid, idle movement of his thumb lightly moving along my lips was calming. Serene. He leaned in, the heat of his breath wispy against my skin.

"When I think of you, death is the last thing that comes to mind," he offered in simple assurance before stepping away and giving me a slow smile.

Maybe it was walking on the heated floors that made it feel like I was getting a hot stone massage with each step, or the multi-head waterfall shower and the soft lights that made it feel like I was showering in the moonlight.

I studied the shirt that Mephisto had loaned me. It was oversized and long enough to cover my naked butt, thankfully, since the only panties I had were drying in the bathroom. I wasn't fond of walking around without underwear, but I didn't have a lot of options.

I found Mephisto in the kitchen. His hair looked darker wet. His suits always looked impeccable on him, but he was decidedly sexier in what he was wearing now: sweatpants and a t-shirt. Over the aromas in the kitchen, I could smell the musky scent of his soap.

"Just in time," he said as I entered the kitchen. He pointed to steaks. "How do you like it?"

"Well done," I said, easing next to him and prepared for the side-eye look of disdain everyone seemed to give the well-done crowd. His jaw twitched but he didn't comment. Instead, he placed my steak in the pan, went to the wine fridge, and returned with a bottle of red wine. He poured me a glass and placed the bottle next to me.

Seriously! I know a standard serving size is five ounces. I reject your recommended suggestion. I picked up the bottle and filled the glass just shy of the top. And then took a long draw from it.

I nodded. Admitting that I barely tasted it while guzzling it down was unnecessary. The cooking food smelled wonderful, but it wasn't the smell of spices and sautéed vegetables that had my interest. On the counter next to the stove was a cake.

"It's white chocolate and raspberry blondie."

The scent of vanilla, chocolate, and raspberries had my mouth watering. It was the only thing I wanted. I attributed it to my horrid day. No longer being bound to Malific didn't seem to be enough. Nolan was gone. In a short-lived moment of foolish optimism, I'd thought Malific didn't want to kill me, and now I had to purchase another car because of her big-girl tantrum at the realization that for a microsecond, she had a bout of humanity. Wine and cake might not be the answer to all my problems, but it was a start.

"May I?"

"It's for dessert."

"You know the wonderful thing about being an adult? You can have dessert for dinner and no one can stop you. They can try to shame you for it, but that's all they have. I'm pretty much shameless. No scolding. No one's going to give you a dessert-first citation. You can just eat it."

He handed me a fork and I cut off a sliver, had a taste. "See? No consequences to eating dessert first." I picked up the plate. "Enjoy your not-white chocolate raspberry blondie. This is what I'm having for dinner."

He laughed and shook his head. "Undeniably Erin," he mumbled. It was good seeing him shrug off the heaviness he had carried since his encounter with Malific.

"I don't at least get to try it?" he asked, turning off the stove.

"Of course I'll share."

"I just want a taste." His soft lips caressed mine as his

tongue explored my mouth. Kissing me harder, he became increasingly ravenous. His need was hot and intense. His hand slipped under my shirt, his strong commanding fingers kneading me as he pulled me against his hardness.

His hands trailed over my hips, the curve of my butt, and then between my legs. His kisses more voracious, his touch fierce as his fingers glided across my wetness. I groaned against his lips, entwining my fingers in his hair, surrendering to desire.

He cupped my ass and lifted me. My legs curled around his waist as he walked me to the island, where he placed me. He tugged at the shirt, yanking it open, spilling buttons onto the island and floor.

He pulled away from me, his dark eyes trailing from my eyes to the curve of my neck where he planted warm kisses, then traveling to the top of my chest to the swell of my breasts. My fingers twined in his hair as he took one breast in his mouth, caressing, teasing the nipple with his tongue until it hardened. His teeth grazed against the sensitive peak, sending a shudder through me. He pressed me flat against the island, continuing his exploration of my body with wet, passion-hungry kisses. Deft fingers strummed my body as he settled between my legs, delivering kisses to my inner thighs before his tongue stroked and laved over my most sensitive parts.

He pulled away, giving me a wicked smile when I let out a low entreating whimper in response. He teased me with his touch, taunting me with the promise of more. My fingers sank into his hair. Pliable under his attention, pleasure rampaged through me. I panted, wanting more of him. A need to feel the weight of his body on me, the heat of him covering me, and him inside me.

He kissed me. My fingers clawed at his shirt in desperation to keep him close.

"Not here, my demigoddess," he whispered in my ear

before pulling me to him, securing me against his body. My legs encircled his waist as he took me up the stairs. He pressed hot fervent kisses to my lips, my cheek, my neck.

He deposited me on his bed, removed his shirt, pants, and underwear. I took in every inch of him, the definition of his abs, the cords of muscle and the way they contracted and bulged with each movement. He slipped the shirt off me. His hands splayed over my body, running over every inch of it and sending more heat through me. He kissed me again, harder, rougher, a raw need in his tongue as he explored my mouth.

He settled between my legs, his hard thickness luring me. His chuckle reverberated in his chest, deep and rough, in response to me groaning and trying to pull him to me. My fingers curled into his back.

His voice was rough and sultry as he murmured against my lips, "My demigoddess," with reverence, need, craving.

I wanted him in a way that I hadn't wanted anyone.

I moaned as he entered me slowly, giving me time to accommodate his thickness. We hit a slow, steady rhythm that quickly escalated into something hard, frenetic, greedy as we gave in to our pent-up desire. Consumed by primal lust, our pace quickened, our thrusts driven by our hunger and desperate craving. We clung to each other as we came closer to our peak. My fingers curled into his back as I shuddered under him, both of us finding pleasure in that moment.

We stayed entangled, his body heavy against mine. He pressed soft, languorous kisses on my skin. When our breathing calmed, he rolled from me, got under the covers, and pulled me close. Face to face, we held each other's gaze.

"I told you there was more than just magic between us."

There was.

He nudged me over and pulled me into him, my back against his chest, his arms firm around my waist. The last thing I heard before I fell into an exhausted sleep was his pleased sigh.

The next morning, after our shower, I slipped on another of Mephisto's borrowed shirts, trying to coax him into giving me my underwear.

"It's just us," he said.

"I still don't want my bare ass sitting on your chair," I pouted, grabbing my panties that he had hanging from a finger.

Grinning, he inched toward me, unbuttoning the first three buttons of the shirt. "A compromise."

Distancing myself from him, I headed downstairs, planning to eat the dinner we'd missed last night. Sometime during the night, Mephisto had gotten up to put everything away, overly pleased that I wasn't woken by his movement.

Food, and the list of other things I had to do included: buy a new phone, search cars, and get more clothes if I was going to accept Mephisto's invitation to stay longer.

Mephisto tugged me to him and turned me to face him. He kissed me, then with a tight-lipped grimace, he buttoned my shirt up again, leaving just the one undone.

"We have company," he explained.

Clayton, who was seated at the kitchen table, looked up from the plate in front of him, eating the final bite of steak. He slid the plate to the middle of the table.

"I like my steak medium rare," he announced.

"I'd care if the steak was made for you. It was for me, and I like it medium," Mephisto said.

"The overcooked one is still in the fridge," he said, his eyes flicking to me. "I'm assuming that's yours, Erin." Clayton smirked, taking in my disheveled hair, bare feet, and me in Mephisto's shirt. It wasn't hard to come to the right conclusion. Whether it bothered him wasn't apparent. His demeanor remained pleasant despite the look that passed between the two men.

Making sense of their playfully antagonistic relationship was difficult. It was obvious that they cared about each other, a brotherhood born of something deep, but it needled me that I might be the reason for the strain that existed between them. An unspoken contention that eroded their jokes and playful sardonic interaction couldn't mask it.

Based on the intense looks they were giving each other, they were engaging in a conversation I wasn't privy to.

"I don't like when you all do that," I admitted. "I'd like to be part of the conversation or at least know it's not about me." I flashed a weak smile, as if I was joking.

"Sorry." Clayton glowered. "It's probably best that you didn't hear M crudely tell me to have carnal relations with myself. It was quite crass."

Mephisto rubbed my back, Clayton attentive to every touch exchanged between us. "I'll get breakfast. Steak and eggs okay?"

I nodded, took a seat across from Clayton, and tried to figure out if they were still having a conversation.

Mephisto glanced at Clayton. "Why are you here?"

"You could be politer about it. I hadn't heard from you since you instructed us to leave. I was worried."

If he was worried, I was a rhinoceros. He made no attempt to sound believable. Mephisto turned from the stove and gave him a look that essentially called him out on his BS.

Ignoring Mephisto's withering glare, Clayton said, "Madison told me this morning that Harrison has returned."

This morning. Phone call? Pillow talk? While cuddling? There were so many questions I had, but they'd be better answered by Madison, so I shelved it.

"You're no longer a suspect in his murder." Clayton took a sip from his glass and gave me a weak half smile. "I'm with you on that," he said in response to my suspicious inquiring look.

"Madison doesn't believe him, nor the excuse of going camping to clear his head and 'recenter' himself. But it has appeased River."

"Is it Dareus?"

"It's all just suspicion, but Madison thinks so. There isn't a spell to determine if someone is hosting a demon."

A murder, with a demon taking over the body, needed to be handled delicately. People wouldn't examine the nuances and intricacies that needed to take place for a demon to inhabit a body after a person was murdered. They would ignore that the person had to have hosted the demon before to form the link, or that the demon had to be summoned and that the body couldn't be damaged. Humans would panic, and it would be another blot against the supernatural world.

"The prevailing belief is that it's Harrison." Clayton gave me a sympathetic look. "Apparently there is still a bounty on you."

Mephisto placed a plate in front of me: steak, eggs, and berries.

"Ketchup?"

They both looked scandalized. *What? It's ketchup. I didn't ask you to garnish my food with the horn of a unicorn.*

"That's a Matsusaka steak," Mephisto told me, his voice and look laden with significance.

"I'm sorry, have I offended the cow on my plate by wanting to make it more delicious?"

Clayton repeated Mephisto's assertion of the type of steak as if hearing the name twice was going to change things. Mephisto seemed to need a moment of reckoning before fulfilling my request.

"Will you try it without ketchup first?" Mephisto asked, placing the bottle in the middle of the table.

"Of course." I took a bite. It was good. I poured ketchup

on my plate, dipped some steak in, and offered him some. Clearly as a polite gesture, he accepted and chewed quickly. I made the same offer to Clayton, cutting a piece and sliding it over to him. He recoiled as if I'd offered him poison and quickly changed the subject.

"The Black Crest grimoire. Is this something we should pursue obtaining?" he suggested to Mephisto. Not to get the powerful spell book out of circulation but on the off chance it might be another option on their quest to return to the Veil. I wanted the grimoire, too, but for the spells that were similar to elven magic.

I needed confirmation that it was Dareus in Harrison's body. And if it was, whoever was responsible had the grimoire.

CHAPTER 32

a wayward smile had settled on Mephisto's lips as he watched me ruminate over the clothes I had tossed on my bed. Two days I'd been with him and admittedly, I'd enjoyed it. Our night activities that spilled into a lot of the day was nice, especially with a god who had spent the last few centuries perfecting his skills. His media wall that gave a view of the house was a comfort, me visiting it occasionally, expecting to see Malific trying to storm the grounds. But the amount of magic needed to break his wards and protection spells would announce her presence before the cameras would.

Instead of giving in to my first impulse of looking for Malific, I practiced my magic and sparred with Mephisto. The elven magic that I'd learned was strong, but remembering that Elizabeth had disappeared on several occasions, I wondered if there was an alternative method of Wynding. But she had that stone with her. Without having gotten a thorough look at it, I wasn't able to identify it in any of the books in Mephisto and Benton's library.

Several unsuccessful attempts were made, using spells I'd

weaved and various stones found among Mephisto's magical objects. Wynding was a magical skill that almost everyone desired and a select few possessed. Vampires could do it, if the person who sired them possessed the ability. Among the Huntsmen, only Mephisto could. A few witches and mages, with a magical boost, could do it, too, which led me to believe it was a combination of bloodlines and magical strength. Because Malific and Elizabeth could, I assumed that I would be able to as well.

The enhanced speed hadn't developed, and to my surprise, spells didn't respond to me threatening to rip them a new one. Cloaking was in my quiver of defensive magic; I was determined to add Wynding.

I spent the first few hours of the morning setting up my new phone and giving Cory and Madison the complete version of being unbound from Malific, my perception of her hesitating, and her retaliation of destroying my car. Completing my rounds of returning calls and texts, I responded to Asher's three texts with a simple, straightforward response, letting him know I was okay. Reliving that day with another retelling wasn't something I could manage.

The remainder of the day was spent trying to Wynd and Mephisto becoming increasingly amused at finding me changing into a cat with each attempt. It wasn't until he was confronted with a righteously irate feline, speculating over whether to treat him to a kitty claw hug, that he suggested we return to my apartment to get more clothes.

"You should pack enough for at least two weeks," he suggested as I tossed a few clothes into a small suitcase.

"Two weeks?" In the car he'd said a few days. A few days meant three—at max a week. Would that two weeks eventually become three? A month? When did staying away from my home and not being a target move from wise strategic maneuver to me hiding in fear?

Drawn into my thoughts, I hadn't noticed Mephisto invading my space. He waited until I lifted my eyes to meet his.

"If you look at it as an act of cowardice, then that's the way it'll make you feel. Protecting yourself, improving your magical skills, exploring your resources, and taking a moment to devise a plan and regroup is smart strategy and nothing more."

My inefficient response to Asher earlier—"I'm okay. I'll call you later"—wasn't enough and was succinct to the point of offense, and that was expressed eloquently on Asher's face as he met us leaving my apartment, my suitcase in tow.

A stony countenance, intense cold steely eyes laser-focused on me, and a painfully clenched jaw. "A text, Erin," he ground out through gritted teeth. Underlying his ire were hints of anguish. Mephisto kept a careful eye on Asher, who simply dismissed him with a look. "Really?"

"I know, it was a grossly inadequate response." I sagged. Asher needed and deserved more. Handing my suitcase to Mephisto, I said, "I need a moment."

Mephisto didn't move, his gaze as hard and fierce as Asher's was cold and dismissive. Ugh. A testosterone-measuring contest. I never had the temperament or patience to defuse a testosterone-driven situation. My first impulse was to start pelting all involved with ice cubes. After all, they were a form of water. But thrashing all involved with frozen water would do the opposite of cooling things off.

No, I wasn't having any of this.

"I need a moment to talk to Asher, please." My tone left no room for debate. "Asher?"

I nudged my chin toward the door, as an invitation and not a challenge. Dealing with shifters was a pain in the ass, an Alpha even worse. It was the delicate dance of being firm but not doing anything that would be perceived as a challenge. Most times I wasn't as cautious about it, but this was a situation that needed to be handled with care. Diplomacy was required to make it right.

He nodded and followed me into the apartment.

"You deserved better," I admitted once we were inside.

Asher's sharp gaze tracked my every movement until I stopped a few feet from him.

"I'm no longer bound to my mother," I told him.

"I gathered that from your informative text of 'I'm okay, we'll chat later.'" Frowning; his tone was frosty. Shoving his hands through his hair. "You didn't go alone, did you?" he asked, his rough, gravelly voice smoothing out and warming.

I shook my head. "I'm sure you know that my father visited." I wasn't under the illusion that Daniel hadn't given him a full debriefing, along with commentary.

He confirmed with a nod.

After giving a brief synopsis of the fight between Nolan and Elizabeth, Asher rubbed his hands over the shadow forming on his jaw. His scowl had eased. "Let her fester in her hate. It has nothing to do with you. You're in the way of what appears to be a codependent relationship. You will never win her affection or kindness," he offered in consolation.

I knew that, but Elizabeth hating me would affect my access to and interaction with Nolan. I wanted Nolan in my life, and as long as she despised me for being me, for being Malific's daughter, she would be a barrier.

Once I had retold everything that had transpired with Malific and the removal of the binding, Asher's face was awash with sympathy and concern.

The stretch of silence between us was punctured by his ragged sigh. "Why didn't you ask me to come with you, Erin?"

Having to navigate around confidences was becoming

increasingly difficult. Asher suspected that Mephisto and the Huntsmen were gods, but it wasn't my place to confirm it. Without giving Asher that information, how could I explain that Mephisto had a longstanding conflict with Malific and a score to settle? He was already enmeshed, and his involvement wouldn't make him an enemy of Malific. Asher's would. Despite shifters' preternatural speed, their ability to shift to their animal with ease, and magic immunity, it was still debatable whether they were a match for a god.

It took longer than I anticipated to sift through the information, culling out what wasn't a betrayal of confidences.

"It's okay," Asher said softly. "I appreciate that you keep my pack's confidences, so I can't ask you to betray whatever his are." His voice tightened at the reference to Mephisto. If I missed the change in his voice, the grimace was obvious.

"I'm going to stay with Mephisto for a few days," I informed him.

His lips quirked into a mirthless smile. "You tend to underestimate my observation skills, don't you?"

It had to be like pulling off a band-aid. Just blurt it out. *I'm sleeping with him and I want to see where this leads.* Once it was said, it would be a rejection of Asher. What happened after? I was used to our banter, our easy interaction—even during hostile disagreements we never had this strained silence.

Gathering the right words, I was about to tell him, when Asher said, "You smell like him. Your scent and his are entwined. Yours is virtually indistinguishable." His voice was level, his expression empty. The heavy, tension-filled silence ticked by. He looked at his watch.

"I should go," he said, backing away.

I lifted my eyes to meet his. "I wish we could go back to the way we were," I admitted.

"Which part? You committing felonies in retaliation for me getting to the Salem Stone first? Sending vulgar balloons?

Randomly destroying my car's tires with caltrops? Or making false reports to the STF that I was in possession of illegal magical objects?"

"First, they were misdemeanors at worst. Second, they weren't false reports. You are in possession of illegal magical objects."

His lips quirked. "Prove it. They didn't find anything illegal in my possession."

"I've been in your vault!"

"And?" he challenged. "You still have the burden of proving I have them."

This guy.

"You deserved that and so much more. We might not have been friends, but we had a mutual professional respect and what I thought was a budding friendship, and you cheated to get the Salem Stone," I told him.

He considered my words then said, "Define cheating."

"Define cheating? Do you think I'm a Merriam-Webster Dictionary? You know damn well what cheating is. Violating the rules of engagement to benefit yourself."

His frown relaxed. "But there weren't any rules of engagement, Erin. And I never cheated." If it involved protecting his pack, there weren't any rules. He was guided by a single-minded motive and would make no apologies for fulfilling his role as Alpha.

I shrugged. "Perhaps you're right, but it didn't make the feeling of betrayal less painful," I admitted.

He nodded. "Okay. It was never my intention to make you feel that way." That was the closest I'd get to an apology.

The uncomfortable silences were getting tiresome. Something needed to change to return to our symbiotic state, but I had no idea what.

Asher finally said, "Erin, this doesn't change anything between us."

"It does."

He made a face. "Not that. You've made your choice. I always abide by your wishes."

"What? No. No, you don't. I say not to send your shifters and you do. I tell you to stay out of situations and you have your little snout firmly in them."

"Well, not those things." He grinned.

"I don't understand your rules, Asher."

"Exactly. Because they are my rules," he shot back. "Erin, I like having you around. Alive and safe. Whatever happens with you and Mephisto doesn't change the fact that I'm here if you need me."

I nodded in appreciation. He leaned forward, stopped abruptly, his jaw clenching with restraint. I started to offer my cheek but instead hugged him. It was long and notably awkward, but despite it, something changed. The easiness between us seemed restored or at least was less tension-riddled.

"So…" I smiled, stepping out of his hold and his hands that had rested on my lower back. "Alphahole? Term of endearment or what?"

He groaned and dismissively rolled his eyes. "Scarlett," he grumbled with a combination of affection and irritation.

"I'm a fan of hers," I admitted.

"So is Evelyn. They've become fast friends and dual pains in my ass," he complained.

"Hopefully the situation with Malific will be resolved soon and Evelyn will be one less pain in it."

Asher gave me a tight-lipped smile before shaking his head. "She won't be returning here."

"Does she know that?" It spilled from me in a surprising rush of vehemence, like water from a broken dam. It wasn't just her leaving, although I wasn't fully prepared for a new world without Ms. Harp in it. With things changing so fast, once again I clung to the frayed tendrils holding together my old life. Then there was Ms. Harp. It wasn't fair for him to take that decision away from her. And a person like her wouldn't appreciate it and definitely wouldn't have a problem telling him.

Asher didn't respond. I suspected he was engaging in similar deliberations to what I had earlier regarding disclosing Mephisto's information.

"I won't betray the confidences we share, despite my relationship with Mephisto," I promised.

The use of "relationship" earned a frown. "You want to believe that."

"Because it's the truth. Asher, you can trust me." I took his hand and gave it a reassuring squeeze. Even if I didn't feel morally obligated to keep his secrets, self-preservation would motivate me to, because betrayal of the pack, despite Asher's feelings for me, would be met with swift and possibly lethal reprisal. It extended further than the quarrel I had with Asher about the Salem Stone. If I betrayed his confidence and endangered his pack, he'd be forced to retaliate.

He looked down at my hand on his, then blew out a breath after considering it for several beats. "Two days ago, I had a chance to observe how Evelyn responds to the full moon. She might not be forced to change, but not changing affects her. She was so tired she could barely move. Her mental acuity was different. And I could sense her distress. It was like that for hours." Because he was forced into his wolf form, he couldn't do anything to help her.

His fingers disheveled his hair when they ran through his thick waves. "Initially I thought it was an evolution, a well-improved adaptation that would benefit us by negating our need to change with the full moon. But it seems to be a defect or some type of mutation. This needs to be studied, and I need to find out if there are others like her. I want her monitored for changes or further adverse reactions. Staying where she is will allow me to keep a closer eye on her and she's happy with the setup."

"Oh." I didn't have much more to offer.

"As a cat shifter, the role of protectorate should fall on Sherrie, but I feel responsible for Ms. Harp. I need to find out what happened to make her the way she is and find a way for her not to suffer during full moons."

"Has the cantankerous, stubborn, bossy woman wiggled her way into your heart?"

He shrugged, directing his glinting gaze to me. "I do seem to have a personality preference."

"Do you have anyone in mind to study her?" I asked.

"I'm vetting some people now. It will have to be someone with a strong handle on science and magic," he admitted with a frown. That would be difficult because science was more objective than magic, which was nebulous. I was living proof of what happened when various magics mixed, and Evelyn was a rebuke that nothing was definitive. The prevailing rule was that if a woman had a child with a shifter, she gave birth to a shifter who changed to their animal form during a full moon. Nothing had prevented that, until now.

Asher had a hard time hiding his concern. He looked down at his watch again. "I should go, I have a meeting."

I followed him to the door. At the threshold he stopped and turned toward me, leaving a hairsbreadth between us. The warmth of his unnaturally hot body enveloped me.

Turning my head, I offered my cheek. He gave it a soft chaste kiss and quickly put several inches of space between us before walking to his car, stopping to look at Mephisto seated in his own car. A look passed between them. It wasn't hostile enough for me to want to pelt them with ice cubes, but there was an obnoxious enough level of testosterone driving it that it gave me a moment of exasperation.

"I don't believe that Alpha and I will be friends anytime soon," Mephisto observed once I got into the car.

"You thought you had a chance after he threatened to storm your house to get to me?" I asked, incredulous, reminding him of Asher's insistence on checking on me after I'd gone missing after being fatally injured.

His lips lifted into a smirk. "Perhaps not," he admitted, placing his hand lightly on my thigh.

CHAPTER 33

*J*gnoring Cory's narrow-eyed scrutiny, I quickly got into his car when he pulled up in front of Mephisto's house.

"Why do I have the feeling that I'm aiding and abetting an escape?"

In the five days I'd been at Mephisto's, he'd continued to remind me that staying with him was "strategizing," which would have been fine if I hadn't spent the morning swimming in a temperature-controlled pool or leisurely reading books while musing over how strangely calming it was watching an okapi eat.

Today, it had become even more challenging to buy into the strategizing theory when it included sitting in the kitchen watching Isley, Mephisto's chef, formerly known as maker-of-the-best-food, prepare me a gyro. I had to do something substantial.

"Yeah, I'm escaping from the land of personal chefs, private pools, waterfall showers, a fascinating library with a druid, and a bed with sheets that make me feel like I'm being swaddled by the clouds," I shot back.

"Now I want to stay." He beamed. "Don't forget what else is swaddling you in bed. Hello." He was still grinning.

I glared at him. "Don't be proud of that. I'm not escaping. I just can't be idle. It's been six days since the encounter with Malific. I feel like I'm hiding."

If not hiding, then Mephisto had enlisted me in some type of protection program. Sparring with him and practicing my magic wasn't enough. I needed to confirm whether Harrison was dead. If he was, I needed to find the culprit and the person now in possession of the Black Crest grimoire. Taking a rideshare to investigate the Harrison/Dareus situation would put the driver at risk.

Cory looked at me for so long I was getting concerned that he wasn't paying attention to his driving. "What do you think you should be doing? Looking for Malific?"

"That's what Mephisto's doing. He goes out every day dressed for battle."

"You think that's bad?"

I kept thinking about Malific's hesitation and that Mephisto was convinced that if she had had a momentary lapse, it wouldn't happen again. That smidgen of hope in me that desperately wanted to believe she didn't want to kill me, wouldn't be extinguished. I needed to reconcile that the woman who gave birth to me didn't possess an iota of the same feelings as the woman who gave me to her best friend and my mother who raised me.

"I keep thinking about her hesitation. I know it's foolish, but I saw the way Mephisto looked at her. He wants her dead." He wanted to be the one to do it. Having been on the receiving end of Elizabeth's and Malific's hate, I knew the look, and what I saw on Mephisto's face surpassed that. It was virulent. Wrathful. In need of retribution.

"I'm chauffeuring you around on this little adventure because after her micro-bout with warm and fuzzy feelings, she was so enraged she destroyed your car. If Mephisto can rid the world of her, good. Because you could have been the car." Cory sounded weary with worry. "He's known her longer, so I think you can rely on his assessment of her. Mephisto's trying to get to her before she gets to you."

"No, he's trying to get to her so he can go home."

Cory wasn't paying attention to the road at all. Realizing it, he pulled into the parking lot of a Starbucks. "Talk to me," he urged.

"There's not anything to really discuss." But I was starting to feel the incipient pangs of emptiness I'd feel when Mephisto was gone. It wasn't wise for me to be spending so much time with him, knowing that the moment he could, he'd return to the Veil. Then we'd go from seeing each other daily to a long-distance relationship. Could something so new survive that?

"I know my safety is part of the equation, but you weren't there when he was ambushed. He was the most alive I've ever seen him. He was exhilarated by the violence. I don't think it's the violence itself, or power-thirst, it's his purpose. Everything he's done since his expulsion from the Veil was so they can return. Setting himself up as this major player in finding magical objects, knowing key people in the supernatural world, it all served one purpose: to return to the Veil."

Cory frowned but remained silent. I'm sure he could hear the quandary in my voice. I didn't try to hide it. He knew me too well and easily suspected there was more to what I'd said.

"Even if he goes back, he'll still see you. I'm sure that won't be an issue," Cory said confidently. Our roles had changed so much over the weeks. He was Mr. Optimism when he used to be Mr. Doom and Gloom. He called it pragmatism, but it often came wrapped in a big box of pessimism.

As we got closer to our destination, Cory looked increasingly apprehensive. Welcome back, Mr. Doom and Gloom. "What's the goal?" he asked, turning into the long dirt road leading to Harrison's trailer.

"Confirmation. Madison is still looking into it, but she can't launch a thorough investigation because there's no evidence that this isn't Harrison."

If I could get a confession as to who had the grimoire, that would be great as well.

"What do you want?" Harrison barked. His eyes were the same as Harrison's, his hair was still straggly and oily, and he possessed Harrison's normal air of indignation. He even directed the same level of loathing at Cory. I kept looking at his eyes, hoping they would revert to the odd snake slits that I was used to seeing on Dareus. The eyes, said to be the windows to the soul. But this could be some form of glamour.

I studied him to the point of discomfort, drawing a withering look from him.

"What part of not coming back did you not understand?"

Now I was second-guessing whether this was Dareus. His attitude, disdain for Cory, and cool disregard for me mirrored Harrison's. Cory gave me a sidelong look.

"I want to help you?" I said to Harrison.

He scoffed. "You didn't kill me, so I guess I could call that help." His eyes flicked to Cory. "But you tried."

There was a sinking feeling. This wasn't confirmation that this was Dareus but more of a verification of Harrison's story. He went away and now he was back.

"Dareus wants you dead. It's only a matter of time before he puts a bounty on you like he did me. There's no official bounty, yet. Maybe we can work together."

He opened the door wider but didn't invite us in. Crossing his arms over his chest, he said, "What do you have in mind?"

"We capture him." I laid out the plan, similar to the one I'd attempted with Cory and Madison, when I offered Dareus my body as host. Cory and I watched his response carefully. As angered as Dareus was during the setup, there wasn't any way he wouldn't respond to us rehashing the plan. All we got from Harrison were indolent nods as he listened.

"If it fails, then I'll just give him more reason to want me dead," he challenged, his look turning smug. "There's still a bounty on you. Striking an alliance with you isn't wise. I'll take my chances alone. From what I've heard, your little threats to the witches have only motivated them to capture you."

He closed the door, and Cory and I looked at each other.

"Is it Dareus?" Cory asked. I shrugged.

This visit had given me nothing. The only thing I'd learned was that people were motivated to satisfy the bounty. That was the last thing I needed.

CHAPTER 34

*Y*esterday, the only thing I achieved was not getting confirmation that Dareus was inhabiting Harrison's body and that people were "motivated" to satisfy the bounty. Malific didn't seem to be actively trying to kill me. Or she hadn't made any new attempt since destroying my car.

Mephisto and I were at an impasse, him wanting to go out, and me wanting to spend the night trying to discover a way to expose who was in Harrison's body and, if necessary, doing what Trace had failed to and making sure that anyone considering taking the bounty knew that it might be a fatal mistake. I didn't have it in me to mince words: "You try to give me to a demon, and I'm going to kill you. Period." Harsh, but people willing to give me to a demon didn't deserve my compassion or leniency. That pronouncement prompted a look from Mephisto that settled into an odd middle between admiration, agreement, and excitement.

I'd spent most of the day with Benton, trying to weave a spell or find a potion that would reveal who was in Harrison's body. That would dictate how to proceed. If it was

Harrison, the bounty was still in effect; if it wasn't, I needed to find who now possessed the Black Crest grimoire.

Mephisto grinned and gave me a reassuring touch. "It's just one night, Erin."

My ivory bodycon minidress with the bandage shoulder straps and network of straps in the back that left parts of my back exposed was in direct contrast to Mephisto's granite shirt and black pants. My sleek high ponytail was done more for functionality than fashion, although the style flattered my face, drawing attention to my heavily lined eyes and mascara-coated lashes. His eyes settled on my peach-glossed lips, traveled over the curve of my neck and the simple silver necklace around it, then it traveled along my legs and three-inch heels.

"You look beautiful," he said before pointing to the sofa. "Please sit."

With eyes narrowed skeptically, I dropped down onto the sofa. He knelt in front of me, his touch light as his hands roved over my exposed thighs, my legs, and to my feet, where he slipped off my shoes. He turned them around and pulled out the blade that was wedged between the heel. His lips pulled into a taut disapproving smile. I'd paid an unreasonable amount of money for shoes with a hidden compartment for a blade. I wasn't about to be shamed for it.

Nice try, Satan. Not this time.

"What?" I asked.

"Revel is safe. I know the owner. It's warded so no one can Wynd in." He seemed exasperated for the third time that night. "If you can't relax and you hate being there, then we leave."

I wasn't just worried about Wynding, but that magic could be used inside. Malific didn't seem like someone who would have a problem attacking me in a crowded room and assaulting anyone who attempted to stop her. Mephisto thought otherwise.

"Clay, Simeon, and Kai will be there, too," he reminded me.

"A whole lot of help that will be. Kai will be distracted by a well-made table and Simeon might befriend a stray cat and forget we even exist. So we're down to Clay, and he'll be more focused on making sure we get nowhere near each other—just for sport." Mephisto fought his laughter but it made his lips twitch. "I'm not wrong!" I defended.

He leaned down. The tip of his nose nuzzled against mine, his hands circled my waist, and his breath was wispy and warm as it brushed along my lips. "You need this, Erin. Nonstop you've been dealing with Malific. Go out, dance, listen to great music, and have some drinks."

I had music and drinks at home and at his home. Along with the ability to have amazing sex with a god. I had fun. But he was right; I needed a reprieve, some normality.

I nodded, took my shoes back from him, slipped them on, and stood. Amusement curled his lips as I clutched my small purse tighter when he looked down at it.

He pressed a light kiss to my lips. "And keeping in the spirit of that"—he looked pointedly at my purse—"do I need to check it?" He stepped back and pinned me with an accusing look. "They do check for weapons."

"What type of seedy, tacky establishment does that?"

As one of the most popular clubs in the city, Revel was far from seedy and tacky. I'd never dared go there, because if you weren't in a who's who of the city, you had to wait in a line that tended to stretch so far it blocked the entrance of the nearby restaurant. Since I definitely wasn't in the former group and I had no interest in being part of the latter, I'd never made an effort to go.

"Fine." I removed the weapons from my purse.

"Shoes?" he asked with a raised brow.

"Shoes stay. But I'll bring a backup just in case they discover the blade. I don't think they will."

"I did."

And? Do you want a prize? But I simply kept my comment to myself, plastered on an acquiescent faux smile, and went to get an alternative pair of shoes.

———

Revel was what I'd expected. It reeked of posh exclusivity, from the dual dance floors, exclusive section, and designer suit-clad security inconspicuously stationed throughout the room. Music was played by a DJ who was just as lively and entertaining as his music. There were bars in three corners of the large space and servers moving between the bars and the VIP section.

Mephisto guided me toward the opposite end of the club, while I was being unnecessarily smug.

"Told you," I said.

"Of course they wouldn't look. It's not typical for someone to hide a blade in their shoe," he shot back, taking my hand and leading me toward a small, hidden-away section of the club that I'd missed on my initial scan. We passed Kai, whose appearance made me do a double take. Leaning against the bar, a drink in his hand, he was dressed in classic-cut slacks and a fitted hunter-green shirt that revealed a physique that was the result of a person who spent a great deal of their time building things. It wasn't unnoticed by the woman in front of him, who placed a proprietary hand on him each time she leaned in to speak to him. His look landed firmly in the politely interested category.

I searched for Simeon, expecting him to be having a chat with an opossum or something. But he was seated in a corner, unconcerned that he was underdressed in his dark-blue Henley shirt and dark jeans, surrounded by people enjoying the company of the two-legged animals.

We moved to the bar. After a drink, I relaxed some but

kept thinking I should be in the library with Benton. Or interrogating Harrison.

"Erin," Mephisto coaxed, "just tonight, have fun. Then we'll dedicate every waking hour to exposing Harrison and getting the grimoire."

The one thing I was confident about was him getting the grimoire. He wanted it just as much as I did.

"What happens once you're able to go back to the Veil?" There. I'd finally asked the question that I'd been agonizing over for days.

He sipped his drink while he considered his answer, keeping his eyes trained on mine.

"I reestablish my life. I've been gone for so long I'm sure there's a lot of work to be done. I have no idea where to start. I was expunged so quickly after Oedeus's death that I don't know what awaits me there," he admitted pensively.

"You know what's here. Maybe this should be your home."

A wry smile overtook his face. "I've never feared or been deterred by the unknown," he said.

Dropping my eyes to my drink, I realized that assimilating back into his old life might consume him.

He placed a finger on my chin, tilting it up until I met his gaze. "There's enough of me for both worlds. And this one has you." He kissed me before taking my hand and pointing to a corner in the club that wasn't as crowded.

Madison was there, in a body-hugging black bandage dress with a sweetheart neckline, accented by a Y necklace. Clayton seemed particularly interested in her necklace. They were *dancing*, or appeared to be when they occasionally remembered to sway to the music. In the few minutes I observed them, they were molded to each other, talking, his arm around her waist and their faces close. The urge to become that annoying third wheel was hard to deny.

With some effort and Mephisto's hand slipping around

my waist and nudging me, we moved to our initial destination, away from the main crowd. The music could still be heard, slightly muted to allow conversation but loud enough that you wouldn't look silly dancing on the dance floor.

He was right, and eventually I gave in to the night. The music was consuming, and the pent-up frustrations and worry had manifested into energy that I used to dance. A half hour later, I was still dancing, shrugging off the drama of the past weeks, enjoying a night of freedom from worry. To Clayton's annoyance, I borrowed Madison to really dance and not do whatever she and Clayton had been doing on the dance floor. Madison made it abundantly clear that she preferred her non-dancing with Clayton.

"Hey! Rude," I shot back after she teasingly asked, "So, how long must I do this before you feel you've had your necessary sister time?" Fifteen minutes in, she traded me for Clayton.

I lured Kai from his admirer and was able to negotiate one dance from him. I realized he was giving me a begrudging politely interested look. His earthbound fluid grace made dancing with him a pleasure.

Eventually I retreated to where I'd left Mephisto. I stood, looking over the room, people watching, when a dark-haired woman dressed in a long cream-colored goddess-style dress with dramatic drapes of fabric and a low-cut V-front showing her sculpted arms came into my line of sight. Long, toned legs slipped out from the slits of the dress with each step. Her severe smile softened as she got closer.

Malific.

Quickly suspicious, I scanned the area, trying to determine who in the crowd were her allies and who were just people out for a good time. With a mixture of humans and supernaturals, the scent of magic tainted and mixed with the Huntsmen, despite them muting it. As she closed in, I kept one hand at the ready to defend myself with magic if necessary and the other to use physical defense. That seemed to delight her and her smile changed to wild exuberance.

She looked past me and her brow rose. She shook her head and I knew she was warning off Mephisto.

"I come in peace," she whispered at him. Then she searched the room for the others, mouthing the same words of treaty. At their distance they couldn't hear her, but her garnet-colored lips could be easily read. Malific's gaze drifted over everyone in the room. There wasn't any ambiguity in what her eyes and expression conveyed. If they didn't stay away, she'd kill the bystanders. I wouldn't risk taking my eyes off her to look at them, but they must have complied because she looked pleased when she returned her attention to me.

"You look beautiful, daughter," she said. Squaring her shoulders, her head lifted slightly, elongating her neck, and she settled into a pose that let her leg slip out from her dress. The voluminous waves of hair framed her face, but the similarities in our features—oval face, angular cheekbones, and sharp narrow nose—could not be ignored. Did she expect me to compliment her? *You can't be a sociopath and a narcissist. Pick one.*

When I didn't return the compliment, she changed position, swallowing every inch of distance between us.

"I will admit, daughter, I am quite impressed by your alliances." She wasn't impressed; envy radiated off her in a minatory wave. "Are you queen or friend of the shifters?"

Was this how she spent her days after our unbinding, determining my reach and my alliances? Before I could answer, her eyes darted to each of the Huntsmen, then regarded Mephisto for a long time before returning to me. "The protection that the Huntsmen provide for you is like nothing I've ever seen. And it is my understanding that you have a special relationship with the vampires. These things alone have proven that if things were different, I would want you to live because you are a worthy adversary. One who would challenge me."

Worthy adversary? Bitch, I'm your daughter.

Instead of letting my thoughts fly out of my mouth, I dropped the insulting part and simply said, "You're my mother." Could I reach that part of her that had hesitated, who, for a fraction of a moment, hadn't wanted to kill me?

"Yes. I am." Her pleasant smile vanished. "Is it maternal, the difficulty I'm having with killing you?" She pondered. A flicker of pride and awareness shone through. It definitely wasn't self-awareness because she would have recognized how bat-crap crazy she sounded.

Don't break out the champagne or buy any cookies yet, mother dearest. Not trying to kill your daughter isn't going to win you mother of the year.

"Maternal." She appeared to be turning the word over in her mind, repeating it several times, determining if it was palatable.

Damn, what would your score be on the personality disorder scale?

A moment of realization hit me. This was the reason it was hard to embrace the plan of killing her. Fear that I could become her. That troublesome feeling of knowing my score, how the desire for magic had consumed me in the manner that power had consumed her. I didn't want to be her. Nor leave room for it to be possible to become her. I didn't make an effort to mask my feelings and felt the frown of abhorrence settle on my face.

"Your Huntsmen killed the remainder of my army yesterday," she informed me in a tight voice. Anger was set alight in her eyes before it settled. That might have been part of the reason we were here. The Huntsmen had demolished the people she had used to fight them and now the two remaining Immortalis were gone. Her eyes shone with the same look of revenge-lust as Mephisto's had when he looked at her for the first time. How would she exact her revenge?

Her admission of maternal feelings wasn't enough to garner any trust from me, and I couldn't risk looking back at Mephisto or the others to read their expressions to gather more insight.

"May I offer you some advice, daughter?" Malific's voice was low enough that I had to shift closer to hear her.

"Is it to not live such a life that people ally to imprison you? If so, I wouldn't call that advice but rather a basic tenet of humanity."

Her lips pulled at a hint of a smile when she reached out to take hold of my hand, lightly pressing it in hers. "Never make an enemy of a demon," she advised.

The prick in my finger came suddenly. Looking down at my hand, there was just a trickle of blood from the sharp prong of the ring she wore. Strange, undeniably dark magic weaved around me, my left arm stung, and the invocation of the spell carried so clearly to me I wasn't sure if it was because I was connected to it or that the music had lowered. Dareus's accented voice was clear in my ear but I couldn't see him.

Frantic, I searched the room, my eyes darting throughout the large space, until they fell on Harrison. In his hand he held a peculiarly shaped aqua-colored object. With Mephisto behind me, it was Kai whose eyes widened on it. He was trying to move toward it, his face strained. Confusion bloomed on his face as his fingers expanded. Magic sparked from them, but he was still immobile.

The sting in my arm continued, and dark satisfaction spread across Malific's face. She waved her hand. I immediately heard thuds and crashes. People screaming and cursing. Bodies colliding and chaos behind me that I had to ignore.

I lunged at Malific, only to rebound against a wall. I looked down and found I was enclosed in a circle. Dark magic—demon magic—brushed through the air. I dropped to the ground, dumped out my purse, and grabbed my eyeliner, quickly creating the sigils for the neutralizing spell, hoping that if I could invoke it around me, it would stop the spell. Scribbling from memory of the paper that Nolan had left for me. Splitting my attention between watching Kai struggle to get to Dareus, scanning the room for Clayton and Simeon who might have been similarly restricted, and working on the sigils. My arm ached as if someone was carving words on it with a hot poker.

Halfway through the sigils, Malific's look of triumph was replaced by something that was hard to categorize.

"Don't you dare," she screeched. Wild eyes moved from me to Dareus.

I continued scribbling, moving in my circle, but it was Malific's shriek that brought me to a complete halt. Her unmistakable appalled look of betrayal. Before I could piece it together, I was tugged into a darkness, my breath whooshing out of me. When the darkness receded and my breath returned to normal, I stood, and found myself enclosed within a demon circle in Harrison's trailer.

Standing in front of me, Harrison's figure blinked, revealing Dareus's slit-like eyes that he'd denied me during our visit the day before. Still holding the peculiar aqua-colored object, Dareus watched me like a specimen under a microscope. I made sure not to show my panic and anger. My refusal didn't diminish the smug look on his face.

"You have no idea how much I wanted to reveal myself to you yesterday." He scoffed. "You thought you were so clever. When you taunted me with your betrayal, I wanted to break your neck. But I refrained because I knew this moment would be so much sweeter."

I followed his eyes to the mark on my arm that no longer throbbed.

"You're demon-marked," he said.

I lunged at him, only to be tossed back, forced to remain in the circle. He dropped the odd-looking object on the ground next to him and grabbed a chair. He placed it in front of me, thumbing through the grimoire that he'd picked up off the center table.

He sneered. "It could have been yours. My request was so simple."

"You wanted me to murder someone."

"Yes, *one* person. Malific had no problem with the request. She seemed disappointed that it was only one. I guess this is not a case of 'like mother like daughter.' Or perhaps there are some similarities. You both fancy yourselves deceitful little foxes, able to outmaneuver anyone. You trying to imprison me in a phylaca urn and *her* promising to bring me an elf, something she had no intention of delivering. All I had to do is this little spell." He turned the book toward me and I skimmed the page. Seemed like another binding spell, but instead of to a person it was to an object.

"The Laes." That was the object that he had just tossed on the floor as if it was insignificant. The thing that kept the Huntsmen tethered to this side of the Veil. The very object that was stored in the box that Mephisto wanted me to find. "You were going to bind me to the Laes. Killing me would have destroyed the Laes."

It wasn't Malific's false claim of some maternal instinct. It was revenge to the very end. What were the Huntsmen willing to do to return to the Veil? Would they go against Mephisto's wishes? Would they kill me? The internal fighting had already caused problems. Something would have to give. I knew Mephisto valued my life enough to stay on this side of the Veil, but I didn't feel that the others were willing to make that sacrifice.

"You're not going to do it, are you?"

He shook his head.

"Never make a deal with a demon. They will always try to find a way to renege." I cited the prevailing opinion.

"I did *not* renege. I have my honor. I said that the person who killed Harrison would get the grimoire. And I plan to honor that."

I knew I'd stopped breathing because I became light-headed and my vision blurred when Elizabeth walked out of the shadows and took the book from him. She didn't even bother giving it the courtesy of a magical destruction.

"I'll never let anyone get access to our magic, or any spells that mimic it," she touted through gritted teeth. She dropped the Black Crest grimoire in the garbage, whispered a spell, and set it on fire.

"Harrison's body is still too human for me and still limits my magic. I want my body here and your mother can't deliver an elf," Dareus explained to me, smiling at Elizabeth who seemed distracted by watching the grimoire burn.

"But I can," Elizabeth declared in a low whisper. "Nolan started this with his foolish goal. It failed. Where he was unsuccessful, I will succeed. The Huntsmen want to go back, and I have the ability to make it happen."

She picked up the Laes. I recalled Kai's face, him trying to get through an impenetrable barrier. I'd attributed it to Malific, when I should have known that the only people who could imprison the Huntsmen were elves. My eyes went to the snake coiled around her arm that she used during the unbinding spell, taking our blood and giving her a way to locate us at all times. While we were focused on the removal of our bond, Elizabeth was planning her next step.

"Madison and Cory will find me." And I hoped Mephisto and the others would join the search.

"Will they?" Her eyes dropped down to the demon mark on my arm. "Demons have to be summoned. Do you know how to answer a summon, Erin?"

I glared at her and Dareus, repulsed by their looks of self-assurance.

Elizabeth scoffed. "You and your mother share some qualities. You both are arrogantly overconfident. I'll be the only one able to summon you, and I have no intention of ever doing so. My promise to my brother will remain intact. I've ensured that you are alive and well, serving your intended purpose. Malific is paying for what she did to us. Because you are still alive, she'll never have the magical ability she once had. As I said before, I'm the justice and the balance needed in a world where magic exists."

She whispered the spell and my stomach lurched. I clawed at the air, trying with all my might not to be whisked away by the magical tug yanking at me.

"No," I hissed through gritted teeth. "Nolan will never forgive you for this."

"He'll never know. You got what you wanted, to be unbound from Malific. I doubt he'd expect you would want any more from him. I've served my purpose to you. Now you'll serve yours to us. Goodbye, Erin."

Stay.

I willed my body not to be snatched out of the circle, not to respond to magic that wasn't inherently mine but the result of a damn marking. My magic had to be stronger. I clung for purchase, trying with all my will to stay grounded, calling out spell after spell without success.

The last thing I saw before being swept away was Elizabeth watching my struggle with obvious satisfaction—my clamoring to stay grounded, my refusal to be whisked away, and her magic overpowering mine. My life had once again been changed. No longer by the mark of a raven but now one of a demon.

MESSAGE TO THE READER

———

Thank you for choosing *Shadowmark* from the many titles available to you. My goal is to create an engaging world, compelling characters, and an interesting experience for you. I hope I've accomplished that. Reviews are very important to authors and help other readers discover our books. Please take a moment to leave a review. I'd love to know your thoughts about the book.

For notifications about new releases, *exclusive* contests and giveaways, and cover reveals, please sign up for my mailing list at McKenzieHunter.com.

CPSIA information can be obtained
at www.ICGtesting.com
Printed in the USA
BVHW050158090223
658191BV00031B/909